Boys I Know

*For anyone who's ever wanted more,
but wasn't sure they deserved it.
You do.*

Published by Peachtree Teen
An imprint of PEACHTREE PUBLISHING COMPANY INC.
1700 Chattahoochee Avenue
Atlanta, Georgia 30318-2112
PeachtreeBooks.com

Text © 2022 by Anna Gracia
Cover image © 2022 by Fevik

Edited by Ashley Hearn
Design and composition by Adela Pons
Cover design by Kelley Brady

Printed and bound in May 2022 at Lake Book Manufacturing, Melrose Park, IL,
USA.
10 9 8 7 6 5 4 3 2 1
First Edition
ISBN: 978-1-68263-371-7

Cataloging-in-Publication Data is available from the Library of Congress.

ANNA GRACIA

Boys I Know

PEACHTREE
Teen

Author's Note

Being part of the Asian diaspora—and "only" half, at that*—has always been a barrier in my life, blocking me from accessing my culture in a way that felt complete. Instead, I snatched at fragments, desperate to assemble something that would reassure me of my place in the world. There wasn't much to cling to in my childhood: Claudia Kishi of *The Baby-Sitters Club*, the Yellow Ranger on *Mighty Morphin Power Rangers*, Michael Chang (the only Asian American to win a Grand Slam title). Then, around the age of ten or eleven, I watched *The Joy Luck Club*. Amy Tan's story about four Chinese mothers and their American-born daughters, one of whom is named June, resonated with me on a different level. Here was a movie in which Asians and Asian Americans dominated *all* of the leading roles, giving varied portrayals of the conflict between first and second generations, as well as what it meant to be Chinese American. I finally saw myself reflected in a way that felt complete and authentic, and I codified that movie into the central vault of my being, like a core memory in *Inside Out*.

In a behind-the-scenes look at the movie written decades later, it was revealed that director Wayne Wang understood the potential impact of such a film on the Asian American community at the time and decided not to limit casting to only ethnically Chinese actors. Instead, he allowed Asians of any heritage (including mixed) to read for the roles, knowing how limited their chances in Hollywood already were. It hadn't occurred to me until then that I had done exactly the same thing with my life. It had never mattered to me that Claudia Kishi was Japanese, or that Thuy Trang, the actress who played the Yellow Ranger, was Vietnamese, or that Michael Chang was Chinese. We were all Asian Americans, and therefore unified in our struggle for visibility and acceptance.

It was with this in mind that I created June Chu, the Taiwanese American protagonist in *Boys I Know*. Like both *The Joy Luck Club* and myself, June grapples with where exactly she fits on the continuum between Asian and American, and the question of what it means to be Taiwanese. And while the story isn't exclusively about a search for June's ethnic identity, I find it impossible to decouple the experience of being a minority in the US with all other aspects of life—especially when it comes to relationships.

Teenage girls are too often reduced to sexual stereotypes and taught to internalize misogynistic double standards, and with the lack of communication and education around these issues in our community, Asian American girls are especially susceptible to these injustices. It is my hope that reading about June's experiences might spare some girls the hurt of learning these lessons firsthand, even if they don't share her exact background. Self-acceptance (whether it be sexually, racially, or otherwise) is a radical act, especially in a society that consistently underestimates and undervalues girls like June. And the journey to discover her worth as a girl is equally as important as the one to untangle her heritage.

Identity can be a tricky thing, especially when trying to navigate the inevitable policing of "authenticity," both from those within and from others outside of that identity. But the real fight lies in the amount of representation we are given in the first place. Every Asian American experience is unique and I wish that we were given space to explore each and every one of those nuances, instead of having to contort ourselves to fit the limited existing media. Our prevalence in the mainstream has grown exponentially since *The Joy Luck Club* was released, but at the same time, it is not enough by any measure. I hope that whoever finds themselves in this book might have hundreds of chances to find themselves in other places too. Because while *my* June is named for *that* June, I am grateful for *all* the Asian American authors who carved out space for me to share my story.

I mean this ironically, as someone who has had that line flung at her a number of times. Please know that there is no percentage threshold or visual requirement for someone to be considered Asian, and that if you, like me, are mixed, you are valid as you are.

—ANNA GRACIA

CHAPTER ONE

"Aiya. You go to school all day looking like jì nǚ? Go change."

I'd barely taken five steps into the kitchen before my mom called me a prostitute. I opened my mouth to tell her the correct term nowadays was *sex worker*, but she wasn't finished scolding me.

"Totally inappropriate." She frowned, the pull of her mouth creating tiny wrinkles around her eyes that made her look closer to her real age. "What people think of you?"

I glanced down at my simple black scoop-neck T-shirt and jeans, trying to figure out why she kept looking at me as though my clothes were see-through. "What are you even talking about? I look fine."

She swiped a bony finger across my chest. "Look. So much skin showing. I can see your bra."

I swatted her hands away, pulling up the neckline of my shirt to cover myself. "You're supposed to, Mom. That's why the straps cross in front, it's the style."

"Looks terrible, like you tangled in string. Looks cheap. No cheap clothes like this in Taiwan. Probably fall apart in the washing machine."

I didn't bother replying that cheap American clothes were probably manufactured in Taiwan to begin with. Instead, I glanced at the clock, wondering anxiously how much longer she was planning to stick around. Rhys was due to show up in ten minutes, and I wasn't exactly looking forward to seeing my mom's reaction when she discovered the AP Biology partner I'd been "studying" with for the last month was a boy.

"I thought you'd still be at work," I said, casually pulling books and papers out of my backpack and setting them on the table like I was a diligent student, ready to study by myself.

"I come home to check on you before I go shopping. Today senior discount day at the fish market."

The only Asian grocer in the area, a full forty-five-minute drive from our house, offered a marginal discount for people aged sixty and older on Friday afternoons. My mom made the drive practically every week despite the fact that she was nowhere near sixty, always hoping she would get rung up by the one cashier who never checked IDs.

Nine minutes.

"Well, everything is great here," I replied with false cheeriness.

"You eat yet? There's xī fàn on the stove."

I eyed the dull, dented gray pot, a fixture in our household from before I was born. My older sister Wendy and I saved up and pooled our money together when we were little to buy our mom a new one for Mother's Day one year, but she continued to use the old one. *Dà shǒu dà jiǎo*, she'd explained. *Big hand, big foot*. Sometimes it was easier just to pretend we understood the Chinese proverbs she loved to spout instead of having to sit through a long-winded lecture. *In Taiwan, everyone talks like this*, she always claimed.

I patted my belly. "I'm saving my appetite for fish tonight." The thought of feeding me a full meal might motivate her to get going. Nothing could spring an Asian mom into action faster than declaring your possible hunger.

Eight minutes.

She frowned again, like she was forgetting to scold me about something before she left. "You practice yet today?"

"I will after I do my homework, which I can't start if you keep standing here talking to me."

I was practically herding her toward the door, my hands anxiously jammed in my pockets so I didn't reach out and just shove her out of the room.

Seven minutes.

"You know," she started. "Wendy—"

"Yeah, yeah, yeah, *Wendy* was never like this. *Wendy* never needed to be reminded to practice." For a moment I forgot all about being cheerful, and the bitterness of always falling short of my parents' expectations that I be exactly like my sister cut through my voice. *Wendy was Valedictorian. Wendy had ten full-ride offers for violin. Wendy is studying premed to become a doctor like Daddy.* Anyone who thought youngest kids were the spoiled ones of the family had never met Asian families, where the first child was revered and celebrated and everyone who came after was watched like a hawk to make sure they lived up to the firstborn's example.

Six minutes.

My mom sighed. "I don't know why you always like this. Daddy say if you put this effort into practicing instead of arguing—"

"Don't call him Daddy, it's weird."

"*You* call him Daddy. I do it when talking to you."

"I don't call him Daddy, I'm not eight."

"See? This is what he say."

I bit my tongue.

Five minutes.

It wasn't enough to get her out the door—she had to be clear out of the neighborhood or she'd see Rhys's car pull into our driveway and my whole plan would be ruined. Sometimes it felt like she lived just to foil my best-laid plans. Like in seventh grade when it slipped out that I'd planned to go to the movies with a group that included boys and she refused to let me go, forcing me to concoct a fake reason for canceling so I didn't have to explain that my parents were weirdly puritanical despite not actually following any organized religion.

"I'll do my practice," I promised. "I always do." *Sometimes at the last minute*, I added silently. *But I always do it.*

She kept frowning at me like she wasn't quite sure whether or not to believe me. Forget that I'd never actually missed a day of practice—apparently my existence itself was suspicious now. Like she could sense I was even *thinking* about doing something she wouldn't approve of.

I kept eye contact, knowing that she'd take my looking away as an admission of guilt and finally she sighed again before making her way toward the door where our shoes and jackets were tidily lined up. She took one last look around, stepped outside, and turned around to add, her eyes squinting, "Go change. Hurts my eyes to look at you dressed like that." With that, she shooed me away and closed the door behind her.

CHAPTER TWO

collapsed back against the closed door, relieved to have actually gotten her out of the house. But doubt quickly creeped back over me. Surely I didn't look *that* bad, did I? My friends would have told me if I looked . . . what was the word she'd used? *Cheap?* If anything, my fancy bra had been not cheap at all—I got a deal by buying it on sale. Not that I could brag to her about that now.

My mom's favorite reminder to me in English was a mangled version of *Why buy the cow if you can get the milk for free*—the irony of which was not lost on me. Regardless of what you called them, sex workers got paid.

I checked my phone again. Rhys was due any second. I didn't really have time to change, but I dashed up the stairs, taking two at a time, and threw on a plain gray hoodie anyway. Just in case. Another minute to smooth any flyaway hairs and rinse my mouth and I was back downstairs as he was pulling into the driveway.

I took two deep breaths, giving myself a full eight count on each exhale. The knock came and I did an extra four count just so it wouldn't look like I was hovering behind the door for him.

"Oh, hey," I said, flinging the door open.

"Hey." As usual, his sharp shoulders were slouched over, as if to apologize for how much taller he was than me. His dark curly hair jumped off his head every which way like he'd just woken up, and a rumpled, faded blackish T-shirt peeked out from beneath his unbuttoned flannel. In other words, perfect.

I allowed myself a momentary fantasy in which he greeted me with a hug and kiss like I was a proper sort of girlfriend instead of waiting until we were halfway through studying to make his move, but I quickly brought myself back to the present before I accidentally said something that might spook him. It had taken him ages to make the first move as it was. I didn't need him figuring out I'd invited him over as a subtle way of establishing myself more firmly in his life.

"What obscure band are you wearing today?" I nodded toward his partially covered T-shirt. He must have owned dozens of different vintage T-shirts, all courtesy of his dad's concert obsession in the nineties. While everyone else bought preworn replicas from Target or Urban Outfitters, Rhys had endless originals, all faded gray with peeling print, like he had worn each one a thousand times himself. They were usually hidden under another shirt or a hoodie or some other innocuous cover-up, but the threadbare edges peeked through at the collar and the waist, which of course I tried very hard not to get caught staring at during class.

He pulled open the flannel, revealing an image of a person in an electric chair, half their body zapped into a skeleton. "Metallica?" At the blank look on my face, his knees crumpled and he threw his head back in a strangled plea. "Come on, June! They're one of the most famous bands of all time. They *invented* thrash metal. You can't live under that big of a rock."

I didn't want to admit aloud that I had no idea who they were, even though it was already pretty obvious I didn't. It was both annoying and impossibly sexy that Rhys was somehow both book smart *and* pop-culture smart, in addition to being cute. People weren't supposed to be good at *everything*; it wasn't fair to everyone else. Why didn't anyone ever want to quiz me on my knowledge of classical composers?

"My rock is actually back here," I said, leading him toward the kitchen, where I had already neatly laid out my materials. "I don't get a lot of sunlight, but they do feed me occasionally."

"Do me a favor, okay?" he asked. "Just look them up. This album especially. It's the best one."

I shrugged noncommittedly, even though I was practically YouTubing it in my pocket. His T-shirt and the words *Thrash Metal* were giving me some very unpleasant screeching electric guitar vibes, but if it gave us something to talk about besides biology, it'd be worth it. "I'll think about it," I conceded. I nodded toward his backpack. "Do you actually have books in there today or is it just for show?"

"Nah, there's definitely a book in there, but I can't guarantee it's the right one." He set his backpack on the table and pulled out a thick textbook wrapped in plain brown paper. "Hey, whaddya know, it is. And look, it opens and everything."

"Watch out, the next step is actually reading it."

He snapped the textbook shut with a loud *thwack* and turned toward me, the faintest hint of a smile playing at the corners of his lips. "Definitely don't want that."

The way he smiled—that little grin that told me we were sharing some kind of inside joke together—made my stomach feel like it was about to levitate out of my body.

I cleared my throat nervously and quickly sat down at the table. "I was just kidding. I outlined the major areas we need to study, with a few bullet points underneath key concepts and terms we should know. I also arranged them by level of importance, so we can work our way down the list." I smoothed the top sheet of my notebook, pressing out the invisible wrinkles.

Rhys whistled and I couldn't tell whether it was out of appreciation or deprecation. "You sure you didn't want to put this into an Excel spreadsheet first so you could color-code it? Maybe add a pivot table?"

My eyes narrowed at the mention of Excel, even though there was no way Rhys could know about my secret spreadsheet of non-parent-approved colleges that were, in fact, color-coded. "That's not how pivot tables work."

He shrugged. "Close enough."

"It's really not. Pivot tables aggregate statistical data and sort it into groups. It wouldn't make sense to use it for this."

Rhys leaned closer to me. "It's a good thing you convinced me to be your lab partner so you could explain all this to me. It's fascinating stuff."

My cheeks flushed at the proximity. This close, I could smell his cologne. It was faint—not like other guys our age that seemed to bathe themselves in scent—but it was definitely there. Sharp and woodsy, like pine trees, but also sweet. Like marigolds. "You picked me, not the other way around."

He cocked his head to the side, his eyebrows creating dark slashes across his face. "Did I?"

I thought back to the first day of class, when our teacher told us each to pick a lab partner for the semester. Never mind that that was a lot of pressure to put on us, but the race not to be left with whoever else didn't get paired off was so great that lots of people made rash choices. Like last year, when I'd paired up with a guy because he'd gotten a 1500 on the PSAT, and he ended up spending the entire semester espousing his personal theories about the link between "Big Pharma" and the rise of cancer diagnoses. *They get you sick, then sell you the cure,* he'd constantly say.

Rhys had turned around amidst the madness, we'd made eye contact, and he'd given a little nod and a crooked little grin—the same one he'd used just now. Then, when we'd been sent to stand next to our partners so the teacher could write them down, he'd pulled my stool next to his so I could lean my back against the wall, our legs bumping against one another as we silently judged other people's choices. Yeah, he'd definitely been the one to pick me.

I cleared my throat again, dragging my brain back to the present and away from the warm feeling creeping through my chest from the memory.

"So like I was saying—"

"Yeah, yeah, I got it. Key concepts." Rhys cut me off, saving me from my own agitated state as he gently lifted my hands and pried the notebook out from under them.

I snatched it back, a little more forcefully than I intended. "Hey, you want notes, you should've taken some. These are mine." I hugged them tightly to my chest, as if ninety-six sheets of college-ruled white paper could protect me from the fact that I might not always be able to identify the fine line between flirty banter and outright hostility.

Rhys regarded me for a moment, as if deciding what to do. One of his dark eyebrows arched higher than the other, the individual features of his angular face always slightly askew.

Maybe this was it. Maybe he'd finally realized how much he liked arguing with me—someone who was actually as smart as him and able to fire off quick retorts—and he'd ask me to do something beyond the confines of our own homes instead of hiding me like a shameful secret.

Without warning, he abruptly leaned over and pressed his mouth against mine, the force of the kiss causing me to fall back into my seat. He followed me, never losing contact as he tilted his head slightly to the left, lips parting, his tongue tumbling into mine and sending my brain into a dizzying spiral. No matter how many times I'd kissed Rhys before, each time made me feel like I was tiptoeing along the edge of a tall building, wanting nothing more than to leap off the side of it but having the good sense not to.

His kisses grew deeper, his hands winding their way through my hair as I suddenly became very aware of how my own hands were trapped between us, desperately clutching the notebook. *Yuàn dé yì xīn rén, bái shǒu bù xiāng lí*, a tiny voice in my head whispered. *When you catch someone's heart, you'll never be apart.*

My hands twitched, desperate to break free and grab on to Rhys's heart as if it were something I could physically possess.

His hands slipped through my long hair and down my back, pausing for a moment longer over the back of my bra. My oh-so-fancy bra with the straps that crossed in front that I was sure he hadn't even noticed during class earlier. Now I felt silly for having covered up with a hoodie. We'd made out a half dozen times, each time his hands inching closer to the more exciting parts of my body, but this was the first time he'd given any indication we might move to the next level. Maybe he really, actually liked me.

The creak of the front door opening followed by the slap of the screen door sent us both scrambling back to our original places. My pulse, already pounding with excitement, was now threatening to send me into cardiac failure from sheer terror. I'd been waiting for the perfect time to have Rhys meet my mom and this certainly wasn't it.

"Mom? Are you back?" I called loudly. I tried to keep my voice light, like I was just curious and not on the verge of a panic attack at being caught with swollen lips and mussed hair.

My mom appeared empty-handed a moment later, the shock of seeing a boy sitting at our table painted all over her unsubtle face.

"Who is this?" she demanded.

Rhys beat me to the punch. "Hey, Mrs. C," he said, rising out of his seat. "I'm Rhys, June's biology—"

"*AP* Biology," I cut in, as if the reminder that it was an accelerated class would magically make her happy to meet the boy who'd just been alone with me in my house.

"Uh, right." Rhys looked flustered by my forceful addition. "AP Biology partner. Nice to meet you." He wavered between offering a handshake or a small wave, his hand just sort of dangling out in front of him for a few moments before he stuffed it back into his pocket.

"You can call me Mrs. Chu." She smiled, but the smile didn't reach her eyes. I knew that smile. It was same the one she used when strangers marveled at her English fluency.

"Oh. Sorry, Mrs. Chu," he mumbled, slumping back into his chair as I silently willed myself to melt directly through the floor, preferably into a grave. If I'd known today was going to be the day my mom was going to meet Rhys, I would have at least given him some pointers beforehand. Rule number one: respect elders at all costs. Forget shortening last names; my mom would die if she knew that Rhys's mom had insisted I call her Susan.

"June, you don't tell me you having someone over to study today," she said, her expression now unreadable.

I cleared my throat nervously. "It was kind of a last-minute thing. We have a test coming up."

"You study a lot, Ryan?" she asked Rhys with a slight nod of her head.

My insides shriveled in embarrassment. "It's Rhys, Mom."

"That's what I say. Rhys."

I silently begged everything holy in the world that Rhys would just think my mom was foreign and confused and not mixing up his name on purpose, which she most certainly was doing. I'd seen her recall the names of childhood neighbors back in Taiwan that she hadn't seen in thirty years with no problems—this was her way of letting me know that she didn't think Rhys was important.

"Not really," he shrugged. "Only when June makes me."

Crap. Wrong answer. My mom was deeply suspicious of anyone who didn't study. *Shǒu zhū dài tù*, she'd say scornfully. *Watching a tree, waiting for rabbits to appear.*

Her mouth turned down into a familiar frown. "I see. Maybe June teach you better habits. Better to dig the well before you are thirsty—wèi yǔ chóumóu."

Oh god. Not the proverbs.

"Hey, Mom, guess what? I got a hundred on my calc test today." I pulled out the stapled packet and waved it in front of her face like a matador, trying to pull her focus from interrogating Rhys.

She took the papers, murmuring aloud as she examined each page. "Only ten questions."

"But each question requires multiple steps to prove. You can see how much writing I have on there." My fingers tapped the test impatiently.

I hated calculus. I hated it even more than I hated trigonometry, and I'd spent most of last year just trying to keep my head above water. I didn't know what I wanted my college major to be yet, but I could guarantee it wouldn't involve upper-level math.

She flipped to the back of the test and looked up at me. "What about extra credit?"

"There wasn't any extra credit. Ms. Chamberlain doesn't offer it."

Her frown deepened, eyes narrowing with the same level of

suspicion she usually saved for people who extolled the health benefits of eating organic foods. "Are you sure? Did you ask?"

"Mom. Are you listening to yourself? I don't need extra credit. I already got an A on it."

She handed the quiz back to me. "Jǐn shàng tiān huā—you can always add a flower to a bouquet. No reason to get A when you can get A-plus. Right, Ray?"

I felt like a slowly deflating balloon, the air inside of me hissing out. Why had I tried to show off in front of Rhys like that? He didn't care about my calculus grades. It certainly wasn't going to make the fact that my mom walked in on us in the middle of kissing any less mortifying.

"Well, we should get back to studying," I said with what I hoped was an air of finality in my voice.

"I just sit here and read my paper," my mom said, settling into one of the barstools at the island and shaking open the newspaper, making sure the two of us stayed within her eyeline.

Great.

My afternoon had gone from hot make-out session to supervised playdate in the blink of an eye. No wonder Rhys hadn't claimed me as his girlfriend yet.

At least it couldn't get any worse.

"Oh, Riley?" My mom called over. "We have dinner early today so you go home at four."

CHAPTER THREE

I sat on the floor of the narrow hallway outside the auditorium—trying not to think about the thousands of dirty shoes that had undoubtedly walked across it—as strains of music came through the doors propped open farther down the hall. Why anyone would install carpet in a heavily trafficked area was beyond me. There was no way to ever get it fully clean.

I paused, my violin and bow suspended over the murky shade of burgundy that had definitely been red at some point, deciding whether I really wanted to put something on this floor that was later going to touch my face. My pocket buzzed and I settled on resting them across my lap while I read the text from my mom:

how much longer? make sure you warm up!!!!

Followed by a string of emojis that didn't totally make sense.

I texted back, telling her the performance schedule had been switched but that I'd just stay backstage. It was easier to lie than admit that sitting on a patch of questionable carpet in a dingy hallway was a better prospect than sitting beside her in the auditorium, listening to last-minute "advice" for the next forty minutes. I wasn't technically allowed backstage until closer to my performance time, which meant I had a whole bunch of time to kill, but I definitely wasn't going to spend it all warming up like my mom thought I should.

I scrolled through my phone, wishing I could text Rhys, but without an appropriate excuse like homework or coordinating a meetup, it would seem weird. What would I even say? *I'm at a violin competition.* Sure, that'd have him texting back right away. Who *wouldn't* want to chat about that?

I called the only person who might want to.

"Hey." Wendy's round face filled the screen as I raised my arm a little farther away from myself to get a more flattering angle. Despite what everyone at school used to say, Wendy and I looked nothing alike. For one thing, Wendy wore glasses, the cat-eye tortoiseshell frames giving her a far hipper look than her personality deserved. For another, she had bangs that were somehow not long enough to be a full fringe and not short enough to be purposeful like those pinup-style girls.

"I'm at Stephens," I replied, referencing the auditorium on the Iowa State campus where the competition was being held. "I'm bored and still have like forty minutes until I go on."

Wendy pushed her glasses up her nose. "Thanks. I'm so flattered."

"We both know you're not busy."

She made a face but didn't refute it.

"What's new?" she asked.

I shrugged. "Nothing, really. Ooh, except that Britney Lee's sister is here," I added with a flash of my eyebrows. "She's competing in my division this year, and get this: she said Britney quit playing violin."

Wendy's face couldn't hide her surprise. "What?! When?"

I paused dramatically, fighting back a sense of smugness. It wasn't often I knew something Wendy didn't, and I wasn't in a rush to default back to our usual positions. "So Britney ended up going to UNC—"

"I know. We're Instagram friends." She made a motion with her hand, telling me to hurry up.

"Okay. Whatever. Anyway, didn't you think it was weird she ended up there when her mom wouldn't shut up about the scholarship offers she had from Indiana or Ohio or wherever?"

"Yeah, but I figured they just made her a bigger offer. Besides, UNC is a better school."

"What does that even mean, a better school?" I mused aloud. "Is there really that big of a difference between like, the number twenty school and the number fifty school? There are really only so many differences schools can have. It feels like those rankings just exist so parents can brag that their kid goes to a higher-ranked school than everyone else's kids. Why else would they sell those tacky bumper stickers that say stuff like *Proud Parent of a Yale Student*? Like, is Yale *really* worth quadruple the amount of the University of Texas or whatever other big state school? Are all the students who go there really the best of the best? Or are their parents just rich and *that's* what lends the school credibility?"

I thought back to my secret college spreadsheet that *definitely* contained schools not on anyone's "best of" list. The problem was, there was no way to apply to them without asking my parents to cover the application fees—which they wouldn't do unless I came to them with scholarship offers first. Not just reversing the normal process, but fully demanding that I push the cart before letting me even apply to get a horse. Maybe there was a Chinese proverb about it.

Part of me felt guilty for spending my warm-up time on the phone instead of warming up like Wendy would have. The other part reminded me that I had already practiced and competed as much as everyone else here, and five extra minutes wasn't going to be the deciding factor.

Success wasn't predicated on who tried the hardest. Rhys certainly proved that every time he aced a test I would bet my life he never studied for. It was too bad I wasn't born with either Rhys's innate genius or Wendy's work ethic. Maybe if I had been, I would be destined for more than the middle-of-the-road existence I was currently living. It wasn't like I *tried* to be mediocre—I just wasn't willing to expend the extra effort unless I was fairly certain it would pay off. The last thing I needed was to waste my life doing a million things like Wendy only to end up exactly where I already was. At least my way allowed some semblance of fun along the way. Wendy never seemed to have fun.

"Focus. *Focus.*" Wendy snapped her fingers at me on my screen like a trainer trying to grab a dog's attention. "I don't need a dissertation on college rankings. Are you going to tell me what happened with Britney or not?"

I took a quick look down the hallway to make sure no one was close enough to eavesdrop before leaning in to continue, my voice dropping to a low whisper. "Her sister said Britney had this huge falling-out with their parents because she wanted to quit violin and now they're not even paying for her college."

Wendy's wide eyes looked even larger through her glasses, magnifying her shock at the news. "She's paying out-of-state tuition? How?"

I shrugged. "Loans, I guess. But her sister said things were so bad she wasn't sure if her parents would even pay to fly Britney home for winter break."

Wendy shook her head in disbelief as I silently congratulated myself on getting the inside scoop. This was the juiciest story to hit the violin circuit since the year Dana Simons changed teachers right before the MTNA regionals and applied to have her previous teacher's name stricken from her submission on the grounds that he had engaged in "inappropriate conduct." The competitive music scene in the Midwest was small enough, it was a miracle anyone managed to keep anything a secret for any length of time, but it was usually the pianists who generated most of the drama.

"Anyway," I said casually. "That's all I have."

Wendy took another moment to recover, shaking her head as if she could dislodge from her brain the idea of being cut off financially by your own parents. "Wow. So that's why you called?"

"I don't know if it's *why* I called, but I figured you'd be interested."

She checked the watch on her wrist. "What time are you performing? Don't you need to go warm up or something?"

"Ugh. You sound like Mom. Don't worry, I have tons of time."

"Then why are you sitting in the—wait, where *are* you sitting?"

I quickly fanned my phone around to show her the surroundings before turning it back to myself. "Hallway. I'm not allowed backstage yet."

"Where's Mom?"

"In the auditorium. I told her my time was coming up."

Wendy frowned the same way my mom did whenever she disapproved of something I was doing.

"Look, she was bugging me, okay?" I said defensively.

"About what?"

I gave a quick summary of my mom's awfulness about Rhys and how she hadn't stopped badgering me about my grades—biology, specifically—ever since, warning me not to zǔo gù yòu pàn, or look left and look right. I was half-surprised she didn't straight up suggest I use those blinders horses wear during races so I could tunnel vision my way to more A-pluses.

Wendy burst out laughing, her hand flying up to keep her glasses from slipping down her nose. "That's hilarious."

"It's not, it was mortifying."

"Why, is he your boyfriend or something?" She said it sarcastically, but I felt heat rush to my cheeks anyway.

"No," I lied. "But that doesn't make it any less embarrassing. She was totally calling him the wrong name on purpose."

"So? Who cares?" She looked at me carefully. "Unless he *is* your boyfriend."

"He's not," I replied loudly. "We're"—I racked my brain for the best description I could think of that didn't actually describe what was going on between us—"friends."

I could've kicked myself for that hesitation. Wendy was going to know I was lying. She was like a shark, smelling weakness like blood in the water, and it was rare she let the opportunity to strike pass her by.

She arched an eyebrow. "Oh, *I* see. *You* want to be more than friends but he doesn't. Yikes. Awkward."

Wendy had the absolutely horrible skill of finding the exact comment that would hurt me most and delivering it as if it were a throwaway thought on her part.

I straightened up, making sure my face didn't reflect the tightness I felt in my chest. "Good one," I said sarcastically, even forcing a smile onto my face like I understood it was a joke and not a shot in the dark that somehow hit a dead-center bull's-eye.

"Let's talk about why he doesn't want to date you." She dropped her voice and leaned closer to the phone, as if confiding something. "Is it because you're not cool?"

"Says the former *student government president*."

"Exactly."

"Yes, exactly," I repeated. "You do know cool people don't join student government, don't you?"

Wendy shrugged off my comment and shoved her glasses up her flat nose. "They did in my year."

I wasn't in the mood to argue about how that was most certainly not true. Cool people played sports and went to parties and had boyfriends, none of which Wendy did while she was in high school. At least I was somewhat close to the third one.

But I couldn't brag about that until I was certain I had something to actually brag about. In the botched words of my mom, *close is for horses' shoes and *explosion sound** because she could never remember the English term for *hand grenades.*.

"Let's talk about you," I said, channeling my best TV anchor voice. "Any boyfriends?" See how she liked being interrogated about her love life.

"No one I like enough to be embarrassed about," she answered in a singsong voice.

Damn it. There was no way I was going to win this conversation. The best I could hope for was to regroup and call her back another day, preferably when I *could* expand on what the hell was going on between Rhys and me. At present, I wasn't willing to offer up a detailed recount of our make-out sessions. Wendy had a habit of offering "help," then holding it over my head whenever it was convenient for her to do so.

But I wasn't willing to concede just yet.

I pulled my brows together in the most concerned look I could muster. "*Oh.* No one ever liked you so you have to pretend you're not interested in dating. It explains why you spent so much time in high school trying to stay busy with other things." I sucked my teeth in mock sympathy.

Surely there had to be some other reason for why she'd never had a boyfriend. No person could really only be passionate about building their college resumé, could they?

"Nice try, but you just can't pull off insults as well as I can." She gave a slight shrug. "Add it to the list of things I'm better than you at."

"Things *at which* you're better than me," I corrected in a haughty tone.

Wendy snorted. "Only you would count better grammar as a win."

"Comfortable living is like drinking poisoned wine," I said solemnly, quoting one of my mom's favorite proverbs. "Maybe being content in your current grammar skills is what will eventually kill you."

Wendy burst into laughter, causing my serious façade to shatter as I laughed too, covering my mouth to try to prevent the sound from reaching all the way down the hall to the stage.

"Okay, you should really go and get ready now." Wendy pushed her tortoiseshell glasses back into place and smoothed her bangs, her pale cheeks still flushed from laughing. "I don't want you blaming me if you don't win."

"Don't worry, we both know I won't win, but that doesn't mean I can't blame you anyway," I said cheerfully.

Wendy tried to put on her disapproving face, but a smile still peeked through. "Don't say that. You have to at least try."

"No one said I wasn't going to *try*. I'm just a realist who knows that I live at *riiiight* about the third-place level." I held up my hand to chin height. "I even have the trophies to prove it."

The smile disappeared from Wendy's face. "It's all about confidence, June. If you *believe* you should win, you will."

Right. Add *confidence* to my list of things I wasn't born with.

I forced a small smile. "Thanks. I'll remember that."

"Don't forget to give me all the credit when you win!" Wendy called out, right before I hung up on her.

CHAPTER FOUR

I thought about Wendy's comments all through the next week of school, especially as Rhys and I dissected mollusks in class, requiring us both to wear scratched-up plastic goggles that smelled vaguely of BO and vinegar. If I wanted Rhys to think I was cool, AP Biology wasn't doing me any favors—the goggles were far too big for my face, so my nose ended up trapped inside like I was wearing a snorkel mask, leaving me to mouth breathe all period. By the time the bell rang on Friday, I was so embarrassed about the goggle indentations across my face and the fact that I'd accidentally eaten shrimp chips earlier that I barely even waved goodbye to Rhys as he left. I'd planned to invite him to watch Liz's volleyball game with Candace and me that night, but couldn't bring myself to, you know, actually do it.

So that night I picked up Candace and drove back to school, the car stuffed with giant foam fingers and oversized pompons, the two of us wearing T-shirts that said *You Just Got Served*. We'd bought the stuff as a joke to embarrass Liz at her first varsity game last year, but it was now our tradition to bring it every time, whooping loudly from the stands with the most obnoxious puns we could think of. It didn't matter that I didn't know most of the rules past "Don't let the ball hit the ground." It was fun *and* embarrassing to Liz, so really, it was a double win for us.

I barely saw my friends now that school had started. Between Candace's work schedule, Liz's volleyball practice, and my parents' insistence that I complete every scrap of homework and practice my violin for exactly three hours before doing anything even remotely fun, we had less and less time together outside of school hours. It didn't help that I'd been spending all my free time secretly devoted to figuring out how to execute *Mission: Boyfriend* under a private browser in case my mom suddenly became tech savvy enough to look through my search history. I'm sure she assumed most of my time was spent writing deeply meaningful college application essays and making notes on my sheet music.

Candace once asked me why I didn't just lie to my parents about my practice time. My parents both worked unpredictably long hours—my dad at the hospital and my mom at the accounting firm—so they weren't usually around for it. But after years of being set against a timer that was paused for every bathroom break or drink of water to ensure not a single minute was wasted, I'd already been conditioned to block out a full one hundred eighty minutes of every day in my calendar to practice.

Besides, Asian moms seemed to have a sixth sense about these things. Kind of like how they could always tell if you hadn't eaten. With Wendy out of the house now, I didn't need to risk extra scrutiny over something as silly as practice time, no matter how much I resented it sometimes. I was better off saving my lies for big stuff.

"We look so cool," I joked as Candace struggled to pull on a white trucker cap that read *Been There, Dug That* because her hand was already covered by a giant blue foam finger.

"Hell yeah, we do. It's too bad your boyfriend couldn't be here tonight to see it," she said, popping up to scream and wave as the players took the court.

We sank back down onto the nearly empty wooden bleachers. "Not technically my boyfriend. But did I tell you even *Wendy* made a comment about how maybe he's dragging his feet because I'm not cool enough?"

I said it casually, like it was a ridiculous suggestion, waiting for her reaction. Candace was always quick to shoot down Wendy's derisive comments, reminding me I always had at least *someone* on my side.

The tiny diamond stud in Candace's nose wiggled as she flared her nostrils in annoyance. "Who cares what Wendy thinks?" she said, and a satisfied smile crept to the corners of my mouth. "Besides," she continued, "it's not like Rhys is the coolest guy. I mean, sure, he has some popular friends, but it's not like he's got tons of other options. He's lucky to even get you!"

I winced. Candace was always committed to telling me the absolute truth, no matter how brutal, but sometimes it would be nice for her to at least sugarcoat things a little. Or at least not make me feel worse by insinuating that getting Rhys to claim me should have been an easy target for success, considering how poorly *Mission: Boyfriend* had been going thus far.

"But it's never a bad idea to play it cool," she continued, ignoring my reaction to her comment. "But if his friends like you, he'll have no choice but to see you for the catch you are. Guys give so much shit to girls about being peer pressured into stuff, but they're exactly the same. It's all just a game. That's how I finally won over Dom."

Candace had been dating her manager at work, a spindly twenty-three-year-old guy with spiky dyed black hair and gauge earrings whose best quality as far as I could tell was that he gave her first dibs on shifts because they were sleeping together. I knew she was trying to be helpful, but she also somehow managed to work him into *every* conversation we had—*Dom loves potato wedges, but not curly fries. Dom is saving up to buy a Kia Optima. Dom hates using emojis in texts.* What kind of monster chooses wedges over curly fries?

"I'll try to keep that in mind," I said. I didn't want to think of "winning" Rhys in the same way Candace had with Dom, but she had a point that all of this wasn't dissimilar to a game. In which case, I was going to need to step my performance *way* up. I might not have any other competitors at the moment, but a third-place finish wasn't going to cut it here. For once in my life, I was determined to be the one on the top of the podium. Well, metaphorically, anyway.

Candace chattered on, straining her short arms around me to try to grab the program I'd snagged on the way into the gymnasium. "It's all about confidence, Juje. I can't believe I'm going to say this, but look at Liz. She just decided one day she was going to play volleyball, took all her confidence from playing soccer, and just applied it. And now look at her! She's . . ." Her voice trailed off as she flipped the flimsy sheet of paper over and back again, searching for something that seemed to be missing in the text.

"She's what?" I asked.

"She's forced her friends to come to a goddamn scrimmage!" Candace bellowed, still flipping through the program in disbelief. "Are you kidding me?"

I don't bother correcting Candace that Liz never actually *forced* us to come, and in fact would probably prefer us not to, which was half the reason we'd started coming in the first place. "Huh?"

"This doesn't count! It's not a real game!"

I looked down onto the court where teams in different-colored uniforms were standing on opposite sides of the net, hitting the ball back and forth. "Are you sure? It looks like a real game."

"I mean it's not a real game in that it doesn't matter who wins or loses. The results don't count. We came to a friggin' practice game!"

"That explains why we're basically the only people here," I said, surveying the nearly empty bleachers.

"And why Liz gave us such a weird look when they came out."

The two of us broke out into laughter at the ridiculousness of the situation, Candace slapping both my thigh and hers with her giant foam finger as her tiny limbs flailed around like the ones on those inflatable tube people at car dealerships.

"All the better for Liz to hear us I guess," I gasped, dodging one of Candace's body blows. "Look, they're in a time-out."

Candace and I jumped to our feet, yelling, and waved our arms wildly, our voices echoing loudly in the empty gym. Liz shot us death glares from the court, but I could tell she was suppressing a smile.

"She loves us," I sighed, throwing an arm—pompon and all—around Candace's shoulder.

"She'd better. I had to ask Dom to switch shifts so I could be here. She could have at least given us a heads-up about it not being a real game."

"Knowing Liz, she might not have known either." I gestured onto the court, where Liz appeared to be boring holes into the net with her eyes. "She looks like she'd body check her own teammates for the ball. She should have been a hockey player."

Candace snorted. "Can you imagine her going one-on-one against Tommy?"

A mental image of Liz hefting Tommy, one of Rhys's obnoxious hockey-playing friends, over her shoulder and chucking him across the ice like a shot put brought a smile to my face. "I would pay to watch that, honestly."

"Do you remember that year we started a petition to try and get student council to sponsor a karaoke night?" Candace asked. "We could do something like that for this. 'The school demands a fight between Liz and Tommy, Principal Blackburn.'"

I laughed. "First of all, it was *you* that started the petition. And I'm pretty sure it was because you wanted to sing eighties ballads in leather pants after watching *Rock of Ages*, which I still haven't forgiven you for making me sit through, by the way."

"*You're welcome*, by the way."

For some bizarre reason, Candace was the only person under the age of fifty who loved Tom Cruise, and she'd made it her mission to watch every single movie he'd ever been in. Why it also had to be *my* mission was unclear, but I'd sat through all of them with her, watching him attempt everything from flashy mixology to poorly executed Irish accents. We hit a rare blip in our relationship after she argued that she didn't see the problem with Tom Cruise being the *actual* last samurai in a movie full of Japanese actors, but we patched things up by yelling "Stay gold, Ponyboy!" at each other every chance we got until Liz threatened to stop being friends with us.

Liz's team won the first set and the two of us initiated another round of obnoxious cheering during the changeover, chanting her name until she gave us a throat-slitting gesture from the court.

We collapsed onto the bench with contented sighs. "It's too bad your violin stuff always has to be silent and polite," Candace said. "It would be so much fun to show up at one of your recitals with this crap, heckling your competition."

"It wouldn't work on me. I'm not nearly as intense as Liz."

Candace narrowed her eyes at me. "Puh-lease. You love to play this whole 'oh whatever violin is just something I do' routine, but you forget I've seen you warm up."

My jaw dropped. "What's wrong with my warm-up?"

Candace mimicked exaggerated alternating shoulder rolls and chopping motions with her arms, her facial expressions making it look more like a terrible dance move than a serious warm-up.

"You're not supposed to do them all together," I corrected her. "And *everyone* has to warm up. It's not like I made up those exercises on my own to be cool."

"Whatever you say, Robot Girl." She continued making chopping motions, her arms flailing in all directions until the foam finger on her right hand flew past me and bounced under the bleachers.

"Yeah. Well. You will definitely be sorry when the day comes and you need someone to individually finger paint circles because let me tell you, I've got that down." I thrust my hands into her face, rotating each of my fingers independently—another one of my very cool-looking warm-up exercises.

"Oh yeah, how could you possibly think Rhys wouldn't find *that* cool? You should do those in front of him."

I shoved her playfully, my mouth gaping in pretend shock. "Rude!"

"What would *actually* be cool is if you'd go and get my foam finger," she said, pointing toward where it had fallen through the cracks. "Seeing as I was copying *your* moves when it fell down there in the first place."

I painted an earnest expression on my face. "But what if I miss some of the game? How will I know who's winning?"

"I hate you."

I laughed, but got up and headed under the bleachers to get it anyway.

CHAPTER FIVE

The next day I was trudging through my usual Saturday morning routine of chores, violin, and a lecture from my mom about how I should be seriously considering Wendy's school, when my phone buzzed with the most important of all-important texts—an invitation to hang out with Rhys and his friends that night.

I talked Liz into coming with me for moral support, and promptly at eight o'clock—a full hour after the time Rhys said they'd be at Grayson's—we showed up. Whatever it was I thought we'd be doing that night, playing poker and drinking forties in a semifreezing garage was not it. But I was determined to be cool. This was, after all, what I'd wanted. Six people, beer, and some weed definitely constituted a party. And Rhys was there. This was my chance to impress his friends.

Grayson pointed to the extra folding chairs in the corner, and Liz wasted no time pulling hers up to Rhys's right side. She motioned for me to put my chair on his other side, but now the table was awkwardly out of balance. Forcing everyone to shift just so I could sit next to Rhys seemed like a bad idea, no matter how many silent admonitions Liz sent me. No one was going to judge *her* for where she sat.

Instead, I pretended to be perfectly okay with sticking my chair into the one empty gap between Tommy, the annoying hockey player Candace and I usually tried to avoid, and Grayson, a heavyset guy who looked like he'd enlisted in the military because he wore nothing but camouflage pants and sported a high and tight haircut. At least I could covertly stare at Rhys from behind my cards at this angle.

The guys been at this for a little while, judging by the number of empties scattered around the cement floor and the pile of quarters in front of Drew, who I immediately recognized as the boy who'd asked out Candace in eighth grade because she was the only girl shorter than him. Suddenly I was grateful Liz had insisted we stop at the gas station to exchange ten dollars' worth of quarters rather than relying on one of the guys to have extras. I imagined borrowing some from the likes of Tommy and shuddered.

"Hey, guys." I waved awkwardly around the table as Rhys nodded to acknowledge me, but he didn't pause in dealing out cards to everyone.

"You two know how to play poker?" Grayson asked Liz and me.

Liz rolled her eyes. "Of course I do."

I gave a noncommittal sort of nod/shrug that could pass for a yes—I didn't have full confidence in my skills like Liz. When Wendy and I were kids, before our lives got too busy with school and violin, we used to visit my mom's parents in Taiwan every couple of years. My ahkong had loved poker and all Western card games. One year he taught us to play, fronting us money for him to win back, before my mom found us out and put a stop to it. That was the last time I'd even *thought* about poker. If I'd known it was an expected life skill I might have brushed up sometime between then and now.

Grayson was starting to explain the basics when Tommy reached over, waving a hand between us to stop him. "She's supposed to be smart; she'll figure it out." He grinned at me. "Right?"

I nodded with as much certainty I could muster. The last thing I wanted to do was make everyone stop playing so someone could walk me through each step. Though it would have been nice if I'd been sitting next to Rhys so I could've used that as an excuse to talk to him. I silently cursed myself for not bringing Candace, who would have made sure to get us next to each other without being obvious. "Choreography," she always called it. Whatever the exact opposite of "if it's meant to be" fatalism was, that was what Candace believed.

I made it through the first couple of rounds okay, my memory of the rules coming back fast enough to avoid any major embarrassments, but sitting across the table from Rhys instead of next to him was growing increasingly difficult. I didn't want to look at him so much that I'd be caught staring, but I also couldn't seem like I was *avoiding* looking at him. So mostly I looked down at my cards, trying to ignore the constant remarks coming from Tommy on my left about how he was definitely going to win this hand.

"Hey, Lara Jean Covey," Tommy said.

"Are . . . you talking to me?" I asked, my hands swirling the pile of cards around the middle of the table to mix them.

"Does anyone else here seem like they'd answer to that name?"

"What are you talking about, Blondie?" Rhys asked.

"Come on. None of you watch Netflix movies?" Tommy stared imploringly around the table to blank stares. I hated that I was the only one who knew what he was referring to.

"What about it?" I asked, my stomach already tightening with regret.

"I knew you'd know what I'm talking about!" Dimples creased both sides of Tommy's pinkish cheeks as he leaned toward me. "See? We have something in common already!"

I gave a tentative smile and the knot in my stomach loosened. I didn't know what was more surprising—the fact that Tommy watched teen rom-coms in his spare time or that he'd openly admit it to his friends. Fitting in could be easier than I'd thought.

"Isn't that the movie about the girl with the love letters that get sent out by accident?" Liz asked. "The previews automatically play on Netflix, it was impossible to avoid seeing it," she said with a wave of her hand to my clearly surprised face.

"You can change that in your settings," Drew piped up, but everyone ignored him.

"Yeah," Tommy replied to Liz. His body was still leaning toward me, but his head now cocked in her direction.

"Why are you calling June that girl's name?" Liz's voice was accusatory. Almost like she knew as well as I did exactly why he was calling me that name.

Tommy's smile didn't crack, his dimples winking at Liz almost like a challenge. If she'd thought he'd be embarrassed at being called out on it, she was wrong. "Because she reminds me of her," he said matter-of-factly.

Never mind that Lana Condor, the actress playing the character in question, was Vietnamese and not Taiwanese. Or that apart from the fact that we both had long black hair and dark eyes, we looked nothing alike. People had been confusing me with other Asians my entire life. At least Lana Condor was prettier than me. And a girl. I'd once been told I reminded someone of Jet Li.

Liz's jaw had dropped open, her shoulders raised like she was ready to stand up and flip the table over on him, but I spoke up before she could. "So you're saying I look like a movie star," I joked, adding in a hair flip for good measure.

All the guys laughed, but Liz's shoulders remained scrunched, her lips pressed together, the muscles in her clenched jaw twitching. "June, can you come to the bathroom with me?" she managed to say through gritted teeth.

"Last door on the left," Grayson called as we left the garage. I heard him chuckle. "Girls, man. Can't do anything on their own."

———

Liz waited until we were safely tucked inside the bathroom before she hissed, "What do you think you're doing out there?"

"Playing poker?"

"This isn't time for more of your jokes. How could you just sit there and let Tommy say that stuff to you about how you look like that actress—who, by the way, you look nothing like? No offense," she added.

How could I possibly take offense at the suggestion that I had absolutely nothing in common with the *one* adorable Asian who'd become a household name while Liz got to be compared to the likes of Florence Pugh, whom she looked even less like?

I shrugged uncomfortably. "It's not that big of deal." Candace's advice to win over Rhys's friends was still buzzing around my head, reminding me to fit in and keep my eye on the ultimate goal. I could ignore a hundred stupid comments from Tommy if it meant I never had to tell Liz that Candace and I had gamified my relationship with Rhys.

Liz's eyes widened in surprise. "Not that big of a deal?" she screeched. "*Not that big of a deal*? How are you not pissed off about this?"

"Because I don't really care what Tommy thinks. He's not worth the fight."

"Don't you think you have a responsibility to speak up? Otherwise he's going to just keep saying that kind of stuff. What if he does that to someone else?"

My eyebrows raised at the word *responsibility*. As if it was my job to speak for all Asian people. I'd gotten it my entire life—teachers looking at me to supplement information when they taught lessons about communist governments or kids asking about which K-pop group they should listen to. Like they didn't understand the *American* part of Asian American.

Besides, it wasn't like if I told Tommy that not all Asians looked alike it would force him to suddenly reflect on his behavior. The only thing that would happen is I would come off like the type of girl who overreacted to everything. Cool girls did not make a big deal about minor, throwaway comments. Cool girls did not dominate a group conversation with heavy topics no one wanted to discuss. Even if Rhys never decided to acknowledge me as his girlfriend, I'd make damn sure it wouldn't be because I was *uncool*.

"Just let it go," I pleaded.

She sighed in defeat but muttered under her breath all the way back to the table, where we reseated ourselves amidst an argument between Drew and Tommy.

"A plastic bag makes way less mess," Drew was insisting.

Tommy threw his hands up in the air. "Who the hell is going to use a giant plastic bag?"

"Not like a trash bag, dumbass. Like a sandwich bag—the non-Ziploc kind. You just spit into it to make it wet and warm beforehand." Drew held out his hand and pantomimed the actual spitting and subsequent motion in case any of us had missed how that worked.

"Pffft, at that point why not use a condom?" Tommy scoffed, pushing up his sleeves and flexing his forearms. Tommy was *always* flexing his forearms. Some guys relied on a hair toss or a smile, but not Tommy. The guy must have owned a hundred different three-quarter-length-sleeved shirts.

"Ewww, you guys are disgusting!" Liz cried, leaning back her chair as if some of their conversation could accidentally splash across the table and touch her.

"It's not the same," Drew said, ignoring Liz completely. "Condoms are expensive. Besides, they're too tight and don't give you the same range of motion."

"Range of motion?" Tommy scoffed. "You're kidding, right?"

"Says the guy who jerks off into a microwaved banana peel," Drew shot back.

"I'll bet you a hundred bucks it feels better than a damn sandwich bag."

"What is wrong with you two?" Rhys asked, his face reflecting the same feeling of horror probably plastered on my face.

"Like you've never tried whacking it into stuff," Tommy said.

"I sure as hell haven't done it with a banana peel!" Rhys exclaimed.

Liz opened her mouth to say something, but Grayson beat her to it. "Enough!" he yelled, his booming voice filling the empty space of the garage. "No one wants to listen to all the weird ways you guys jack off. Do that shit on your own time, you're holding up the game. Blondie, it's your turn to call. Rhys, how many forties did your brother get us? I'm out."

He held up his empty bottle and rattled it for effect. It looked like just a regular-sized bottle in his oversized hand. If Grayson were even remotely interested in athletics, he would have been a shoo-in for the football team. He could probably block half the opposing team single-handedly.

Rhys tipped his flimsy folding chair back onto two legs, straining to reach the cooler behind him before fishing out a beer and tossing it to Grayson. Grayson wiped it on his pants, twisted it open, and promptly guzzled down half the bottle.

"Hey, why do you guys call Tommy 'Blondie'?" I asked suddenly, hoping to pivot the conversation away from the previous topic. "Is it because he's not a real blond?" Tommy, like a large number of girls at our high school, had light brownish hair that he most certainly highlighted and pretended to pass off as natural.

The guys exchanged amused looks around the table, like they were all in on some hilarious inside joke that was somehow funnier than tough hockey player Tommy getting highlights.

"Dang, June, you really are straight edge, huh?" Grayson laughed, his body shaking the table and causing Drew's tower of quarters to topple over.

I stiffened at the accusation. I hadn't sat through that entire masturbation conversation only to be called "straight edge."

"It's a strain of weed," Rhys offered, as if that explained everything.

I looked to Liz, who shrugged helplessly. She probably knew less about weed than I did, and my knowledge began and ended with the fact that they didn't call it "stoned" for nothing. The kids who managed to smoke it in the bathrooms or the parking lot during lunch tended to shuffle into their afternoon classes like slowly moving statues.

"You wanna try some?" Grayson asked, offering his slim vape pen to me.

I waved him off. "No thanks. I like my brain cells."

"You calling me stupid, Covey?" Tommy asked, taking a puff off his pen and blowing a cloud of vapor toward me.

Across the table, I heard Liz snort.

Tommy pushed his sleeves up to his elbows again as he blew another stream of vapor at me. "You could really use some of this. It'd loosen you up, if you know what I mean." He gave me a little wink, the dimple in his cheek laughing at me.

I could feel heat rising to my cheeks and I hurriedly buried my face in my cards before any of the guys could see it. Was it possible Rhys was holding back with me because he thought I was uptight? What if he'd told his friends that? The thought of Tommy having intimate knowledge of what Rhys and I had or hadn't done made me wish for a swift death.

"No, Tommy, what *do* you mean by that?" Liz's voice rang out clearly, her eyes fixed on his.

His attention shifted away from me and back across the table at Liz, who was now giving him the same look she used anytime our PE teacher asked for "a couple of strong boys" to volunteer to move equipment around the gym.

But just like before, Tommy refused to be goaded into feeling embarrassed. Or who knows, maybe he just wasn't smart enough to realize what Liz was doing. He cupped his hands around his mouth like a megaphone. "I mean that Rhys only wants his girlfriend tight where it counts."

My throat constricted, forcing up a swallow I'd been intending to go the other way. But a tiny thought popped into my mind, pushing its way past my disgust at Tommy's remark.

Did he just call me Rhys's girlfriend?

There was dead silence in the garage for a few seconds after Tommy's announcement, both Grayson and Drew blinking slowly like they hadn't quite heard him correctly. Rhys looked as mortified as I felt, his eyes somehow both open wide in shock and squeezed shut at the same time, while Liz sat there looking around at each of us, imploring us with her eyes to say something.

I was a hopeless cause. My mouth wouldn't have worked even if I'd wanted it to.

Liz turned her focus on Rhys, who was still sitting next to her, his mouth curled open in shock. "Are you really going to let him sit there and talk about your girlfriend like that?"

That snapped me out of my daze.

What the hell was she doing? Tommy using the word *girlfriend* was not the same thing as her using the word *girlfriend*. Now Rhys was going to think *I* referred to myself as his girlfriend. And hadn't I told her to ignore Tommy?

Sure, Tommy was an asshole. But Liz and I both knew that coming in. I'd brought her with me for moral support—not for her to go off script on a solo crusade to end all sexism. And now she'd brought Rhys into it, all under the guise of saving poor, helpless me. I'd worked so hard to get to this point and she was going to ruin it all with her selfishness.

My mind spun in circles, desperate to find something— *anything*—to say before Rhys was forced to answer Liz. Anything that didn't remind everyone of Rhys and me, the word *girlfriend*, or anything having to do with *tightness* of any kind.

"We should play some music," I spluttered, and all eyes came to rest on me. I could feel heat starting to creep up my neck, but I held my head perfectly motionless, as if I'd absolutely meant to change the topic in such an abrupt and forceful way.

Liz threw daggers at me from across the table for interrupting her interrogation of Rhys, who looked even more relieved than I did about it, his eyes returning to a normalish size instead of the wide saucers they'd become when Liz had turned on him. But my attempt at a distraction seemed to have worked. Grayson cleared his throat and started scrolling through his phone for songs, while Drew quickly busied himself with shuffling and dealing another hand.

Tommy, meanwhile, gave one final smirk at Liz, probably feeling pleased that he'd managed to goad her into reacting. Guys like Tommy were all about the kind of reaction they could get. Sometimes I wondered if he even believed half the shit he said or if he just wanted attention.

Grayson cleared his throat again and thrust his phone toward me. "Here. You pick. Since you're the um, you know, the guest or whatever."

Okay, so Rhys's friends weren't exactly comfortable with me yet. But there was still time to salvage the night. I quickly scrolled through his choices and selected a song I knew Rhys would like.

Grayson gave me an appreciative nod. "Metallica. Nice choice."

"What is this?" Liz asked, a look of *who the hell are you* on her face.

Rhys, however, broke out into a smile, and I knew I'd made the right choice. "It's this little-known band June recently discovered," he said with a crooked little grin at me.

All the anxiety that had been twisting my insides since Liz's outburst finally began to recede, and I allowed myself a slow, silent four-count exhale. *This* is how the night was supposed to go.

I gave a shy smile back, letting him know I understood his joke, and our eyes latched on to each other. Suddenly I no longer cared what any of his friends or even my own friend was doing. It was like I'd found a tiny little space for just the two of us to exist in.

To my left, Tommy let out a low grumble of disgust. "Get a room, you two."

CHAPTER SIX

After the awkward poker night at Grayson's, things seemed to go more smoothly between Rhys and me. I'd made it through several more get-togethers with his friends and even managed to make jokes when Liz would get up in arms about whatever offensive comment Tommy made. Luckily it was still football season, which meant we sometimes got to enjoy time without him.

AP Bio was still a challenge, what with our recent foray into sheep brain dissections, which meant more goggle lines on my face, but at least now I knew Rhys and I would see each other outside of class more often. Without necessarily meaning to, I'd also spent the past several weeks obsessing over what Tommy had said about me being uptight. I could only be so relaxed when having to stay on guard at all times to make sure it didn't seem like I was more into Rhys than he was into me, which resulted in my chest feeling like it had developed some kind permanent knot inside of it.

Hopefully I could relax soon. Liz's birthday was fast approaching, and between Candace and me, we'd managed to convince her that a "fun night away" at her dad's cabin would actually be *more* fun if it wasn't just the three of us. And while probably none of us wanted Tommy there, it was sort of impossible to just invite Rhys, Drew, and Grayson, so we also got her to compromise by promising the boys would be in charge of bringing the alcohol.

Candace, who had been sworn to secrecy about my ulterior motives for the sleepover, also helped come up with a name for it: *Mission: BJ.* After watching all 712 *Mission: Impossible* movies, she'd begun dubbing every idea of ours "Mission" something. *Mission: Tacos* whenever she craved Mexican food, *Mission: GOOP* the night we made our own face masks with brown sugar and honey, even *Mission: Danger Zone* for a double nod to Tom Cruise the time we snuck out during a sleepover to go cruising.

"I'm so glad you're here," I whispered to her as we huddled together in the compact kitchen of the cabin, shoving candles into a sheet of grocery store cake that was decorated with lumps of what were supposed to be soccer balls.

She dropped her head and leaned into me, her hand holding out the rest of the candles we needed to put in. "You didn't tell Liz about *Mission: BJ*, did you?"

"Please. Can you imagine?" I pretended to stab myself in the heart.

It wasn't that Liz was totally unsympathetic to my situation with Rhys. She just didn't seem to have any grasp of what high school relationships were supposed to look like or the kind of effort required to maintain them. There were entire days when she didn't respond to texts in our group thread, and we were her best friends. The chances of her understanding my fear that Rhys would get bored of me were less than zero. She seemed to have the same idea about relationships as my mom—that one day you'd just grow up and get married without ever having had any kind of physical contact with another person. No muss, no fuss. Literally.

"Are you nervous?" Candace whispered.

I managed something between a shrug and a head shake. "I just need some drinks first. I'm sure it'll be fine."

So what if I'd never come close to doing anything like this before? According to Candace, I just needed to go into it with confidence. And covered teeth. *If Savannah could do it with braces, anyone can*, Candace had reassured me.

Savannah was Liz's next-door neighbor, whom Candace and I had been friends with since middle school. When Liz moved next door to her, we all became close friends—until Savannah got her braces off, made the cheerleading squad, and became obsessed with things like football games and spray tans. I'd always assumed Liz stayed friends with her out of convenience because she relied on Savannah for rides to school, but who knew why any friendships worked. After all, Rhys was friends with Tommy for some reason. High school didn't sort itself out into tidy little cliques based around one common interest like it did in the movies.

Candace and I eventually finished placing all the candles and lit them, carefully walking the cake over to the table, where Drew had portioned out eight cups of sour apple Pucker for us to toast with. After a rousing rendition of "Happy Birthday" and Liz taking a solid two minutes to come up with her wish and blow out the candles, I cut up the cake and handed out pieces to everyone. It was a weird juxtaposition, green-and-pink-frosted birthday cake with alcohol. Like I was somehow still a kid at a birthday party while also adult enough to drink and give my sort-of boyfriend a blow job later.

After toasting Liz, I tipped my cup back, the neon green concoction sloshing against my lips like liquid sugar. I nearly spit it out as the cloying sweetness threw my throat into spasms. If I had thought beer was an acquired taste, this melted Jolly Rancher drink was so much worse. I squeezed my eyes shut and gulped down as much as I could without puking. The faster I could get this drink down, the better.

Looking at everyone else's faces around the table, it was clear most of us felt similarly.

"Jesus, what is this?" Tommy grimaced, staring at his cup like he expected it to read *Nuclear Waste*.

"Gray said to get something sweet," Rhys said, pouring himself another cup and passing the bottle around.

"I meant like orange juice and rum," Grayson said with a "don't blame me" face.

Rhys shrugged. "Blame Paul. He's the one who bought it. There're other flavors in the kitchen. Next time you're all welcome to buy your own stuff."

No one dared complain after that. Rhys was the only one with a sibling both old enough and reckless enough to buy alcohol for a bunch of high school kids. Even if Wendy had been able to, something told me she wouldn't be the type of sister to do such things.

"I like it," Savannah piped up, her squeaky, high-pitched voice always cheerful. "I think it goes well with the birthday cake."

Tommy set his cup aside and clapped his hands together mischievously. "Speaking of birthdays . . . what kind of games are we going to play at this party?" He wiggled his eyebrows suggestively. "Spin the bottle? Truth or dare? Strip poker?"

My stomach gave a flutter at the thought of confessing secrets of any kind or taking off my clothes in front of Rhys's friends. Then again, I'd already gulped down two glasses of the sickly sweet alcohol. I could count this whole experience as checking a box on my Recently Revamped™ high school experience Bingo card. At least then I'd know for sure I wasn't uptight.

"I'm down to play whatever," Savannah said with a pointed look at Tommy. She wasn't one for subtlety. Or taste.

I'd heard Savannah and some of her squad mates giggling before as they discussed the finer points of Tommy's physique. Clearly they'd never had any kind of extended interaction with him. There was only so much a pretty face and cut abs could compensate for.

Liz made a face. "Ew. It's not that kind of party. And if any of you start taking off your clothes, I'm kicking you out."

"Come on," Tommy protested. "I gave you other choices. Let's liven this thing up. You're eighteen. If we can't take you to a strip club, you could at least have the decency to let people take their clothes off here." He rubbed his hands together, flexing the forearms already exposed beneath the green sleeves of his baseball tee.

"Don't be that guy," Rhys admonished him. "Can't we just sit here and drink? Why do we have to play anything?"

Great. So Rhys didn't want to see me naked either.

I drained another cup and went to retrieve a new bottle from the kitchen. This one was cherry, giving me hopes that it might taste better. It didn't. I drank it anyway, ignoring the screams of revulsion coming from the back of my throat.

"I could put on some music," Drew volunteered.

"No one likes that hee-haw country shit you listen to," Tommy said. He pointed at me. "And we're not listening to whatever boring violin shit you like either."

"I'm curious, can you even name another genre of music outside of what *you* specifically listen to?" I asked from the kitchen, pouring myself another cup. I'd come here determined not to let Tommy get under my skin and ruin my night, but it got tiring to always listen to him loudly proclaim his useless opinions. Even if I'd never admit that to Liz.

"What the hell is a 'genre'?" he asked.

I smiled sweetly. "Exactly."

"Enough!" Liz's voice silenced even Tommy. "This is *my* birthday. I'm glad you're all here, but we're going to do what *I* want."

She took a deep breath. "We're going to play a board game." She held up her hand before Tommy could add anything. "I'm choosing the game. And everyone is keeping their clothes on." She gave an extra pointed stare at Savannah, who'd just pulled off her socks. Either Savannah had anticipated that it would come to this or she kept her feet impeccably maintained all the time, with sparkly toe rings on the second and fourth toes of her right foot, a silver chain linking the two to her unnaturally tanned ankle. How that could have been comfortable to wear under a pair of socks was beyond me.

Drew tasked himself with starting a fire while Liz rooted through the game cabinet. There were shouts from everyone as Tommy and Grayson took jabs at Drew's small size and whether he had the ability to lift the logs into the raised fireplace and Candace shouted over *them* to veto Mille Bornes as the chosen game. Eventually Liz settled on Trivial Pursuit.

There were lots of groans and protests from the group, especially Grayson and Drew, who generally refused to play anything that didn't involve a deck of cards, but we all settled in to play anyway. Candace stepped in and quickly assigned the teams, making sure to pair me with Rhys before anyone could argue we'd be too strong of a team. Thank god for Candace.

As the game went along, Rhys and I settled into a groove, much like we did in AP Bio, sorting out clues and answers together. It was sort of weird to be almost comfortable with him around his friends without having to play the role of the cool girl. Then again, I'd lost count of how many cups of the diabetes drink I'd had. Everything felt more comfortable when the sharp edges of my brain were dulled.

By the time the game finished, everyone was either fully buzzed or drunk, and I was sitting so close to Rhys I was nearly in his lap, our knees and elbows bumping constantly, sending tiny waves of happiness through me. We celebrated our victory with a chaste high five while the second-place team of Candace and Drew booed raucously, Candace's loud voice overwhelming Drew's.

I had been wrong. This was so much better than strip poker. My cheeks were beginning to hurt from smiling so much. I almost wished I hadn't answered the last question correctly so we could have kept playing.

But I only had one night to execute my plan. And unlike Liz, Candace understood the importance of my getting time alone with Rhys. She'd offered to sleep in the living room with the guys so I could have him sleep with me in one of the two bedrooms, but there wasn't a way for me to ask him that didn't involve, you know, actually asking him, and I sure as hell wasn't going to do that in front of all his friends. So instead, Candace and I had worked out a signal for her to send him in after me in a way that appeared less orchestrated and more . . . romantically unexpected. Candace was a master choreographer.

"I'm tired," I fake yawned, head lolling against the overstuffed couch behind me and arms stretching above my head. I wasn't quite as tipsy as I pretended to be, but I couldn't stomach the thought of another glass of the synthetic-tasting liquor. I also didn't want to be sloppy drunk in case I did something embarrassing like throw up when his penis was in my mouth or something.

"You're red," Grayson whistled.

"It's hot in here," Savannah piped up, taking the opportunity to peel off her paper-thin shirt in slow motion to reveal a low-cut, spaghetti strap camisole beneath. Disregarding the target of her efforts, I had to applaud Savannah's approach. I should have studied her more before deciding to attempt my own seduction. She certainly seemed to have had more practice at it.

Sadly for her, Tommy didn't seem to notice. "Your face looks sunburned, Covey."

I could feel my cheeks growing hotter as everyone swiveled their attention toward me. I knew my face turned red when I drank, but I didn't need Tommy pointing it out in front of everyone. Who gave him the right to nickname me, anyway? Even Rhys didn't have a nickname for me.

I pressed my hands against my forehead, absorbing the warmth that radiated from it into my hands, as if that would also take away the color. I wasn't going to look very alluring and sexy if my face was the color of a beet.

Rhys leaned toward me. "You *are* really red." His sharp eyes zeroed in on me like a doctor evaluating a sick patient.

"Like Savannah said, it's really hot in here," I replied more loudly than I intended.

"Do you want me to get you some water or something? Maybe you shouldn't drink anymore."

Oh god. I looked so bad my own boyfriend was cutting me off.

"I'm fine," I insisted.

"You should go lie down," Candace suggested, her eyes signaling to me that it was really more of a command than a suggestion.

This wasn't how I wanted to make my exit—under a cloud of suspicion that I couldn't hold my liquor as well as everyone else—but I wasn't exactly convincing anyone it wasn't true at the moment. And at least it would be dark and cool in the room, unlike the sweltering living room, where Drew kept throwing logs on the fire like we were the Ingalls Wilder family fighting for survival in the middle of winter or something.

Jesus. Maybe I *was* drunk. The entire literary canon of log cabin dwellers and I somehow settled on a semifictionalized account of someone's life I read once in second grade. Abraham Lincoln. Paul Bunyan. Henry David Thoreau. The grandpa in *Heidi*. The precogs in *Minority Report*. Even Kathy Bates's character's house in *Misery*. Was that a log cabin? It was sort of cabin-y. It was remote, anyway.

Wait, what I was I thinking?

"Rhys, maybe you should take June in there to make sure she's okay," Candace said sweetly, continuing to shoot me covert messages with her eyes. This one was warning me, *Get it together*.

I gave a hard blink to reset my brain and grabbed the waiting hands of Rhys, who pulled me up from the floor with ease. He was tall, but I'd never really thought of him as being particularly strong. I just figured his long limbs gave him an advantage because . . . leverage . . . or something.

"Easy there, Wobbles. I've got you." Rhys scooped me up and headed toward the room.

I blinked again and looked at the floor wavering far below me. I wasn't imagining things. Rhys was actually carrying me, his arms cradling the middle of my back and behind my knees.

My heart floated and fluttered like a helium balloon in a breeze. This was it. This was really it. I needed to unfog my brain because *this was it*.

Mission: BJ. Tom Cruise had nothing on me.

———

I kicked the door shut as we walked in, plunging us both into the inky black of the unlit bedroom. Even with him literally carrying me, I couldn't see anything beyond my own face.

I wasted no time. I flung my arms around his neck and spun my body so that my legs wrapped around his waist while my lips dove at him like a cat trying to tackle a laser point. Only in this case, the cat was intoxicated and my attempt to pull his head toward me in the dark was met instead with a crashing of his nose into my chin as we tumbled backward onto the ground.

"Ow ow ow!" I yelped, rubbing the back of my head where it had hit what felt like the corner of the bed frame.

I could hear Rhys stumbling to his feet a foot or so away, my vision starting to adjust enough that I could at least identify him apart from the rest of the darkness.

"Uh, are you okay?" he asked.

Mortified and possibly concussed. Thanks.

I scrambled to my feet. "I didn't realize you were such a lightweight."

"I didn't realize I was going to be required to do gymnastics exercises in here."

Shit. I couldn't afford to fall into our usual friend-zone banter right now. I needed to strike first to gain the upper hand. Xiān fǎ zhì rén.

Those Chinese philosophers really had a proverb for every situation.

I dove in again, more carefully this time, and looped my arms around his neck—really just my fingertips, since I didn't have the benefit of being hoisted several feet in the air this time. But it was enough for me to be able to lock on and sway my body toward him, and he mercifully held on to me without us falling.

His arm moved to encircle my waist and I felt a tingle crawl up my spine. "You feeling all right?" he asked.

"I'm *excellent*," I purred. He probably couldn't see me batting my eyelashes at him, but there was no mistaking the flirtation in my voice.

"Why don't we get you to bed?"

"Yes, why don't you?"

Rhys said nothing but shuffled me a couple of steps toward the bed, yanking back the covers on one side.

"Aren't you going to join me?" I asked in my most innocent voice, sitting on the bed and tucking my legs under me. I piled all my hair over my right shoulder, running my thumb and forefinger over the pieces closest to my face, as if my always-straight hair needed additional straightening. The room was still too dark to see anything more than outlines, but it at least helped me *feel* more alluring.

Rhys cleared his throat twice, the floor creaking as he shifted his weight from foot to foot. "I, uh, should probably get back out there. Let you get some rest."

"I'm not tired."

"You said you were tired and that's why you came in here."

Jesus Christ. He could not be this dense, could he?

"I wanted you in here with me," I said. It was surprising how easily the words came. The Pucker turned out to have been a good choice.

"Why is that?" Rhys's voice sounded unsteady in the dark, his imposing figure only an outline in front of me.

I inhaled a gulp of air. It was now or never.

Still perched on the bed, I reached over and brought his hand to my mouth. Slowly I bit the tip of his middle finger before sucking it into my mouth. A small yelp escaped from Rhys.

I took it as a sign to continue.

I lavished more attention on it before adding in his ring finger, grazing them with just the lightest touch from my teeth. Rhys's breathing had increased to a ragged pant, and the only indication of the party still going on outside our door was the tiniest sliver of light on the floor.

I had him. I could feel it.

I couldn't see his face, but the way his hand stayed raised when I ran my tongue down it a final time told me I'd finally achieved what I'd set out to do.

He wanted me. Me. Only me.

I was no longer June, the smart girl from class who occasionally made funny jokes. I was no longer the girl who was good enough for kisses behind doors, but not good enough for kisses in public. I had the upper hand now. He wanted *me.* And I was the only person who could give him what he wanted. I could bond him to me. Catch his heart.

"Holy shit, June," he breathed. His hand was still raised, hovering mere inches from me. Looking for a place to set it, he found the top of my head before gently running his fingers through the length of my hair. Adrenaline coursed through my body, sending hot waves downward toward a single point of interest.

I loved the feeling of having his hands in my hair. He knew that. He was telling me, in the best way he knew how, that I was special to him. That I meant as much to him as he meant to me.

His hands kneaded the sides of my head, his fingers gripping handfuls of my hair as he tried to steady his breathing. I leaned forward and slipped one hand into the waistband of his jeans as my other hand went to unbutton them.

He jumped back like I'd electrocuted him. "Whoa. Hey. Wait a sec."

"What happened?" I reached out to reassure him, to bring him closer to me, but he was out of reach. Only the lower half of his body was illuminated by the sliver of light coming in from under the door, leaving me to guess at his mental state. It didn't seem like a good sign that he'd physically jumped away from me.

He paused a beat, letting the silence linger between us. "You should go to bed. I'll see you in the morning." Before I could protest, he shuffled toward the door and went back outside.

CHAPTER SEVEN

I returned home from the cabin exhausted and mortified. In all the worst-case scenarios I imagined, I'd never considered the possibility that Rhys just wasn't interested in hooking up with me. At least, not in the way he and his friends apparently talked about.

I gave my parents the briefest of hellos after dropping off Candace, Liz, and Savannah, pretending to be too tired for any further details of my weekend and trudging up to my room amidst shouting reminders from my mom to practice the piece for my competition next month. Like I had energy for that.

I collapsed into my desk chair, opened my computer, and began surfing for PDFs of sheet music instead. I needed something that would distract me from the disaster that was my life; something that wasn't Paganini or Mendelssohn or Brahms or someone else who'd been dead for a hundred years. Pop music, no. Jazz, definitely no. I scrolled past pages and pages of Top 40 hits, Latin hits, and dozens of other songs that were far too upbeat for my sour mood.

I needed music to hide in; music to distract me from the fact that my de facto boyfriend practically sprinted out of a room to avoid being alone with me—that I was so awful, so intolerable, I couldn't even get him to stay for the promise of the one thing every guy claimed to want.

I slouched over my computer and banged my head on the keyboard several times, hoping it would knock me unconscious and I could wake up to find out this had all been a dream. Instead, Metallica came pouring out of the speakers. My head shot up in surprise.

Great. My forehead had managed to queue up the playlist I'd created the day after Rhys told me they were his favorite band. The entire world was mocking me.

Screw it. Metallica was right. Nothing else mattered. My life was falling apart, I could never face Rhys again, and the only distress my parents could possibly imagine was my not getting in enough practice time.

I did a quick search for the sheet music to the song that was playing, tightened my bow, and began to play along to the music. It wasn't the same as listening to it on full volume with headphones on, but adding a violin to it made the song sound more melancholy. One violin, all alone and out of place. Just like me. Nothing else matters.

My fingers bore into the fingerboard harder than they should, as if I could squeeze the life out of my disappointment just by pressing the right combination of strings. My anger poured out of me, binding each atom of my feelings to an atom of music and setting them adrift into the air, away from me. It was cathartic.

I sank deeper into the music, no longer worried about hitting every note precisely, but feeling the rhythm of the music and my connection to the emotion of it. It had been so long since I'd played something I loved deeply. Instead, playing had become almost clinical—something I executed with robotic precision, counting down the minutes until I could stop. Like everything else, it was just something I needed to get through. Another hurdle.

This—this song, this music—felt like a scenic road, winding through hills and valleys; a journey in its own right. The crescendos and decrescendos were less like obstacles I had to clear and more like a gentle roller coaster I'd chosen to ride. And to think, if James Hetfield had stuck with classical piano, he might never have created this.

Just as I hit the beat when the drums kicked in, my door flew open. My mom entered, no knock necessary, hefting a basket of clean laundry that was almost as big as her.

"What are you doing?" I demanded, dropping my violin to my side and quickly muting the volume on my computer. She didn't deserve to be a part of my private moments.

"Clean clothes," she said, holding up a stack of folded clothes.

"You couldn't have done that earlier? Like before I got home? Or literally all day yesterday?"

"Lots of laundry to do. Dān qiāng pī mǎ—single gun, single horse."

I gave an exasperated sigh. My patience was already raggedly thin from having to pretend everything was fine on the drive home from the cabin. I didn't have time for her nonsense proverbs. "No one knows what that means."

"Take on difficult task alone."

"A little dramatic for laundry, don't you think?"

She said nothing, but continued to pull open drawers and place stacks of folded clothes in them. She never bothered to take note that I separated my shirts by sleeve length and weight—she just dumped them all in and I had to go back and sort through them.

"Mom, just leave them on the bed. I'll put them away later."

She held up a thong. "Why you wear this underwear? It covers nothing!"

My eyes widened at the scrap of black fabric dangling from her fingertips. "Mom!" I jumped up from my chair and snatched it from her grasp.

"I just ask. Where you get this kind of underwear? Like dental floss! You like the feeling of something in your crack?"

"None of your business! Can you just get out of my room? You're interrupting my practice!"

The truth was, Candace had given me the underwear as a gift a week ago to wear to the cabin because she said I'd feel more confident if I had on sexy underwear. But they were new, so I'd thrown them in the wash and forgotten all about them until my mom was holding them up like something she'd fished out of the drain. It was just as well. The night had been uncomfortable enough. I didn't need underwear "in my crack," as my mom said.

She peered across the room and over my shoulder at my open computer screen, because of course she did. That was the real reason she'd come in. That way she could ask me personal questions under the guise of being *concerned* since she just happened to be here dropping off laundry instead of the nosy mom who barged into my room with no excuse.

"What you playing?" she asked, moving her head to try to see around the blockade I'd fashioned with my body.

"Music. Are you done here?" I asked. I was impatient to get back to being alone before she could launch into one of her speeches about responsibility or something Confucius said or who knows what else. I wanted to wallow about the state of my life, and her incessant questions were getting in the way.

She frowned. "That doesn't look like your practice piece. You know Wendy say her program only have one spot left for violinist. They going to be looking for first-place winner, not third place. You want them to give to another player instead?"

"Yes, Mom, that's exactly what I want."

"Then where you go, huh? Northwestern top school for doctors. You and Wendy go together. Better to have you both in one place." She said it as though we'd discussed it a million times instead of just her saying it AT me. As if she could declare her way to a more studious daughter—one who didn't slack off on practicing her competition pieces because no matter what she did she always ended up in third place anyway.

I exhaled loudly, my emotions barely held together by Scotch tape and threatening to spill out and drown the both of us. "Did it ever occur to you I might not want to be in the same place as Wendy?"

My mom scoffed. "You think everything about what you want? You go where they take you. You lucky you have Wendy there so they see interest in you. No one else going to offer you full ride."

I didn't want to rebut with the two partial offers I'd gotten from schools on the East Coast. My mom wasn't going to be impressed with a school tab that cost forty-five thousand dollars a year instead of sixty and required that I major in music instead of premed. Especially if a school like Northwestern dangled the possibility of practically no cost. Analyzing numbers was literally what she did for a living.

The only problem was that my mom refused to consider the possibility that just because Northwestern took Wendy didn't mean they'd take me. I'd been dragging my feet on applying, not only because I didn't really want to go there, but also because I couldn't imagine the humiliation I'd feel if I wasn't actually accepted. After all, I hadn't spent my four years of high school padding my resume with student government and volunteer groups like Wendy had. I'd counted on distracting my parents from their all-Northwestern dream with an acceptance to a decent midtier school—preferably far away from here—only I hadn't managed to tempt anyone into extending me an offer for a full ride on either the academic *or* music side yet. Everything was a half measure, worthy only of someone who was *near* the top but not actually *the* top of anything. My third-place legacy was finally coming home to roost.

I'd already worked my way through half my spreadsheet with no luck. If I couldn't get somewhere like Creighton, stuck in the middle of nowhere Nebraska, to offer me a vast sum of money, what chance did I have with a school like Northwestern? My parents just refused to see the writing on the wall.

"And what if they don't offer me a full ride, huh? What then?"

I hadn't meant to give voice to my deepest fear—that I'd not only fall spectacularly short of Wendy's ten offers, but that I might end up with *no* offers, not even from the place where I was supposed to have an "in." At the same time, I was desperate for an answer—a backup plan for my backup plan. I didn't want to be left alone in free fall like Britney Lee, staring down a hundred thousand dollars in future debt and cut off from my entire family.

My mom nodded confidently. "You get full ride. Northwestern will offer." She announced it the same way she announced all her expectations. There was only one result she'd tolerate and it was my job to figure out how to make it happen or suffer the consequences. "But not if you don't apply."

"Okay, okay, I'll send it in."

My usual annoyance with this conversation was being overshadowed by my unstable emotions. I'd held off the urge to cry until now, but the stress of arguing was too much for me to handle. If I didn't get her out of here in the next five seconds, I'd break down sobbing and have to listen to some proverb about how tears were tools of the weak or something. I drew in a shallow breath, my entire torso clenched to keep it all inside of me.

"Can I get back to practicing now?"

She eyed my computer again. Maybe she couldn't see clearly enough across the room to spot the jagged Metallica logo printed across the top of the sheet music and she believed I really was about to diligently practice my competition piece without another reminder. Maybe she knew me well enough to understand that

I hadn't just been wandering aimlessly and that I'd put together a whole spreadsheet of options more viable than banking on a unicorn scholarship from a school that declined 81 percent of its applicants. Or maybe, for once, she would just remain silent and trust me to figure things out without her hovering over me, critiquing my every step.

I sent a silent prayer to any possible deity currently spying on me, regardless of their religious affiliation, promising to submit my application to Northwestern today if my mom would leave my room. I had even come up with the title to my personal essay within the last thirty seconds: Smash the Pots and Sink the Boats—the Chinese proverb about Qin dynasty general Xiang Yu, who cut off the possibility of retreat during battle by destroying his own troops' supplies. I'd effectively done the same this past weekend at the cabin, and now had to find a way forward or succumb to my humiliation.

Obviously my essay wouldn't mention blow jobs explicitly, but I could easily find a way to wax poetic about the larger implications of choosing a school to attend and how it irrevocably shapes your future path. It didn't matter that I had no idea what I wanted that path to look like—school administrators ate that kind of stuff up.

I could feel the pull of Metallica calling me back to my chair, where I could disappear from prying eyes and drown in self-pity for a little while longer before having to face the inevitable. A last supper before the illusion of a limitless future was destroyed. *Just let me finish the song and I'll write my stupid application*, I pleaded silently. *Today. Right now. I swear.* Anything to get her out of my space.

She finally turned to leave, murmuring, "Gàn huó bú yóu dōng lèi sǐ yě wú gōng—working without obeying the boss bring only hard work and no merit."

She shut the door behind her.

CHAPTER EIGHT

As it turned out, I didn't need to worry about facing Rhys on Monday. Or Tuesday. Or Wednesday. Or Thursday. For four days he didn't show up at school. Sure, maybe he was sick. Maybe he'd gotten the flu. Or the plague. Or mono. From not kissing me.

Or, more likely, maybe he was avoiding me. It wasn't like his parents paid attention to whether or not he came to school. He could easily skip an entire week or two before an administrator would sound the alarm. They had enough kids to worry about who *weren't* easily passing all their classes.

So when Candace issued an invitation to go ice skating with her and Savannah after school that Thursday, I took it. I still had a practically new pair of white figure skates from the time my parents decided to have Wendy and me try figure skating. My mom was convinced at one time that one of us would grow up to be the next Michelle Kwan—but an Olympic gold medalist. *What a waste, all that practice just for silver*, she would say, shaking her head anytime Michelle Kwan's name came up. Apparently World Championship golds weren't worth anything. When neither

Wendy nor I showed any particular talent for it and my parents realized how much indoor daily ice time cost, they quietly hung up our skates without another word and doubled our practice time for violin instead.

"Who you go with?" my mom asked, poking her nose into the laundry room as I fished through the bin of miscellaneous hats and mittens that had accumulated over the years.

"Just Savannah and Candace," I replied.

"Who is Savannah? I know her?"

"Mom, I've known her since middle school. She used to come over. She had purple braces? Squeaky high voice?"

She nodded, even though it was clear she still didn't remember. "When last time you use those?" She nodded toward the pristine white skates laced together and slung over my shoulder.

"I thought you'd be happy I'm getting more use out of them. You were the one who complained about how much they cost."

My mom sighed, the weariness of my insolence weighing heavily on her drooped shoulders. "Why you always accuse me of complaining? I just tell you the price of things so you know. Bù dānjiā bù zhī chái mǐ guì—you have no idea how much rice and fuel cost without being head of household."

"I don't think ice skates count as a household necessity."

My mom arched an eyebrow. "You know how much your violin cost?"

Oh god. She could bring anything back to the price of our violins. The lessons, the equipment, the mileage expended driving us to lessons. It was like she saw us as endless expenditures that only drained her bottom line. I never asked to play violin. It's not like I was begging her for new bows or expensive rosin or literally anything. Wendy was the one who had always gone to the exclusive camps and national competitions my parents deemed "not worth it" for me because I wasn't as good as her.

It was like I was a prisoner, chained to my instrument against my will, then being charged for the privilege of owning it. The fact that so many other Asian kids happily accepted their fates only made me more seem ungrateful in comparison.

It wasn't worth delaying my plans to have an argument I'd never win.

"I'll be back before curfew," I said, squeezing past her to grab my shoes from the hallway.

"It's only afternoon. You come home for dinner."

"I told Candace I'd have dinner at her house. She's giving me a ride."

"You ask me to go there for dinner?"

I bit my lip. "No, but I didn't know you'd be home today."

For some reason my mom always happened to be around lately. Like she was just hovering, watching my every move, waiting for me to screw up. Good thing she didn't know how badly I'd already botched my love life.

She nodded with finality. "I see you home for dinner. Daddy is working late at the hospital so just you and me. I make your favorite, mapo tofu. Extra spicy."

I twisted my grimace into a tortured smile. "Just you and me. Great."

I turned to leave, but I could feel her frowning gaze on my back, boring a hole through the Sam's Club no-name puffer jacket she swore was "just as good" as the North Face one I'd asked for.

I whirled back around. "What?"

"I don't say anything," she said.

I tapped my foot impatiently. "I know you're thinking something critical. Just say it already."

"Why you think all I do is criticize? I say things to help you. Liángyào kǔ kǒu—good medicine tastes bitter."

Even with the proverbs she used often enough for me to memorize, she still always repeated the English translation afterward as if she were reading it from a textbook. Those were our entrenched roles: her as the wise teacher, me as the ignorant student whose only job was to memorize these proverbs and absorb them as gospel. "Yeah yeah, whatever. Just get it over with."

She shrugged innocently.

"Fine. Whatever. I'm going outside to wait for Candace." I turned to go.

"You not going to be cold with those pants?"

There it was.

I sighed loudly. "What's wrong with my pants?"

"They don't look very warm."

"They don't need to be very warm. I'm going ice skating, not sledding. My legs will be moving."

She pursed her lips. "They so tight I can see the outline of your butt."

"They're yoga pants, Mom. They're supposed to be fitted."

"You not going to do yoga."

"That's just the name of them! They're not only for doing yoga. You can use them for any kind of workout."

"So you want people to see your butt when you work out?"

Good Lord, it was like she had a particular knack for making literally anything about what I was wearing.

"Yes, Mom. I'm wearing these pants especially *for* Candace and Savannah, who most definitely want to look at my butt while we ice skate."

She shook her head at my insolence. "I think you going to be cold. No butt to show if you freeze it off."

"I'll be fine."

"You don't know how cold it will be. Change into warmer pants, just in case."

I stayed rooted to my spot. "I'll be fine," I insisted.

She rushed back to the laundry room and grabbed a pair of my dad's waterproof windbreaker pants and thrust them into my hands. "Here. You take. You thank me later."

There was no use in arguing. I would just leave them in the car and tell her I had put them on. But that didn't mean I had to thank her for them. "Fine," I said. "I'll see you later."

I walked out the door as my mom called after me, "We eat at five thirty."

————

I slid into the back seat of Candace's ancient Buick. Savannah was already in the front passenger seat. "Your car is looking shiny.

What'd you wash it or something?" I asked, quickly closing the door to keep more heat from escaping into the cold November air.

Candace turned to me, the pointy red winter hat on her head giving her a distinct garden gnome vibe. "I work at a car wash? What's with the extra pants?"

"It was a joke, darling. And don't ask." I tossed them into the empty space next to me.

"Hey, June," Savannah chirped. "You ready for some hockey?"

"Hockey? I thought we were going ice skating."

Candace and Savannah exchanged glances, Candace's pierced nose wrinkling. "We are," Candace said, trying to clear the guilty expression from her face. "We just might also have hockey sticks in our hands while we skate."

I stretched my seat belt so I could lean forward, my arms resting on the center console. "Why do I get the feeling you two are keeping something from me?"

More glances between them. Finally, Candace spoke.

"We're going to this guy on the hockey team's house. He has a rink in his backyard. There might be a couple of guys there."

My eyes widened. "Hockey players?" I shrieked. "Like Tommy?"

If I wasn't ready to face Rhys yet I certainly wasn't in the mood to face Tommy and his inevitable barrage of questions and comments about our relationship status. I hoped Rhys hadn't told his friends about what happened at the cabin, but I wouldn't put it past Tommy to ask me about it anyway.

"We don't know that he'll be there!" Savannah exclaimed, her voice shrill with defensiveness. "He might not be."

"*Might* not?"

Candace cut in. "We didn't want to tell you because you might not come and I think it's good for you to get out and get your mind off . . . last weekend," she finished judiciously.

Savannah nodded sympathetically, causing me to punch Candace in the arm. Savannah and I might have been close in middle school, but she was more like an outer-circle friend now. Not someone I wanted to confess to about my sort-of boyfriend literally running away from me.

"Oh, relax, I didn't say anything," Candace said with a wave of her hand.

"She didn't have to," Savannah chirped. "I was there, remember? No guy walks out of a room with his girlfriend in it unless there's something seriously wrong with him. You could do so much better." She leaned forward to change the radio station, adding airily, "It's not a crime to keep your options open. No one wants to get stuck in one place too long. High school is too short."

I opened my mouth to protest, but there wasn't really anything I could say to refute what Savannah had just said that wouldn't totally incriminate me. I slumped back into my seat, no longer looking forward to my afternoon. This was supposed to be a fun distraction. Instead, I'd been betrayed by my best friend, all so I could go and make a fool of myself in front of a bunch of guys I didn't know or care about. As if I didn't feel uncool enough as it was. I sulked the rest of the way there while Candace and Savannah happily sang along to the radio.

When we arrived, we were greeted by a gigantic professional-looking ice rink complete with boards, boxes, and painted lines in the side yard of an otherwise normal-looking house. There was even a giant manual scoreboard hovering over the far side of the rink with a narrow deck encircling it and a ladder stretching down to the ground some twelve feet below. The entire structure was a monstrosity, like a volcano that had risen up from the ground in the middle of an otherwise normal suburban neighborhood. It was jarring.

"This is Marcus's house," Savannah whispered as we climbed out of the car, pointing to one of the boys already on the ice. "He's only a sophomore, but Tommy said at the cabin that he'll probably make varsity this year."

Impressive. Maybe Marcus had tiger parents, judging from the amount of money they must have sunk into building this personal rink. Back when my mom considered pushing figure skating as our future, she'd had Wendy and me create an ice rink in our backyard by carting buckets of water from inside to dump on the snow and stamp it down until it froze. I could only imagine the tab for what we would have "owed" our parents in scholarship money if she'd paid for something like this. The only things missing were the announcer's box and championship banners hanging from nonexistent rafters.

"Hey, Marcus, great house!" Savannah called out, her voice rising in pitch like it did whenever she was flirting. "I can't wait to get out there and do some spins around you!"

I gave Candace a look like, *Really? A sophomore?* Not that I was on the most solid relationship footing at the moment, but at least I had the sense not to lower my standards to someone who wasn't even old enough to drive. I could only imagine the comments Wendy would have for me about that.

Candace shrugged. "He's not bad-looking."

At least Tommy wasn't here. There were three guys on the ice, accompanied by two girls I recognized from Savannah's cheerleading squad. We laced up our skates on one of the two players' benches installed just outside the rink and headed out to the ice.

A blur of neon orange skated past before backtracking toward us, his skates sending a spray of snow several inches into the air as his blades scraped to a stop along the ice. "Oh, *hello*, ladies," he said, as if our sudden appearance was the most interesting thing in the entire world. His muddy green eyes took us in for a moment before they settled directly on me. "I'm Brad," he said with a grin, a small dark spot in the corner of his mouth where a tooth should have been, peeking out like a hidden secret.

A sudden flush came over me, like I'd been sent here to find the most rugged outdoorsman and stumbled across Brad in his neon orange stocking cap. Even his nose was a little crooked, with a red slash across its bridge, like he'd gotten into a fight with a bear and emerged with only minor injuries.

Another spray of snow flew into the air as a second body stopped in front of us. "Hey. I'm Justin," he said. This guy had no hat on, the cold air turning his pale cheeks and the tips of his ears the same reddish color as his hair. Next to Brad, Justin seemed sort of sickly, like those pale kids whose parents had to chase them around to slather on sunscreen. Not that Brad was any darker than Justin—just more . . . hardy.

"June," I said politely, trying very hard to look at both guys equally and not just the one favored by Darwin to propagate the human species in case of the apocalypse.

Candace introduced herself, then added, "You must not go to Pine Grove, because there are only two guys at our school who can pull off that bright-ass orange color, and I don't recognize either of you."

Candace. Never one to mince words.

I wondered which two guys from our school she had in mind. That hat was aggressively orange. Not that Brad couldn't pull it off—the blond waves escaping out the bottom of the hat softened the overall look.

Brad smiled, the dark spot in his mouth flashing again. "Cedar High. We're both seniors. But we grew up playing with Marcus and a bunch of the other guys from Pine Grove, so we all know each other."

"You're seniors who hang out with sophomores at other schools?" Candace asked, her eyes narrowing, like he would lie about such a thing. "That's not weird."

Brad jerked a thumb at the redhead. "Justin lives two doors down. The district line splits the neighborhood in two. Marcus invited us over to practice before the season starts. There were supposed to be more guys from your team coming, but they're not here yet?"

Ugh. The reminder that Tommy's arrival was still a possibility clouded the five seconds of relief I'd had from thinking about last weekend.

"Then again," Brad added, "it looks like you ladies could put up a good fight. Anyone who wears those pants to play hockey knows how to create a distraction." He winked at me.

Oh god, my mom was right about the pants. I could feel the heat rising to my cheeks as a buzz went through my body. But it also wasn't the worst thing in the world? I mean . . . he'd noticed. And commented.

I swallowed uncomfortably and fixed my eyes on the ice, determined not to be the one to turn my back first. Then it would just look like I was sticking my butt out there to be stared at.

"Guys! Come on! Let's get started!" Savannah's hot-pink-gloved hand was waving wildly from the other side of the ice, where she'd managed to hook her other arm into Marcus's. From the scowl on his face, he didn't seem overly pleased about it.

"We should split into teams," Candace announced as we assembled, ready to take over like she always did. It didn't matter that she was no sportier than I was—Candace just liked being the boss, and people usually just listened to her.

But before she could start assigning people to one side or the other, Brad slung an arm around my shoulder and called out, "Old-school NHL All-Star rules! North America versus the world. I call China."

He leaned down toward me. "How far off was I?" he whispered in a husky voice.

"Close enough," I squeaked.

Usually explaining to people that I was Taiwanese led to a frustrating exchange wherein I had to convince people that yes, Taiwan was a real country and no, I didn't mean Thailand. I didn't want to have that conversation while his face was three inches from mine.

"What part of the world are you from, Hoffman?" Marcus challenged.

"My grandpa's Swedish. That counts." He gave me another wink, his green eyes twinkling in the light.

This guy was seriously cute. And seriously flirty. But he also just could have been one of those people who flirted with whoever was closest and had a pulse. Like Savannah.

Candace rolled her eyes. "Yeah, and my great-great-grandma was from Estonia. That doesn't make me international."

"You can join our team," Brad said to her, his arm continuing to rest across my shoulders. My knees were uncomfortably locked into position and the muscles I'd admired earlier were far heavier than I anticipated, but I didn't dare move. *Be cool*, I reminded myself firmly.

"Guys versus girls," Marcus said firmly.

"No fair! That puts all you guys on one side." Savannah pouted.

"Not to mention there are three of you and five of us," I added. Not that I was lobbying for Brad's plan for me to stay on his team. If that was the way it worked out, and I had to constantly keep my eyes on him in case he needed to pass me the puck, so be it. I didn't make the rules.

"And all of you play hockey!" Savannah protested. "We can't compete against that!" Her voice became increasingly high-pitched with each word.

Marcus shrugged. "I guess you'll lose then. My rink, my rules."

Everyone mumbled in begrudging agreement. It was clear no one wanted to play this way except Marcus, but it *was* his rink. He had a lot of conviction for a sophomore.

Brad's arm lingered on me a moment longer before he broke away and began skating backward, still facing me. "I guess you'll have to do your best to cover me," he said with a glint in his eye, pushing a lock of blond hair back into his hat.

Oh my god. I was supposed to be taking a break from my boy problems, not creating news ones. But Brad was so cute. And the way he kept smiling at me sent little jolts of electricity up my spine. I'd never had someone flirt with me quite so blatantly. It felt nice.

I joined the huddle with Candace, Savannah, and the other cheerleaders while Candace barked instructions on passing and scoring. It wasn't like she was an expert on the sport, but Savannah was clearly only here to flirt with Marcus, and the other two girls were more than willing to let Candace take the lead.

We broke apart and scattered, mostly chasing the guys around the ice as they passed the puck back and forth a million times, using every fancy trick they could think of before scoring to make it seem like we had a chance. Every time Brad had the puck, he would skate close to me, passing the puck between my legs before zipping past me with a coy smile. I was starting to see why people liked sports.

Finally, Candace got her stick on the puck.

"Jujubee," she called out and whacked in my direction. I could see Brad skating toward me, his broad shoulders squared and ready to block me. I wouldn't be able to get past him, but I didn't mind the idea of him having to get close enough to stop me.

But before he could reach me, Savannah shrieked, "June, look out!" just before I felt the full force of a body colliding with my right shoulder.

I hit the boards with a loud *thud* before crumpling to the ice, an explosion of pain bursting through my body. My throat garbled a noise somewhere between a grunt and a moan.

"Marcus, what the hell is wrong with you, man?" Brad sounded angry. "You *checked* her!"

"She had the puck."

"This isn't a real game!"

"They wanted to come out and play with us, so I'm playing."

Brad skated over and crouched down next to me. "Hey there China Doll, you broken?" he asked softly, removing his hand from his glove before pushing the hair out of my face.

My cheeks flushed at the term of endearment even as I could feel bruises starting to form on both my hip and my right shoulder. And thanks to my not-warm-enough pants, it felt like the ice was burning straight through to my skin. Thinking about the water-resistant warm-ups I'd left in the car only added insult to my injury. "I'm fine. I'm totally fine," I choked out, trying my best to sound breezy and casual.

"Here, let me help you up." Brad grabbed my hands and pulled me to my feet.

"Marcus is an idiot," he grumbled, reaching over and briskly brushing the snow off the front and back of my pants. "I know he's only a sophomore, but damn, you'd think he'd have *some* kind of awareness of how to act around hot girls."

Either he was the slickest guy in the universe, spouting compliments as he slyly felt me up, or he was completely clueless to the fact that he just *touched my entire butt*. I was now blazingly aware of just how thin my yoga pants were.

"Are we playing or what?" Marcus demanded from the center of the ice, holding up the puck.

Savannah giggled. "I'll face off against you." Jesus. I couldn't believe she was still into him after seeing what a jerk he was.

Brad eyed me with concern, his hand now much more appropriately placed on my shoulder. "Are you sure you're okay? I could sit down with you for a while."

I shook my head. I didn't want to seem like the kind of girl who couldn't hang in a friendly little game of backyard hockey. Well, semifriendly.

"Aw shit, you're here?" Tommy's unmistakable voice rang out.

"Doerr!" Brad yelled back in surprise. "Long time no see."

Tommy made his way over to us. "Since when do you play hockey, Covey? I thought your little stick arms got tired from holding up your violin." He laughed at his own joke.

Brad looked at me. "You know this loser?"

"We go way back," Tommy said. "She's my buddy's girlfriend. She didn't tell you?"

Tommy said it casually, like it was an afterthought and not a pointed remark. Like there was any way he could have known that the entire lower half of my body still hadn't stopped tingling since Brad brushed the snow off me.

I turned my head away, my cheeks already starting to flush. I didn't want to see Brad's reaction to Tommy's helpful addition.

He *flirted with* me, I reminded myself. *There's no law against liking it.*

"Thank god she's smart enough to stay the hell away from *you*," Brad joked. But he'd scooted a few steps back, putting more distance between the two of us.

"Say that to me on the ice, you pussy," Tommy shot back.

"I'm already on it, what the hell are you waiting for?"

The two of them continued to talk trash back and forth and I slipped away, skating straight for Candace to make an impassioned plea for leaving. She asked no questions.

Savannah, on the other hand, asked a million. "Why do we have to go right now? I was just about to convince Marcus to play one-on-one with me," she whined, not picking up on the fact that Marcus would sooner skate over her face to score than participate in the kind of flirty hockey she was envisioning. Clearly she'd been living in a different world than the rest of us for the past hour and a half.

"Then get a ride home with someone else," Candace said dismissively. "I need to go."

"But *whyyyyyy*?" She drew out the word into a long wail like a literal squeaky wheel demanding grease for her needs.

"Savannah, I'm not your mom. Either get in the car or get a different ride. It's not difficult."

Savannah sulked back to the ice, presumably to find a way to stay and have another run at Marcus. She was nothing if not persistent. In eighth grade, she begged her mom for a tongue piercing for six months straight until she caved.

"Thanks," I said to Candace after Savannah was out of earshot.

"I'll be in the car," she said with a nod behind me.

I turned to find Brad making his way over.

"China! You ditching the team already? And taking Estonia with you?"

I did a quick scan to see if Tommy was close by, but he was across the ice with a group of hockey guys. Not that I wasn't allowed to talk to other people.

"Candace needs to go," I said, repeating the same lie she'd given Savannah. Candace was ride or die and I loved her for it. She didn't care if leaving early made her look uncool—she took the fall without me having to ask her to do it.

"I could have given you a ride home," he offered.

Gulp.

"You don't know where I live."

"I'm guessing you could point me in the right direction?" He rested his arm atop the boards and leaned casually against them. "That is, unless your boyfriend would have a problem with you being alone with another guy."

My throat caught at the word *boyfriend*.

"He's not really my boyfriend," I said.

I felt a stab in my gut the moment I said it, but there was no taking it back. I'd disowned Rhys—the exact thing I'd been trying to keep him from doing to me for the last two months.

Still, it wasn't totally inaccurate. We'd never used the terms *boyfriend* or *girlfriend*. I was just being . . . factual.

Brad's face perked up as he leaned toward me. "Really?" He pulled off his hat, revealing a matted head of blond hair that he quickly raked his fingers through. Christ Almighty, he was even hotter without the hat, with soft waves of light blond hair framing his grass-green eyes and charmingly crooked nose.

"Does that mean you'll give me your phone number?" Brad

held out his phone to me, his smile wide enough to reveal the space where his tooth was missing.

Holy shit.

This had escalated quickly. This was no longer light flirting on the ice or incidental bumps while jockeying for the puck. This was a hard do-not-cross line.

Or was it?

What was a phone number, anyway? Lots of people had my phone number. Even Tommy had my number. It wasn't like I kept it a secret. Was it that big of a deal if some guy wanted to text me now and again? It wasn't like I would be cheating on Rhys. If that was even a thing, considering we'd never made our relationship official.

Rhys and I were like a river with no source or a tree with no roots—wú yuán zhī shuǐ, wú běn zhī mù. We existed in the middle of no-man's-land—no relationship to betray because it had never been there to begin with. Kissing wasn't a contract, and Rhys had no reason to take me seriously because there was no threat that he would ever lose me. Tommy being here could turn out to be a blessing in disguise.

"Sure," I said as casually as I could, typing and retyping my name into his phone as my fingers struggled to hit the correct keys. I handed it back to him and fished out my own phone. "I guess that means you owe me yours."

"I'll do you one better," he said, tossing me his hat.

I knit my eyebrows in confusion. "How is this better?"

"I'm letting you borrow it. That way I know I'll see you again."

My heart jumped into my throat. So it wasn't just texting he had in mind. He wanted to see me.

Everything was a blurry jumble in my mind, but one thought jumped out at me: *I wish Wendy could see this.* Wendy, who was so sure I was some nerdy shut-in like she was, would probably die if she saw someone who looked like Brad asking for my phone number.

I felt my confidence shoot back up. "I don't know if I'm allowed to fraternize with the enemy," I said with a disinterested look. "I hear Cedar High is our biggest rival."

He grinned at me, his blond locks falling expertly over one eye. "You could always switch teams."

Maybe we were speaking in euphemisms or maybe we weren't. I glanced over at Tommy, who just stood there watching the two of us like he was recording the entire interaction in his mind.

"I'll think about it," I told him. "Thanks for the hat."

He saluted me, one arm resting on the ledge, his athletic body tilted with unimaginable swagger. "See you at the next game, China. Or sooner." His green eyes winked at me, outshining even his smile.

Whew. I'd barely made it out of there alive.

CHAPTER NINE

The next day, Rhys was at school. No explanation as to where he'd been the previous four days, no acknowledgment that he hadn't texted, no apologies for leaving me to complete our cat's eye dissection alone. He sat through class, one earbud in, listening to music and tuning out the rest of the world like we didn't exist.

I may have held strong by not contacting him after the cabin incident—though I'd considered more than once just blaming the alcohol and pretending I didn't remember—but my resolve was cracking. I just wanted him to say *something*.

"You haven't said anything about my hat," I said, rifling through my backpack for a pencil.

"Huh?" Rhys pulled out his earbud, like he'd just realized I was sitting next to him.

"You haven't said anything about my hat," I repeated.

I'd worn Brad's orange hunting stocking cap in school all day like some kind of hipster, daring Rhys to comment. He hadn't even noticed.

I dropped my backpack onto the ground with a loud thud.

"What's there to say?" Rhys asked.

"Maybe like, how does it look?"

Rhys shrugged, his face giving no hint of interest in having a conversation with me. "It's a hat for deer hunting. You don't hunt."

"So you don't like it?" My pencil remained poised above my paper, as if I was ready to document whatever answer he gave instead of the dissection wrap-up questions we were supposed to be working on.

His eyes looked heavy. "I don't know, what do you want me to say? It's a hat."

"Aren't you curious where I got it?"

For a moment I wanted to ask him how he felt about the fact that while he was hiding from me, some other guy was flirting with me and asking for my number. I wanted to ask him why some guy I'd just met was comfortable talking to me even when his friends were around, when Rhys clearly thought it was too much commitment. I wanted to ask if he even cared that some other guy wanted to see me, or if it didn't matter because after two months of making out with me and over-the-bra groping, he still couldn't bring himself to use the word *girlfriend*.

Rhys gave a deep sigh, his chest heaving out, then in—his body going slack like a violin string that had been unwound. His eyes fluttered shut as he shook his head from side to side, the curls on his head shaking with the same sense of weariness.

"No, June. I don't want to know where you got it."

All the energy I'd pent up thinking about how my argument with Rhys was going to go fizzled like a deflated balloon. He didn't even care. Tommy had probably told him everything and he couldn't even be bothered to *pretend* to care.

I used to think my mom held the title for most passive-aggressive sigh. She'd do it after every one of my third-place finishes. Every time I got a 99 on a test. Every time I attempted to compare myself favorably to Wendy. I was a constant disappointment, and her sigh was the quickest way of reminding me of that.

But even the persistent ache of those blows couldn't compare to the searing pain slicing its way through every single one of my internal organs, my lungs at half capacity and filling with the blood pouring from my heart. Rhys's sigh had been so much deeper, so much more defeated than anything I'd ever experienced before. Like he was tired. Tired of me always wanting more. Tired of me.

I dug my teeth into my bottom lip, willing myself not to tear up. Crying would make all of this so much more embarrassing.

"Go back to your music," I said, my voice devoid of any emotion as I snatched up his copy of the worksheet. "I'll do everything like I always do."

Rhys didn't argue.

———

By the end of the day, I'd gathered my wits about me. Rhys did not want me. Or if he did, it apparently wasn't enough for him to even try to prevent my slow death of embarrassment after our disaster at the cabin. If he'd at least pretended everything was normal, I could have convinced myself he cared enough about my feelings to pretend it never happened. Instead, he was acting like I barely existed on his radar.

I took a deep breath and straightened my spine as I marched over to him. I'd already smashed the pots—I might as well prepare myself to sink the boats too. It was funny how a college essay I never even wanted to write would serve as the inspiration for this totally unrelated situation, but damn it if those Chinese philosophers hadn't gotten under my skin. I was determined to provoke a reaction from Rhys one way or another.

Planting myself behind the opened door to his locker, I stared at him, daring him to say what he wouldn't say earlier. His eyes flickered toward me for a moment, but quickly resumed shuffling the books in his locker, stuffing some of them into his backpack. I didn't know why he bothered. It wasn't like he was planning to open them at home.

I cleared my throat and he glanced at me again but said nothing.

"You can't just ignore me forever," I said, hating how pouty my voice sounded. I had been going for coolly detached.

His eyes had the same irritated look he got whenever a teacher called on him in class. "Who's ignoring you?"

Anger flared inside of me. How dare he stand there and feign ignorance after I'd already done 90 percent of the work to even get us to this conversation? "You are!" I exploded. "You're not saying anything."

"You're the one who came over here and just stood there."

"You barely talked to me in class. And I haven't heard from you in five days. For all I knew you were dead." I mentally counted backward to the night at the cabin. It seemed like a lifetime ago. "*Six* days!"

"No one was stopping you from texting me. You usually do."

He didn't say it in a way that made it sound like he was in any way hoping that I would have texted him at any point over the past six days.

His words smacked me across the face and I sank back into the metal lockers, reeling from the hit. I was such an idiot. How could I have missed it? Rhys didn't just not want to date me; he didn't even *like* me. Why else would he act this way after I'd tried to seduce him? Clearly I'd repulsed him to the point that he couldn't even talk to me with any kind of civility. There was no conversation to be had—only escape.

My cheeks struggling to contain the embarrassment burning inside of them, I blurted out, "This isn't working."

Rhys continued to fiddle about in his locker, the only sound between us the thud of his books being rearranged. Around us, students talked and laughed, lockers jangled, and people walked past.

"I think we should break up," I said, a little louder this time to make sure he heard me.

Rhys blinked twice, zipped up his backpack, and slammed his locker shut with a metal clang.

I held my breath, waiting for his response. A tiny part of me clung to the hope that he'd be angry—confused, even. Anything that would let me know he felt one single, solitary emotion about me and the fact that I was calling it off.

But true to form, his face showed nothing. It was as if I'd just suggested we write our labs in blue pen instead of black. "If that's how you feel, then I guess we're breaking up," he said.

I stiffened, suddenly aware of the cold metal digging into my spine. What did he mean *if that's how you feel*? If *he'd* bothered having any actual feelings, we wouldn't have been in this position in the first place. I wasn't about to apologize for not wanting my boyfriend to ghost me for a week after I humiliated myself to try and get closer to him.

I straightened my shoulders, perhaps as a vivid counterpoint to his constantly hunched posture. I wasn't going to let him think I was walking away from this with anything less than relief at having gotten it over with. I tossed my hair over my shoulder, my chin raised like a haughty princess. "I guess I'll see you later then."

He didn't reply and I made my way toward the exit, convinced his eyes had already shifted away from me.

I texted Brad the next day and just like that, I had my first *official* boyfriend.

CHAPTER TEN

I shifted my legs until they stuck out straight ahead of me, my butt throbbing from the hard carpet in Candace's room. Once upon a time, her parents had installed thick, fluffy blue carpet—the exact kind I'd begged my own parents for—only for it to pill and flatten within a few years' time, just as my mom had predicted it would. I stubbornly remained where I was, ignoring the protests from my tailbone as I ran my fingers through my long hair. One hand still firmly on her phone, Candace handed me a small trash can with her free hand so I could deposit the nest of black hair I'd just pulled out.

"Here's another picture of the view at the top of the trail—ooh, and another one of us," Candace continued, swiping across her phone to reveal several nearly identical selfies of her and Dom outdoors, their faces oversized and glossy from the close exposure. "Liz told us about this trail, actually. She said her soccer team took a trip there last year for a workout."

"Since when do you hike?" I asked. When Candace and I were in middle school, it had been a struggle to even get her to walk half a mile to Dairy Queen because it was slightly uphill.

She shrugged. "Dom likes it. Besides, he still lives at home, so it's one of the only times we get to be alone *if you know what I mean*," she said, her eyebrows shooting up and down suggestively.

The thought of the logistics required for what she was suggesting sent a mental image of the two of them through my mind. "Good Lord, woman, have you never heard of doing it in a car like normal people?" I wrinkled my nose in distaste.

Candace's eyes widened. "Does this mean you and Brad—"

"No," I quickly cut her off. "Just um, the other stuff so far."

She squealed and pretended to throw a handful of confetti into the air. "Really? Ooh, it's official then! Jujube, I'm so excited for you!"

My face flushed with embarrassment. On one hand, I was proud of me too. On the other hand, it was something entirely different to be *congratulated* on it.

Candace dropped her phone, abandoning the rest of her hiking pictures with Dom. "Tell me everything! When? How many times? Why did you wait so long to tell me? How was it?"

I shrugged shyly. "I didn't want to make a big deal over it."

It was at least partially true. After what happened with *Mission: BJ* at the cabin, I didn't want to run the risk of reliving the indignity of having to explain to her what happened if things went sideways again. Besides, she was busy with Dom most days now, and the school cafeteria wasn't the ideal place to discuss such matters.

"But it *is* a big deal! This is a huge step for the two of you," she insisted.

"Right. The two of us," I echoed.

It felt strange to think of it in those terms. Obviously he'd been there each time it happened—a key participant, even. But I was always so focused on my end of things that I hadn't really stopped to think of it as something we were doing *together*. Did it count as a joint activity if only one of us was doing all the work?

But I couldn't deny the effect it'd had on our relationship. If Brad had been openly affectionate before all of this, he was downright smitten now. For the few minutes I had him at my mercy each time, it felt like I was the most powerful person in the world. It was unclear why men thought they ruled the world when it seemed like they would give it away in a heartbeat just for the chance of getting a blow job, but it was satisfying to do it for someone who was so appreciative nevertheless. It was weird now to think about ever using this as a ploy to get someone to commit instead of as a reward for someone who already had.

My phone buzzed, jolting me back to the present. I checked the screen. "It's just Wendy," I said. "Give me a sec."

I swiped up the incoming call to reveal Wendy's round face in my screen, her bangs pinned back, the dark tortoiseshell glasses floating atop her ivory skin like a Snapchat filter.

"Hey, can't talk, I'm at Candace's," I said.

She wrinkled her nose. "Rude. Then why did you answer?"

"Wouldn't it be ruder to screen you?"

"I only had a couple of minutes to talk anyway. I have spin class soon." She pulled her hair up into a long ponytail as if to illustrate the point.

I tried to imagine Wendy on a bicycle. "Since when do you *spin*?"

"I started a couple months ago. It's great for stress relief."

If Wendy had ever been stressed in her life, her perfect façade had never shown it.

"How often do you go?" I asked.

"I used to only go a couple times a week, but then they asked me to teach a couple of the introductory classes, so now it's more like four or five days while I work toward my certification."

Jesus. She was so good at everything she couldn't even take an exercise class without being asked to lead it.

Candace leaned over, pushing herself into view. "Hey, Wen," she cooed.

"Hey, *Can*," Wendy replied, signaling her displeasure.

"How's college? June said you're in nerd heaven."

I elbowed Candace in the ribs off-screen while trying to keep my face as innocent looking as possible. It was one thing for me to make little comments about Wendy—it was quite another for Candace to tell her about them.

Wendy's lips curled up into a smirk. "June probably needs to be *more* of a nerd if she wants to get into *my* school."

"Oh please, I'm taking *one* less AP class than you did!" I burst out.

A satisfied smile spread across Wendy's face, happy she'd effectively gotten a rise out of me. "I still think it was a mistake not to take AP Music Theory. Mr. Hartsough loves me. It'd be an easy A. You're not going to be valedictorian without the extra grade weighting."

"I don't care about being valedictorian anyway," I said.

Wendy cast a doubtful look at me, snickering. "No kidding, *Intro to Ceramics*."

A laugh tried to escape my mouth, but I forced it back, clamping my teeth down into my tongue hard enough to draw blood. I'd realized it was a mistake to take the class by about the third week, when I was still trying to properly center a bowl—something I still couldn't do though the end of the semester was rapidly approaching—and the minuscule freshman sitting next to me was churning out pots half the size of himself. Adding insult to injury, my hands seemed to retain the dry, chalky feeling of the clay no matter how many times I washed and moisturized them.

But Wendy didn't need to know that.

"At least I tried something new," I said with as much dignity as I could muster.

"Maybe June's planning to make something for her and Brad's six-week anniversary," Candace cut in with a sly smile.

"That's not a thing," Wendy and I said at the exact same time.

Candace burst out laughing, her hands hitting both me and my phone as they flailed through the air in her typical dramatic fashion. "I swear, you two are exactly the same person sometimes."

"No we're not," we both replied in unison again.

It was hard not to see at least a little bit of humor in that.

"So," Wendy said after we'd all settled down, shoving her glasses back up her nose. "You're still dating that hockey player, huh?" I noticed she'd stopped grimacing when she said the words *hockey player*, but her face hadn't yet morphed into a convincing smile when talking about him.

I straightened up a little at the mention of Brad. "Mm-hmm."

"I thought you'd have blown through him by now, like . . ."

Candace's eyes grew considerably wider before she collapsed into a fit of giggles beside me, her arms flailing up from the floor as she tried to muffle herself on the blue carpet.

Wendy gave her a confused look, her voice still stretching the last syllable before deciding to finish her thought. ". . . like you did with the last one."

She was eyeing the space Candace had been in, but Candace was now on the floor gasping loudly for air through ragged coughs as I gave her a swift kick with one of my socked feet.

"What exactly is her problem?" Wendy asked me.

I pressed my lips together, trying not to let my face give away anything as I gave a helpless shrug.

Wendy looked unconvinced. "Okay, well, she sounds like she's about to blow chunks over there, so you might want to get her to a bathroom."

At the mention of "blow chunks," Candace broke down again and I was in deep danger of not being able to keep a straight face anymore.

"We should probably go," I squeaked out, my lips pressed tightly together to keep a laugh from escaping.

Wendy gave us a final exasperated look. "Yeah fine. I have spin anyway. Talk to you later."

"Quick!" Candace gasped from the floor. "Before she *blows the whistle* on you!"

I hung up as quickly as I could—without returning Wendy's farewell—as Candace and I disintegrated into hysterics.

CHAPTER ELEVEN

Wendy called me again the next day as I was on my way over to Brad's house.

"Hey," I said, Wendy's round face grinning at me from the place my phone clipped into the dashboard.

"Are you driving right now?"

"No, I'm sitting in my car, taking selfies with my seat belt on because it looks cool."

Even without looking, I knew Wendy was rolling her eyes. "You really shouldn't answer your phone while you're driving. Especially video. It's not safe."

"Okay, Mom," I replied.

She pushed her glasses up her nose. "Anyway, I was calling you back since I didn't really have time to talk yesterday and had to get off so quickly."

I chanced a quick glance at the phone to see if this was one of her weirdly sarcastic jokes that weren't actually funny, but her face didn't give any hint of it. Was she so used to being in control of every situation that she just assumed *she* was the one to let *me* go?

"I don't really have a lot of time today," I said airily. "I'm on my way to Brad's."

Wendy frowned. "That's what I wanted to call and talk to you about. Don't think I didn't get what you and Candace were laughing about."

Took you long enough.

"I don't know what you mean," I said simply.

"I don't think that's true, but I'm just—I'm just going to say what I called to say anyway."

I flashed my eyes toward the screen again, waiting expectantly for what big, important thing she'd come up with in the past twenty-four hours. "Well?" I prompted. "The suspense is *killing* me."

She glared at me, but she did speak. "I know Mom and Dad don't know about Brad so I feel like it's my responsibility to say something."

I sighed inwardly. Whenever Wendy anointed herself as my replacement guardian, it was like the ending of *It's a Wonderful Life* but in reverse, so an angel somewhere lost its wings.

"I—well, um, I think you're moving too fast," she blurted out in a rush.

I paused, waiting for her to continue, but she said nothing. "Is that all?" I asked.

"What do you mean 'is that all'? June, this is serious!"

"Mmm-hmm." I nodded with an insincere look of seriousness on my face.

"I mean it! You've barely started dating this guy and now you're . . . you're *doing* stuff with him?"

I almost burst out laughing at the sight of Wendy, red-faced and stammering, trying desperately to avoid saying the words *blow job*.

"Didn't you hear Candace yesterday? We have a six-week anniversary coming up."

"June, this isn't funny!" Wendy was practically shouting into the phone now. "You can't just go around—like, you know—you need to be careful! Is he pressuring you?"

The novelty of witnessing Wendy awkwardly try to discuss sex was quickly wearing thin. As if I weren't a whole autonomous human being capable of making my own choices. "I'm not *going around* doing anything, not that it's any of your business," I snapped. "But anything that I *am* doing, I'm choosing to do, thank you very much."

"It *is* my business," Wendy insisted. "I'm trying to help you make good decisions. I don't want to you regret this later."

Ha. Good decisions. As if the only decisions worth making were the same ones she made.

I pulled my car into Brad's driveway and turned off the ignition. "I have to go. I'm here. Off to make some more bad decisions."

"June—"

I never heard the end of Wendy's sentence. I'd already hung up.

———

God, Wendy could be so infuriating. Every time it seemed like she might be approaching anything resembling a normal sister, she immediately backtracked into whatever "big sister" role she'd concocted for herself. I'd never expected to actually be able to talk to her about the stuff that was going on between Brad and me, but she could at least have the decency not to bring it up in the first place. Especially if all she was going to do was tell me how wrong I was about everything.

"You've gotta work with me here," Brad whispered in my ear as we lay together on his bed, his kisses trailing down the side of my neck.

My brain was still spinning so furiously I'd barely registered the fact that his hands were making their way toward the waistband of my jeans until I felt his tugging at the button.

I clamped a hand over his to stop him. "Not right now," I whispered. Even though his door was closed and his dad was a floor below us, I always felt uneasy about the possibility he would walk in on us doing something. I'm sure if his dad were really concerned, he wouldn't let us be in here alone. My mom didn't even let girlfriends she didn't like go upstairs at my house. Either way, having his had in such close proximity didn't exactly set the stage for feeling sexy.

"Come on," he urged. "I haven't seen you in days. You've been so busy."

A pang of guilt fluttered through my stomach. Between school and violin and a mom who insisted we eat dinner together every night, even though my dad was rarely home for it, it was a monumental task to arrange time to see him. We talked every day, but it wasn't the same as actually *being* together.

"Your dad is home," I whispered.

"He'd understand how much I need this," he murmured, his lips nipping at my earlobes.

A flush of heat raced down my body the way it did every time his breath hit anywhere near the sensitive spots on my neck and ears. Sometimes I would give in because I couldn't help myself, but I was still upset about my conversation with Wendy and wanted to vent about it before doing anything else.

"Hey, wait, I'm mad about something," I protested, even as his tongue lined the underside of my jawline and caused me to giggle.

"That's terrible," he said between kisses. "I should probably try to cheer you up. Get your mind off things."

His hand slid around to my back and began its descent inside my pants.

The coarseness of his hands gave his grip a primal feel, and slowly his desire began to rub off on me. My fight with Wendy receded to the background, drowned out by the tingling between my legs.

"Your dad is downstairs," I hissed as he began tugging my pants down, still zipped and buttoned.

He ignored me, his hands and lips melting my resistance inch by inch.

"Mmm, I love the way your body feels," he murmured into the nape of my neck. "I love how soft you are. I love the way you smell."

I tingled with warmth as his bulky arms squeezed me, pressing me more tightly against his solid frame. His hands were everywhere now, the places he touched burning with awareness. I decided to give into it. This was my decision, and I was making it. Besides, I had better things to do than sit around and think about something annoying Wendy had said.

"Okay, let's do this," I whispered fiercely. "I'm ready."

"Ready for what?"

"*Ready* ready," I repeated with as much insinuation as I could muster.

Brad's head whipped up, his eyes lit up like a traffic light. "Really? Are you sure?" He looked as though I'd just told him he'd won tickets to the NHL All-Star Game.

"Yes. But not here."

Brad looked around his room like there might be a secret portal we could go into to escape his dad. "Okay, let's go," he said, jumping up from the bed and pulling me with him.

"Go where?"

"We'll figure it out."

We stormed downstairs, pulling on boots and jackets and rushing outside before the hormones could wear off.

I looked up at the tiny flakes drifting down from the sky. "It's snowing."

"Barely. Come on." He tugged my hand as he headed toward a small playground down the street, next to an empty soccer field and away from any houses.

"Shouldn't we have taken your car or something?" I asked timidly, my courage waning in the bright light of the outdoors.

"This'll be more fun," he replied, his familiar grin widening enough to reveal the spot where his tooth was missing.

I straightened up, trying to get myself more excited about my decision. I'd come this far. We'd have sex sooner or later, the way things were going. It might as well be now. All it lacked was a proper name to give it the feeling of accomplishment it deserved. *Mission: Risky Business*, I thought. Candace would have been proud.

I raced ahead of Brad, sprinting straight onto the swings, where I pumped my legs back and forth to build momentum. Brad reached them a few moments after me, the two of us racing to see who could reach the highest peak. Finally, on the count of three, we both jumped.

Brad stuck his landing, while I tumbled over, unhurt and giggling.

"You win," I conceded as he pulled me up.

"You ready to do this?" he asked.

My eyes scanned the plastic fixtures, beaded with water where the snow had melted off in the sun. "Where exactly do you have in mind?"

He pointed to the bright green tunnel in the middle of the structure.

"Won't it be kind of"—I paused to hug myself—"cold?" I asked, tiny snowflakes continuing to fall around us.

He gave a coy smile, the little space in his mouth winking out at me. "I can keep you warm."

He led me across the slightly springy rubber mulch floor and up the recycled plastic stairs until we reached the tunnel. It looked even more cheerful than usual, the bright sun bouncing off its shiny exterior like a beacon of fun. The makers of this playground probably had a different idea of *fun* in mind, but now that it was winter, no one else was using the playground anyway. Besides, hiding out inside was better than doing it out in the open.

I crawled into the tunnel first, awkwardly flipping over onto my back to make space for Brad to fit on top of me. Our legs stuck out the end of it, but at least our heads and bodies were covered.

He wasted no time.

The moment he positioned himself, he leaned in and kissed me. Forcefully. Like he was ready to move things along.

I reached down to unzip my jeans, bumping his bulge in the process. Jesus. Was he really already ready? Had he gotten that within the last four seconds or had it been like that since I suggested we do it? Maybe it wasn't an exaggeration that teenage guys were walking around with hard-ons 24-7.

I lifted my hips and yanked my jeans down to my knees before setting my butt back down on the cold plastic. A cold, stabbing pain shot up my spine, forcing me to bite my lip to keep from screaming in his ear. It felt exactly like what I imagined an epidural would feel like, but without the benefit of numbing my entire lower body in a timely manner. The frozen tunnel showed no sign of warming against my exposed skin.

I should have volunteered to be on top.

Brad started to lower himself onto me, but I stopped him. "Wait. Do you have a . . . condom?"

I nearly whispered the word. Like it was something we weren't supposed to talk about. But the first time Candace had had sex back in tenth grade, her boyfriend convinced her they didn't need one because "they were in a relationship" and she ended up with gonorrhea. No matter how embarrassing it was to ask about condoms, it was infinitely better than ending up with an STD. Even one of the curable ones.

Balancing his weight on his left hand, Brad used his right hand to grab his wallet out of his back pocket and pull out a condom. Seamlessly he replaced his wallet, ripped the wrapper off the condom with his teeth, and slid it onto himself. It all felt so coordinated. Like he'd executed this move a hundred times before.

I squeezed my eyes shut, willing myself not to think about that.

The tunnel was simultaneously both stuffy from the heat of our bodies and freezing from the cold air rushing in at our heads. I wondered if it was possible to get frostbite and heatstroke at the same time.

"You sure you're ready for this, China?" he breathed, the visible puff of warm air lingering, then dissolving between our faces.

I nodded.

No matter that his body weight was pressing me into the still-frigid cold plastic, its unforgiving shape pressing into my spine and sticking to my bare skin like a tongue on a frozen flagpole. I just needed to get through this.

"I'm really glad we're doing this," he whispered in my ear, lowering himself onto me.

"Me too," I managed to whisper back.

I didn't know what to expect. Candace had warned me it might hurt if I wasn't into it enough, but books and movies always made it look effortless, like everything just fit together. That was not the case. I could feel Brad dutifully trying to make his way inside of me. It felt like he was trying to push through a brick wall, the head of his penis just ramming up against me. It was just a thin piece of skin. Surely it couldn't take this much effort to break through. Hadn't he done this before?

My mom had insisted Wendy and I not use tampons for fear of breaking our hymens. Wendy had tried, rather exasperatedly, to explain that the hymen had nothing to do with virginity, but my mother wouldn't hear of it. My dad refused to get involved. Eventually Wendy began hiding illicit boxes of tampons in her closet for us both to use, purchased with whatever funds we could scrape together. It was the only time I could remember Wendy rebelling against our parents.

By the time I reached high school, my mom had given up the fight and we didn't have to hide menstrual products like drugs, but she only bought the slimmest tampons "just in case."

I opened one eye and peeked at Brad, who stared straight ahead with a look of determination as he thrust his hips back and forth. The pressure on my very-much-intact hymen was beginning to hurt, and just when I considered asking Brad to stop, his penis jammed inside of me with a rough jolt.

I yelped in pain, biting down on my lip so hard I nearly drew blood.

Brad didn't seem to notice me wincing; instead, he excitedly increased the speed of his friction-filled thrusts, the light lubrication of the condom having long worn off. It felt like I was being filed down from the inside with an emery board. I squeezed my eyes more tightly, hoping it would all be over soon.

I asked for this. It was my decision. I kept repeating the phrases over and over again to myself, as if they would make this whole ordeal less uncomfortable.

For some reason I was reminded of a pair of tall, shiny black wedges that I'd begged my mom to buy me for a performance. She'd insisted they were impractical but eventually got them after days of me begging, warning me that she wouldn't buy me another pair if they hurt. We'd gotten to the competition only to find that they didn't provide chairs for performers, and I'd had to suffer through my ten-minute presentation while my feet felt like they were on fire.

"Doesn't this feel good?" Brad panted, his breathing heavy and his arms trembling from the exertion of holding his body above mine.

My mind drifted back to the burning sensation below my waist as I tried to muster an enthusiastic smile and an *mmmmm* that could both double as a "yes" response and some kind of sound of pleasure. If I pretended to enjoy it, it might be over sooner.

Mercifully, after a few minutes, it was. Brad made a pained face, his entire body convulsing as he finished. Afterward, he wiped the sweat from his forehead, kissed me lightly on the lips, and climbed backward out of the tunnel with his jeans around his ankles.

The cold came rushing in and I scrambled to pull my own pants back up. I didn't want him to see me half naked, even though we'd just done something far more intimate.

Except it hadn't *felt* particularly intimate. Granted, the circumstances weren't ideal, but I'd imagined my first time at least feeling a bit more romantic. Like Candace had said, something we did *together*. Not just something he did *to* me, which is very much how it had felt.

Maybe I'd done it wrong. Or maybe it was just the fact that we'd been squeezed into a freezing-cold playground tunnel. But surely sex wouldn't be so hyped up if this was how it felt for everyone.

I climbed out of the tunnel and stood up, looking for Brad to see if he had similar mixed feelings about what had just happened. He was disposing of the condom in the garbage, but he caught my eye as he wiped his hands on his jeans and smiled.

"God, I love you," he called out, the dark spot in his mouth visible even from this distance.

I love you. The words echoed in my ears as my knees weakened and I grabbed the railing to stabilize myself. I'd never had anyone say those words to me before. Not my parents, not Wendy, certainly not Rhys. Candace, maybe, but not like this.

"You can say it back, you know," he said, still grinning as he walked back toward me, his gait bouncing from the springy floor.

"I know. Yes. I do," I spluttered, my disappointment from only a few minutes ago now wiped from my memory.

He climbed the stairs back up to me, gently brushing the hairs that had blown across my face with his familiarly calloused hands. "That's more like it." He leaned over and gave me a kiss, which turned into another kiss, his tongue prodding its way back into my mouth.

"God, China," he whispered. "The things you do to me."

I flushed with pride, the sting of the cold air around us dimming just a bit.

His forehead stayed connected to mine, his face tilted and hovering just above me. "Do you want to go back in there for a second round?" he asked, his voice low and suggestive.

For all the satisfaction it brought me to know he wanted me again so soon after he'd just climaxed, I also felt like I'd swallowed one of those shrink-wrapped expanding towels, the fabric rapidly unfolding in my stomach as it took on the weight of my insides.

"I think I might need a little . . . rest first," I demurred, making sure to keep my face as pleasant looking as possible.

Brad grinned, his missing tooth suddenly a gaping chasm at this distance. I'd never noticed just how large the hole really was. Why had he never gotten a replacement tooth? Was it really possible to just get used to having a void where something should be?

Brad kissed me again—this time on the forehead—before slinging his arm around me as we made our way off the playground and back to his dad's house. I snuggled into the crook of his shoulder, hoping his warmth would be enough to quell the chill that had worked its way back under my skin. If I hugged him a little tighter, I might be able to recover the feeling I'd had back when we were safely tucked in bed, before I'd discovered his kisses were less romantic and warm when produced in the process of other activities.

Brad squeezed my shoulder. "You okay?"

"Mmm hmm."

"Good. Because I gotta make sure my girl is taken care of. Make your first time special for you."

My girl. I was someone's girl now. I'd been claimed.

The words echoed in my head all the way back to the house.

CHAPTER TWELVE

I sat at the kitchen table, shoveling down a bowl of xī fàn and ròusōng for lunch—the saltiness of the dried pork stinging the spots in my mouth that had already been singed by the hot porridge—as I scrolled through my texts to assess my options for the first official day of winter break. They weren't great. Brad had gone ice fishing with his friends from Cedar High last night and wouldn't be back until the afternoon; Candace and Dom were going to the movies; Liz and Savannah were bowling with Rhys, Grayson, and Drew. I didn't know which was worse: being the third wheel to Candace and Dom's endless inside jokes about work or having to go do sports while pretending like things weren't awkward between Rhys and me. We had settled into a sense of normalcy during labs, but that usually died the minute we stepped out of class. It was like we could only function in our little bubble, where he didn't have to pretend I didn't exist because he still hated me for dumping him for Brad. Or who knew, maybe he did hate me. It was always impossible to tell with him.

I helped myself to a second serving, wondering if it was possible to eat my way out of boredom. It'd been less than half a day since break started, and yet it felt like I'd already read the entirety of the Internet. Even Wendy had interesting things to do since getting home over the weekend: running errands to prepare for her trip to Central America, where she was going to be volunteering with a medical mission for some nonprofit that gave kids free orthopedic surgeries. Not that I particularly wanted to go to Nicaragua right now, but at least it was *something*.

Was this what my breaks would look like when I came back from college? All my friends would be busy going about their lives, and I would be stuck at home with my mom because I didn't fit in anymore? They would all probably go to the University of Northern Iowa. And after they spent a year living together and hanging out every day without me, how could I be sure I'd be welcomed back into the fold? I barely fit in now. Ironic, considering Liz wasn't even friends with Rhys and those guys before me. And now she was off *bowling* with them like she hadn't accused them all of being unapologetic misogynists just a few months ago. It didn't matter that Liz had never held a grudge against me or Candace when we argued—she could have at least *tried* to hold one against the guy who practically forced me to break up with him. Even if I'd acted like I was fine about it.

I never would have needed to explain this to Candace.

I angrily toggled away from the pictures Savannah had posted of Liz and Rhys posing with their bowling balls, my right hand still clutching my chopsticks as if their happiness might accidentally float through the phone and I could pop it like a balloon. When had they replaced me with the likes of *Savannah* anyway? I mean sure, I'd been spending more of my time with Brad lately, but that didn't mean they couldn't invite me. I'd texted Liz about doing something and she'd replied she was already on the way to the bowling alley with Savannah but that I could "totally join if you want."

I heard my mom's light footsteps shuffle into the kitchen, followed by a disapproving cluck of her tongue. "You ruin your eyes, always looking at that phone."

Two beats too late, I thought of a quip about how luckily we had excellent vision insurance. It was just as well. Wendy wasn't around to laugh at it and Mom never found anything I said funny.

She peered over the table into my bowl and gave a little frown. "That not fill you up."

"It's my second bowl, I'm fine," I reassured her.

"I make you eggs," she said, heading for the refrigerator and pulling out a carton of eggs.

"You should save them for Wendy, she'll be back soon. Oh! That reminds me!" I exclaimed, my mood already lifting by the story I was about to relay. "She was telling me about how she's been talking to some of the previous volunteers and they said that since it's a volunteer mission and everything is funded by donors, they try and spend as little as possible on overhead so apparently they eat nothing but rice and beans for the entire time." I grinned expectantly at my mom. The one and only food Wendy truly hated was beans.

But instead, her frown deepened. She held out an egg at me. "You want fried or scrambled?"

"Mom! Are you even listening to me? I told you an entire story and you didn't even react."

"What, beans and rice story? How you want me to react? Ha ha, so funny. You like to see your sister unhappy. How you want your egg?"

"I don't even want eggs."

She turned back to the stove, where a pan was already out and waiting. "Okay, I fry it."

I slumped back down over my bowl, my mood souring again. This was for sure going to be my future, destined to go through life alone and misunderstood, with even my own mom not enjoying my company.

"What you do today?" she asked.

"Contemplate my boring existence and feel sorry for myself," I mumbled, my words garbled by the fact that half my face was smushed into the hand propping it up.

My mom looked at me carefully for a moment before briskly returning to the stove probably to cook something else she'd force me to eat. "Daddy and I work hard our whole lives. Study, work, study, work. Barely time to think. No time. Now? We are lucky. Daddy still works hard, but I have time. Time to think. I give that time to you. Cháng jiāng yǒu rì sī wú rì, mò jiāng wú shí xiǎng yǒu shì—when one is rich there is time to think all day, when one is poor there is no time to think."

I lifted my head a fraction of an inch off my fist—just enough to be heard in case the snotty face I was making didn't quite convey my reaction. "What?"

My mom shook her head at me, jabbing a wooden spoon in my direction, as if to prod me from across the kitchen. "You always accuse me, say I don't listen to you. When you listen to me?"

"I'm listening to you; I just have no idea what you're trying to say."

She gave an exasperated sigh and turned back to the stove, but she didn't stay that way. With a louder than usual bang of the wooden spoon against the side of the dented gray pot, she whirled back around to face me. I flickered my eyes up from my phone but didn't set it down.

"Time!" she exclaimed. "You have so much time! What you do with it?"

"Geez, relax, when you asked me what I was doing today I didn't realize I needed to have an entire itinerary. It's the first day of break."

She clucked her tongue again like I was purposely being infuriating. "You say trust you. You say you figure out your future. Where that get you? No school, no scholarship, no nothing! But you have *so* much time for friends. You always going here, going there with this friend, that friend." She swooped the wooden spoon back and forth in big arcs, little bits of wet rice flying off the end of it without her noticing. "Now you have no friends, but you still do nothing. Just sit around."

I dropped my phone—accidentally toppling my chopsticks off the side of my bowl in the process—as I sat up in indignation. *No friends? Do nothing?* Where did she get off accusing me of being lazy when I'd only had half a day off?

"For your information, I already got my acceptance letter from Northern Iowa."

My mom snorted, half a laugh caught somewhere between her nose and her throat. "You go to high school in Iowa—of course they take you. They take everyone. You think someone get into Northwestern and choose Iowa instead? I tell you don't apply there and waste money."

Like Rome, all my mom's roads led to Northwestern. It was as if she was a pushy MLM consultant, earning fees on every person she convinced to attend or something. But I refused to give up that easily. I hadn't bought any of Jenny Lipinski's mom's mascara and I wasn't about to buy my mom's BS about Northwestern being the only viable option for my future.

"I'm sure UNI would give me a scholarship," I countered. "I might not even need to play violin. I could just be a regular student there. You and Dad always said school should come first."

I mentally high-fived myself for throwing her own advice back in her face. And the idea of maybe not having my life revolve around practice times gave me a tiny thrill, even if I had no clue how plausible my suggestion really was. I could always research it later.

My mom stared at me, her mouth barely suppressing a mocking smile. "You want to stay in Iowa? Throw away years of hard work to be like everybody else? Go ahead. Shǔ mù cùn guāng—mouse's vision only one inch long." She held up her thumb and forefinger in front of her eye an inch apart, as if to illustrate the insult.

She was so damn smug. As if she could provoke me into backing down.

Well, screw her. I hadn't planned out every step of my future for the next ten years like Wendy had, but that didn't make me a shortsighted loser. She acted like I had no future other than the one music would provide for me. As if I was worth nothing without the violin.

I'd never made a secret of the fact that I resented my parents pushing violin on me from an early age. Maybe if I'd been allowed to choose my instrument I would've ended up with it anyway. But the point stood that I'd never been allowed to choose. Not that they cared.

They already had their golden child in Wendy—there was no reason for me to keep torturing myself to stay in second place. It wasn't like I could drop any farther at this point. If I was going to be shunned for being the loser of my family anyway, I might as well go somewhere I could at least decide my own schedule.

She set down in front of me a bowl of xī fàn with a fried egg and a sprinkle of furikake across the top. I hated how delicious it looked and smelled. "You'll see. This is best," she said confidently.

"You have no idea what's 'best' for me. You've never even bothered to ask." I jumped to my feet, shoving my untouched bowl away from me as if accepting it would mean conceding the fight. I didn't want to accept a single thing from her ever again. "This family sucks," I hissed.

I expected the usual admonishment for my language and for daring to claim she was anything but altruistic, but as I stalked out of the kitchen, I heard her call after me happily, "Jiāng bù zhǐ shì zhòng yào de dōngxi, èr shì suǒyǒu de yíqiè—family is not important thing, it is everything."

CHAPTER THIRTEEN

I sat in my car just off the end of the driveway at Brad's mom's house for over an hour, waiting for him to return from his ice-fishing trip. It was difficult to sit still, my blood running hot from the confrontation with my mom. I had to keep readjusting my seat, sliding it back and forth as I tried to find a comfortable position to curl into.

I hadn't seriously considered going to UNI before this, but that didn't mean I *couldn't*. After all, safety schools were supposed to provide just that—safety. I had a perfectly good life right now. I had someone who cared about me and my feelings, which was more than I could say for the people I lived with. And while I wasn't exactly happy about how chummy Liz had been with Rhys and the guys lately, it wasn't like I'd been completely cut out, which is probably what would happen if I left all together. At least if I stayed here, I wouldn't have to start my entire life all over again. Northern Iowa didn't have to be my dream school—it just had to be good enough.

That was my entire brand, really. Good enough test scores to get the A but not the A-plus. Good enough skills to get a trophy, but not first place. Good enough to be someone's girlfriend, but not their first choice of company. Just Good Enough™.

The rest of my thoughts were interrupted by Brad's return, his face brightening into a wide smile the moment he caught sight of me in my car, curled into a ball with my fingers outstretched toward the heat pouring out of the dashboard vents. I don't know how well he could actually see through my fogged windows, but after the day I'd had, it was incredibly validating to have someone react like that to my mere presence.

I jumped out of my car as he parked, flinging my arms around him the moment he'd stepped onto the driveway. And exactly as I'd hoped he would, he wrapped his arms around me and carried me into the house, creating the sense of safety I was so longing for. I told him about my fight with my mom, about how she practically dared me to go to UNI, and how she accused me of doing nothing with my life.

"You're not doing nothing, you're doing me. Or at least you're about to," Brad murmured into my neck, his hands already making a beeline for my waistband.

I gave a snort of laughter. "I'll make sure to mention that to her next time."

His face remained buried against the base of my neck, and, trying to untangle my hair as he went, he asked, "Can we stop talking about your mom now? It's making my penis feel awkward and confused."

I laughed again, brushing my hair out of his way as we staggered down the hallway toward his bedroom, pressed together like two halves of a sandwich cookie. "Should we talk about *your* mom and where she is right now?"

"Gone," he replied, pulling my shirt up over my head before resuming his assault on my collarbone area. "Now I swear to god, if you mention either of our moms once we set foot in my room, I am going to . . . well, I don't know, but I'm sure I'll think of something."

After we were finished, a contented drowsiness settled over me. Between the sheen of sweat on my skin and the warmth of the late-afternoon sun that streamed through the blinds like it was June and not December, I was all too happy to dive back under Brad's cozy sheets to create a cocoon for myself to take a nap. I knew I was supposed to get up and go to the bathroom afterward, but the emotional drain of the day plus the sex had made me sleepy. Maybe I'd take a little nap first, then pee later. Was there a time limit on how long I had to expel the bacteria before developing a UTI? I nearly chuckled to myself, thinking of my dad's reaction if I asked him.

"Am I allowed to talk about my mom now?" I asked Brad's naked backside as he crossed the room to throw away the used condom. "If so, you should know that she explicitly told me she's more important than you, so technically I should be able to talk about her at any point."

Brad gasped.

"You can't really be surprised by that, can you?" I asked. "I mean, the Chinese literally invented the concept of filial piety. It even has its own character that combines the words for *old* and *son*. You know, because girls mean nothing." I paused for a moment, pondering—not for the first time—how much more insufferable my parents' behavior would be had Wendy been a boy.

Brad let out a string of curse words under his breath.

"Don't worry, I'm not that bugged about it. As the second born, I was never going to be important either way. You should see what my grandparents did to my mom in their will." I yawned again and rolled over onto my side, fluffing the pillow several times to get the right distribution of filling.

I was just winding up, ready to tell Brad all about the unfairness of customary Chinese distribution of assets when he looked over his shoulder at me, his face even paler than usual and stricken with panic. It was clear he hadn't heard a word I'd said.

"The condom broke," he said in a shaky voice.

All thoughts of my mom, Confucius, and whatever else I was mindlessly jabbering about a second ago disappeared out of my mind, along with most of the breath from my lungs.

"What?" My voice was barely audible.

I yanked the comforter up to my chin, as if it could extinguish the wave of cold that suddenly washed over me. Brad kept talking, but my brain blocked out any reception of words and the sound hit my ears like waves crashing on rocks.

This couldn't be happening. If I squeezed my eyes tight enough—if I could just fall asleep like I'd planned—all of this would go away.

ANNA GRACIA

I could hear Brad pacing around the room, his heavy footsteps accompanied by the scratching sound of his hands furiously running over his hair—something he did whenever he was uncomfortable. He muttered an impressive string of expletives to himself over and over, every few syllables punctuated with a louder f-word than the rest.

No no no no no. I pulled the covers over my head to muffle the sound of Brad's voice. If I couldn't hear him, all of this wouldn't be real. I couldn't get pregnant. What would my parents say? What about college?

People had accidents all the time. Condoms broke. Even when they didn't, they weren't 100 percent effective. I silently ran through every reproductive fact I could remember from tenth-grade health class, as if there would be a secret answer in the notes to prevent all this from happening in the first place.

It wasn't fair! We'd been safe! We'd been smart. Pregnancy scares were for stupid people who didn't use protection. It was bullshit. I didn't deserve this.

The bed rippled as Brad sank his weight onto the side of the mattress. A moment later, a rush of cool air and bright light hit my face as Brad peeled back the covers. "Can you talk to me, babe? I'm freaking out here. What are we going to do?"

I kept my eyes squeezed shut as my hands pawed around, searching for the covers to pull back onto myself. I wasn't ready to face his questions. I wasn't ready to face any of this.

"June! Stop ignoring me!"

My eyes flew open in surprise at Brad using my actual name. His face was filled with exactly the amount of fear that was currently twisting its way around my heart and into my stomach. His hands were fidgeting in his lap, up to his head, and back onto his lap in a loop. Twist, scratch, rest, repeat.

"What do we do what do we do what do we do?" He bounced a little with each question, bouncing waves of panic off his body and onto mine.

Why was I supposed to be the one who knew what to do? We'd both been through the same state-mandated health class. And it had been *his* condom that broke.

I pushed myself up into a sitting position, my head slumped over into my hands. I couldn't look at Brad yet. He was expecting me to say something—to know the answer, as though I should know the answer to everything.

Except I didn't know the answer. Not here, not anywhere. Why had I even started having sex in the first place? Why hadn't I considered this as a possibility? Why couldn't I go back in time and undo all of it?

I hit the heels of my hands against my forehead. *Stupid, stupid girl.*

Brad grabbed my arms and gently pulled them away from me. "Babe. China. Please. Say something. Tell me what to do."

Something about the cutesy nicknames irritated me, the words scraping against an already open wound. But the fear of not knowing what to do crowded out all other thoughts and I raised my eyes to meet his, ready to confess that I had no more idea of what to do than he did.

"Isn't there some kind of test you can take?" Brad asked. "You know, to find out if you're pregnant?"

A light bulb went off and I could finally look at him with a spark of relief. "We can go to Planned Parenthood." *Thank god for Planned Parenthood.* I couldn't risk trying to go see a doctor. What if they told my dad about it? Pine Grove wasn't exactly a big city.

"Planned Parenthood? For what? Can't you just buy a test at Walgreens?"

"I'm not going to take a pregnancy test. I'm going to get the morning-after pill and I'm not about to risk running into someone we know, buying it at the store."

Brad blinked several times, his wrinkled forehead clearly trying to process the information I'd just given him. "The morning-after pill? What's that? Like an abortion?"

"What? No. It's a pill that keeps you from getting pregnant in the first place."

"But how? I thought once my uh, sperm, you know, hit your—" He awkwardly crashed his gathered fingers together and mashed them against each other.

I held up my hand to make him stop. "Yeah, no. There's no guarantee that even happened. But either way, this pill is made for accidents. It'll fix everything."

Well, it would fix this, anyway.

"Hand me my phone," I commanded. "I'll look up where the closest Planned Parenthood is and make an appointment." Finally. Something actionable.

He grabbed my phone off his nightstand but pulled back from handing it to me. "Shouldn't we talk about this some more?"

"What is there to talk about?"

"Well, what if you *are* pregnant? Shouldn't we talk about our options?"

"That's the whole point of Plan B. So I don't get pregnant in the first place."

"But I came inside you. Like, a lot. And my dad always said he got my mom pregnant on their first try. So my dudes are just like, swimming around in there looking for stuff, you know? You could get pregnant before you even get that pill. Then what? Besides, I don't even know where a Planned Parenthood is."

I will not get pregnant.

I will not get pregnant.

I will not get pregnant.

I will not get pregnant.

It wasn't even a question. I refused to entertain it. I would go to Planned Parenthood. I would take the morning-after pill. And everything would be fixed. All of this would go away.

I snatched the phone out of his hand. "I'm making an appointment. I don't care how far I have to drive."

CHAPTER FOURTEEN

As it turned out, the closest Planned Parenthood was only a thirty-minute drive. So the next morning, I waited until my mom left for work and drove to pick up Brad for my appointment. *Our* appointment.

"Morning, China," he said, sliding into the passenger seat and leaning over to give me a kiss.

My annoyance from yesterday crept back in, the shine of a pet name having long worn off. Why had I let him start calling me that in the first place? Had he really been *that* cute?

I stiffly accepted the kiss but didn't return a greeting of any kind. I just wanted to stay focused and get this whole ordeal over with.

I typed the address into my GPS, clipped my phone into the holder attached to my windshield, and set off for what was to be my first ever ob-gyn appointment. My mom always insisted we didn't need to go because, as she said anytime the subject arose, *You don't need to go unless you're having sex, and you're not having sex, right?* Even with my dad's medical degree, he refused to overrule my mom when she told us her nonsensical beliefs as if they were facts. Like when she told Wendy and me that putting hair binders around our wrists would cut off our circulation and make our hands fall off. Or that using tampons would make us not be virgins. Or that showing our belly buttons—even in summer—would make us sick.

The silence that hung in the car between us was broken only by the occasional directive to turn left or right from the authoritative female British voice on my GPS. Even my hands, which usually fiddled between the radio, window, mirror, and whatever else, now gripped the steering wheel like it was a life preserver thrown to me in the ocean.

My eyes remained laser focused on the road ahead. Each minute that counted down on my estimated arrival time meant I was a minute closer to erasing this mistake. If I could make this problem go away, everything could go back to normal. Everything *had* to go back to normal.

Without realizing, I'd shifted into my breathing exercises: eight counts in, hold for four, eight counts out. Eight in, hold four, eight out.

In the silence of the car, my breathing sounded unnaturally loud, like I was shouting at myself to relax. I reached over and switched on the radio to the classical station. Mozart. Thank god. Mozart always calmed my nerves.

Brad reached over and switched off the music, the silence barging back into the car like an uninvited guest. "I've been thinking," he started, before clearing his throat. "It's not the worst thing in the world if we have a baby."

My head jerked in his direction, taking my hands—and the car—with it. With a yelp, I swerved back into my lane and adjusted my rearview mirror, as if the driver behind me had caused me to nearly drive off the road.

He continued talking, unnerved by our near-death experience with a dirty snowbank on the side of the freeway. "We love each other. That's the most important thing. And you said yourself yesterday that you're thinking about going to UNI. I wasn't really sure about the whole college thing anyway, so I can just get a job and take care of the baby while you're at class. We can figure this out together. It can make us stronger."

My stomach revolted and I could feel acid stinging the base of my throat. It was true. I had told him I was considering staying here for college. And yesterday, I was sure I'd meant it. But hearing him now—hearing the future he'd planned out for us in the space of an evening—shook me awake in the most violent way possible to the fact that it was absolutely *not* what I wanted in any sense of the word. I didn't want to stay here, I didn't want to move in with Brad, and I certainly didn't want a baby. Nothing about what he proposed was anything I wanted for my future.

He was still talking, something about how we had our parents to help us, but all I could think was that I needed him to shut up. Or I needed to find a way to shut him out, at least. I would have covered my ears and shouted at him to stop if only I could pry my fingers from the death grip they had on the steering wheel. Surely it was on the brink of snapping in half from the pressure I was exerting on it.

I cut him off midsentence. "I don't want a baby, Brad. I'm in high school."

"I know it's not great timing," he said. "But hey, neither was the start of our relationship. You had a boyfriend when I met you and we managed to work *that* out."

"Jesus Christ, do you really think that's the same thing?" I exploded. "You seriously think that taking care of a living, breathing human being together for the rest of its life carries the same complications as flirting on an ice rink."

I didn't pose it as a question.

Brad's face showed the wounds from my words, as if they'd physically slashed him. "You don't have to yell at me. You always complain about how your family talks to you, but you do the same thing. You treat everyone around you like they're stupid and it's kind of an asshole thing to do."

I opened my mouth to protest, but bit back the words *I only do it to you because you are* before I could say them. Here I was, dealing with a crisis that could literally upend my entire life, and the only thing he could focus on was how impolite he thought I was being.

When I said nothing, he added, "Besides, babies grow up. You only have to take care of them for the first few years until they get a little bigger, then it's not as much work."

I strangled the steering wheel even tighter, my fingers beginning to ache from the strain. *This* was the person who wanted to be responsible for keeping another human being alive. Someone who thought raising a baby took all the effort of planting a tree.

I stared straight ahead at the road, my eyes practically boring holes through the windshield. "Raising kids is a lifelong commitment. It's not just *a few years* and then everything goes back to the way it was before. I'm not willing to sacrifice my life for—"

"You're being kind of selfish, you know," Brad cut me off, crossing his arms in front of him in a huff. "I'm your boyfriend. I should have a say in this. It's not all about you. You're sitting there talking about it like you're the only one whose life is impacted. Like it's *such* a terrible thing to want to bring a kid into this world."

"It is terrible!" I shrieked. "It's terrible because I don't want to do it!"

My outburst seemed to have silenced him at last. He didn't say anything, but he continued to sulk the rest of the way there.

When we arrived at the center, I checked in at the desk and slumped nervously into a hospital-waiting-room-type chair in the corner, my anger at Brad practically radiating off my body. I didn't want to be alone but at the same time didn't want him anywhere near me. He didn't try to talk to me, but he did sit down in the chair next to mine, and I found myself leaning so far over the armrests on the opposing side I was practically taking up both seats.

During the wait, I started checking out the other patients, looking for other teenage girls and their boyfriends who might be in the same predicament. All I saw was a couple of middle-aged women reading magazines with toothy, smiling faces splashed across their shiny covers. As if there were anything to smile about right now.

When it was finally my turn, I nearly dashed to the exam room, Brad trailing behind, where I was asked for a brief medical history and a urine sample. Within minutes, I had my answer.

The test was negative.

I breathed for the first time in what felt like a day, my chest nearly collapsing upon itself with relief.

Then came the bad news. "It's too soon to tell from a urine test whether or not you're pregnant from this incident," the nurse told me. "We have you take it anyway in case you've had unprotected sex previously because we can't administer you the emergency contraceptive if you're already pregnant. Sperm typically survive up to three days in your cervix but can last as long as five days in the right conditions, so you should take another pregnancy test. They're most accurate when taken no sooner than seven days after a missed period."

Another pregnancy test? What the hell had I come here for then?

The nurse continued, "A blood test taken by your doctor can detect pregnancy much earlier—"

"I want the morning-after pill," I cut in. I'd sat through enough of my dad's medical lectures to know that health professionals were required to cover every conceivable option and risk, but nothing was going to change my mind and we were wasting precious minutes that could be used to prevent this disaster in the first place.

"You're probably not even pregnant," Brad argued.

"I can't afford to take that chance," I snapped.

The pill wasn't free. Something about funding cuts. I wasn't absorbing much information. I asked Brad if he would split the cost with me.

"That's a lot of money," he said, squirming. "I don't even think you need it. And you're the one taking it, so . . ."

I paid for the pill and swallowed it on the spot.

———————

The two of us didn't talk on our way back, but the side effects began to kick in before I even reached my house.

First came the dizziness. I dropped him off as my head started to feel light, then pulled over to the side of the road to puke my guts out. Hopefully, experiencing side effects meant I'd absorbed enough of the meds that throwing up didn't matter. It wasn't like I could ask my dad.

I wiped off my mouth and glanced at my reflection. It was sallow and clammy, like I was sweating out a hangover or going through a violent withdrawal. I couldn't risk showing up at home in this state, not with my family being the way they were.

I pulled out my phone and through the blur of my watering eyes, I dialed Candace.

Voice mail.

I dialed again.

Voice mail.

Damn it.

I tried for a slow exhale, hoping to calm the turmoil in my stomach, before pulling my car door shut and driving a few blocks farther. When I could hold it no longer, I pulled into a park and vomited out my car door, my stomach retching nothing more than acrid bile until my throat burned. I unclicked my seat belt and collapsed back into my seat, weak and sweaty from the exertion. I slid my seat back as far as it would go, propping my feet up on the steering wheel to try and calm the spinning in my head.

Nausea, vomiting, dizziness, and cramps—all the same side effects as pregnancy. Nature must have been having a good laugh at my expense.

"June?"

My eyes flew open at the sound of my name. Rhys was standing a safe distance away from my car—and the puke puddle next to it.

I scrambled up to a sitting position and subconsciously wiped my mouth, as if it weren't already obvious where the puke on the ground had come from.

"What are you doing here?" I asked, looking around the deserted park.

He held up the handle of an empty leash, a large golden retriever happily trotting between trees and stopping to sniff them. I'd completely forgotten his family had a dog. I mostly avoided the thing, its huge paws and slobbery mouth prone to leaving marks on my clothes I didn't appreciate. People acted like you were some kind of monster if you didn't immediately get emoji heart eyes at the sight of a dog, so I had told Rhys I was afraid of dogs and let him assume I'd had some kind of nebulous past experience. He never asked for specifics.

Rhys ambled over to the passenger side of the car, presumably to avoid the mess on my side, and opened the door before I could wave him off.

"You feeling okay?" he asked, his head peeking in the door.

I saw his eyes glance down to the Plan B pamphlet poking out of my purse. The nurse had insisted I take it, along with a handful of condoms, which were, with my luck, completely visible from where Rhys was standing.

A look of surprise passed over his face and I quickly snatched up the purse and shoved it into my back seat. "I'm fine," I lied. "Just getting some air."

Rhys climbed into the passenger seat uninvited, his weight shaking the car as he plopped himself down. "So. Things going well with the boyfriend, huh?" His voice had a hint of a teasing tone.

I was too sick to be embarrassed. "What do you want?" I asked flatly.

"Geez, okay. I'll back off," he said, raising his hands in surrender. "Sorry to check on you when you're puking by yourself in a public park on a Tuesday morning. I should obviously know everything is completely fine and normal here."

He didn't leave, however, reclining his seat to give his long limbs a bit more space in my compact car. I concentrated on my breathing: eight counts in through the nose, hold for four, out through the mouth for another eight. Surely the nausea couldn't last much longer; I didn't have anything left to puke up at this point.

"You want some water or something?" Rhys asked.

I looked over eagerly. "Do you have some?" My mouth tasted like a sewer.

"Uh, no."

"Then why would you offer?" I snapped.

Rhys shrugged meekly in response to my cutting tone, sinking back into the seat as he mindlessly wound the leash around his hands. My hands clutched the base of my abdomen, the cramps in my uterus growing with intensity like it was preparing to expel the very sperm that threatened to get me pregnant. Forget taking home plastic crying babies—schools should just make kids take the morning-after pill. Then they'd never have sex.

"Aughhhhhhhh!" I wailed in frustration. It wasn't fair that I was suffering through this. Why was I the only one bearing the brunt of the consequences? Brad was able to get off with nothing more than passing panic and was now safely at home, blissfully unaware that I had ended up here—puking my guts out on the side of the road. He cared more about the chance of a baby *I* was taking away from him than whatever pain I was going through.

Anger rose up inside me like a volcano. This was bullshit. All of it was bullshit.

"I hate you, you know that?" I spat at Rhys.

This was all his fault. If he hadn't been so . . . so . . . Rhys-like while we were together, I would never have been swayed by the appeal of Brad. I would have never been put in this situation. I'd still be safe in the land of making out and over-the-bra touching, wondering why my boyfriend didn't want anything more from me. Surely this had to be a lower level of hell than that.

He turned his head to look at me, unruffled by my outburst. "Wow. Okay," he said.

The most Rhys-like response of all time.

It was like there was nothing he cared about enough to get upset over.

"Why are you here?" I demanded.

"Because I was out walking my dog and saw you and thought something was wrong? You're right, I'm such an asshole. I should have known it was my fault you're going through something here that involves a shitload of condoms and some kind of morning sickness. Clearly you've got this under control." He snapped the door handle angrily, trying two times before he successfully pushed open the door.

Damn it.

Brad was right. I was an asshole. And not just to him, even if it felt like he'd deserved it this morning.

"Wait," I said before he could climb out. I squeezed my eyes shut, as if it would make saying the words easier. "I'm sorry. I'm just . . . having a bad day. It's not your fault."

Rhys sat back again but left the door ajar, letting his long legs dangle out the side of the car.

We sat in silence—the thick, awkward silence of two people who were trying very hard to avoid the topic we were both thinking about.

I blew out a puff of air, the stray hairs that had stuck to my clammy face belatedly set free. It was easier just to tackle the topic head-on. "I'm not pregnant, FYI."

Rhys shifted uncomfortably. "I never said you were."

"You made a morning sickness comment."

"You were puking."

We lapsed back into silence, Rhys fiddling with the leash by winding and unwinding the thick black nylon around his knuckles.

The nausea had subsided, but my head was still buzzing, swimming with a million thoughts. After today, nothing would be different and yet everything would be different. I felt like I'd unwillingly entered some club of girls who had to take the morning-after pill—like we were marked, tattooed with invisible ink as though people could pass a black light over us and judge our choices. Fundamentally, my life was exactly the same as it had been twenty-four hours earlier. I was still not pregnant and perfectly happy about it. But I was now someone who'd had a pregnancy scare. Even knowing it was statistically reasonable that I'd eventually have one, it still had the capacity to make me feel like it reflected negatively on who I was as a person.

The expression on Rhys's face when he saw the pamphlet— even though it passed in a fraction of a second—was clear. I was not the type of person he expected to have this problem. I was expected to behave better. Or smarter. I'd dealt with the problem, but if only I'd somehow been better, I'd never have run into it in the first place. He saw me like my family saw me: disappointing, perpetually failing to meet expectations.

Maybe that's how he'd always seen me.

A wave of lethargy passed over me, the weariness from the morning's events seeping into my bones and weighing me down like lead. I was tired—too tired to sit here and convince Rhys that despite the fact that I felt zero regret over my choice to take the morning-after pill, that didn't make me a bad person.

145

"I'm going home," I announced, my voice full of the fatigue I felt inside.

Rhys unwrapped the leash, pulling it taut between his hands. "You sure you're okay to drive?"

"I'll manage."

With some effort, I managed to sit up and scoot my seat back into its proper position. I shut my door, the immediate smell of puke waning, though not totally disappearing from inside the car. Rhys heaved himself out like a giraffe climbing out of an egg, the metal fastener on the end of his leash clanging loudly against the side of my car.

He turned like he was going to say something to me, but seemed to think better of it and shut the door behind him without a word. I drove straight home, collapsing facedown onto my bed with my arms outstretched, as if I could hug the one space that was free of judgment.

CHAPTER FIFTEEN

I awoke hours later, bleary-eyed and dehydrated, my head vibrating like it'd gotten stuck in a bass drum, but the sickness in my stomach was gone. I was tucked neatly under my covers, a glass of water and two aspirin on the nightstand next to my bed, the room lit by the lamp on my desk.

Instantly my heart surged and I leapt out of bed toward the spot I'd remembered dropping my purse, which remained slumped on my desk chair, the Plan B brochure and condoms safely zipped inside and away from view.

Thank goodness.

I collapsed back onto my bed, gratefully swallowing the two pills with a swig of water and placing the glass back down with a louder bang than I'd intended. But who had left them for me?

As if in answer to my question, my door opened with a light knock and Wendy's round face peeked through. Her voice was gentle as she made her way across the room to me. "You're up. How are you feeling?"

"What time is it?" I croaked, my throat not yet healed from the acidic bile I'd thrown up earlier.

"Almost six."

Shit. I'd slept through most of the day.

"Did Mom send you to check on me?"

She shook her head. "I told her you were busy with college essays so she wouldn't bother you."

"Oh." When we were younger, Wendy and I used to cover for each other all the time, but it'd been a long time since Wendy had lied to my parents for my benefit. I took another large gulp of water before adding, "Thanks."

I sat all the way up now as a cue to show that I was indeed recovered, but Wendy made no moves toward the exit.

"I wasn't feeling well," I said, offering the barest of just-plausible-enough excuses.

She gave a slight nod giving only the vaguest sense that she was even listening to me.

"Okay," I said, making to swing my legs off the edge of the bed. "Well, I should probably—"

"You know you can talk to me, right?" she cut in, her voice pressed with urgency.

"What?"

"You can tell me what's going on with you. I'm your sister. I won't judge you."

I highly doubted that last assertion, but her eyes were pleading, her fingers twisted up into knots of anxiety. She certainly *seemed* convincing.

Still, I hesitated. She already didn't approve of Brad, or of what we were doing in our relationship. There was a chance I'd end up with a lecture and not the sympathetic ear I needed right now.

Then again, it was nice to see she cared enough to check on me. She obviously knew something was up but hadn't put on her disapproving face yet. So that was something.

"I had some stuff happen with Brad. It's not a big deal, I already took care of it," I said.

Wendy chewed on her bottom lip, seemingly torn about whether or not she wanted to say anything. "So . . . what's going on with you two now?" she ventured.

Something about her demeanor and the way she so gently tiptoed around the topic made me think she very likely already knew what had happened, but funnily enough, I didn't feel outraged at the intrusion. It was almost a relief not to have to say the words aloud.

I shrugged. "I'm not sure yet. It's complicated."

She chewed her lip some more, her hands fidgeting into her pockets, up to her glasses, then back again.

"I leave for Nicaragua in the morning," she announced, her voice suddenly back to its normal volume, her hands now clasped tightly together in front of her.

"Yeah, I know," I said, trying to brighten my tone to match hers. "Have fun."

"Just um . . . just be safe while I'm gone, okay? You can text me anytime."

I nodded. "Thanks."

She gave me a final smile—a smile that looked like the kind of encouraging smile you'd give a gravely ill person after reassuring them that everything would be okay while knowing it wouldn't; a smile that said while she hoped for good things for me, she didn't

ANNA GRACIA

really believe they would happen; a smile that said everything about how she saw my future if I continued on my same path.

"Mom said dinner will be ready in about twenty minutes," she said, closing the door behind her.

I flopped back down on the bed, my arms over my eyes to shield them from the light that now seemed so bright it was blinding me.

———

I spent the subsequent days hidden in my room, replaying both "the incident," as the nurse at Planned Parenthood had called it, and Wendy's reaction afterward. She'd been so . . . nice about it. Come to think of it, so had Rhys. Something was definitely in the air if the two people who usually managed to torment me the most were both acting friendly. Maybe I was just that pathetic lately.

My phone buzzed, pulling my attention to the source of my current misery.

I love you.

Call me.

Still busy?

Is everything okay?

I miss you.

I miss your face.

Earth to China.

Come in, China.

tap tap is this thing on?

I threw my phone across my bed where it would hopefully disappear, the insulation of the pillows swallowing any further sound from it. I'd started what felt like a million texts to Candace and Liz, but there wasn't a succinct way of summarizing everything that had happened over the past few days. I wasn't even sure I *wanted* to tell them. It was, essentially, a nonissue. I had taken care of it, and I didn't have unresolved issues about doing so. But I also didn't know how to explain the sudden change of feelings I had toward Brad. Why I suddenly felt a knot in my stomach every time he called me "China."

I could hear muffled buzzing coming from the pillows, and the guilt of ignoring Brad started to creep back into my chest. It was perfectly reasonable, I'd told myself, to take a day to process what had happened. Then one day stretched into two, two into three, and now here I was, four days later, dreading every buzz of the phone because I knew it would be him, texting yet again to check in on me to make sure I was okay.

I was a crappy girlfriend. Like he'd said in the car, this was something that *both* of us were dealing with, and I'd shut him out completely. Granted, he had had the absolute worst take on the situation, but that didn't give me the right to just ghost him.

I knew what it felt like to be ghosted, and yet, I couldn't bring myself to answer any of his texts.

Everything he was doing right now that grated on my nerves—the constant texting, the check-ins, even the cutesy nicknames—was exactly the same stuff I loved about him before this. He'd given me exactly what I'd wanted, right down to the slightly over-possessive way he insisted on always walking with one arm around my shoulder, like he wanted everyone to know I'd been claimed. I'd wanted someone who adored me, and now that I had that someone, I couldn't stomach the thought of ever seeing him again.

The music blaring out of my speakers switched to the next song, and I jumped off my bed in a hurry to change it before the Metallica song had made it past the opening notes. The last thing I needed right now was another reminder of Rhys.

Somehow the knowledge that he knew what had happened was worse than Wendy knowing. Like the fact that he hadn't wanted to sleep with me made it look like I'd jumped the first available person after him.

Another muffled buzz came from my pillows, and with great reluctance I flopped back onto my bed, stretching across to rescue my phone from its fluffy prison.

If you don't feel like talking, you can call me and I'll just talk.

I need to see you.

Please.

I'm going out of my mind over here.

No one had ever *needed* me. Not my friends, who were so busy with their jobs and indoor soccer practice and whatever else that they hadn't even noticed I'd gone MIA for four whole days. Not Wendy, who had texted me twice since she left, but only to remind me that she was there for me if *I* needed *her*. And definitely not my parents, who'd spent the past few days reminding me that *néng zhě duō láo—the talented are kept busy—*and pointing out that I was decidedly *not* busy at the moment.

But Brad's need weighed me down, like I was trying to swim across the ocean and he'd disguised himself as a life preserver only to turn out to be a heavy rock. As much as I'd wanted to believe that my mom's insistence on excellence in all things was bullshit, I couldn't deny the pull I still had toward at least *attempting* to reach it, even if it wasn't in the way or at the level she expected me to. Going to UNI just because I'd already been accepted seemed like giving up. Had I really, honestly put my best effort into finding a good school my parents would approve of? Or had I unwittingly sabotaged the process, knowing my parents would be unhappy with whatever I chose so not bothering to try too hard? After all, I'd been doing that with music for years.

My phone buzzed again, pulling my thoughts out of the theoretical and back to the practical. I swiped at the screen, another barrage of messages from Brad stacked one on top of the other like a never-ending soliloquy of need.

Hey.

It's me again.

I can't fall asleep without hearing your voice.

China Doll.

I need you.

Call me.

I love you.

You are getting these messages, right?

Please answer.

I threw my phone across my bed again—this time not because of fatigue, but frustration. He didn't need me because I made him happy or because he liked talking to me or even because I made him laugh or smile; he needed me like a scuba diver needs oxygen. Like he didn't know how to live without me. Even miles away— even without answering my phone—I could feel that his need was so palpable it stretched across the space between us, its greedy fingers reaching into my lungs and stealing the oxygen to take back to him.

This wasn't about love or emotions; he wanted to possess me. He wanted to keep me, like a literal china doll—never mind the fact that I wasn't actually Chinese—that he could hold and adore and who would never leave his side. The fact that he'd never bothered to properly identify me was just an added insult. Had he ever actually loved me? Maybe he didn't know what love was. Maybe I didn't either. But whatever it was, it sure as hell wasn't this.

Spurred by my sudden realization, I launched myself out of bed and into my desk chair. Being with Brad had lulled me into such a sense of complacency that I hadn't made any further progress on my college spreadsheet. Thankfully I'd had the foresight to add a column for the schools that had notable music programs. Whether or not I really wanted to commit to playing violin for another four years didn't matter anymore—it was going to be my ticket out of here. Early admissions windows had long passed, and while my grades were perfect, colleges weren't likely to be falling all over themselves to snag yet another Asian with straight As. I needed actual, substantial scholarship money, not just admission—unless I wanted to end up like Britney Lee. I certainly wasn't banking on my pending application with Northwestern.

My fingers flew across the keyboard, drafting emails listing my accomplishments with a file of myself playing to each of the music directors, asking if they had space in their program and if they'd be interested in making me an offer. It was probably too late to expect much, but if the school wasn't too expensive and I got at least half of it covered, I could take out loans to subsidize my first year and bargain my way up once I got there. Or I could apply for residency and get in-state tuition. I'd get a job if I had to. Anything to keep me from winding up at UNI.

I drafted email after email to the various music departments, espousing my deepest desire to go to *their* school. My love for music. My unfettered dedication to perfection, as exhibited by my rigorous daily schedule. I lied and lied and lied, over and over and over again, until I'd finally checked off the final box. My back screaming and my fingers stiff, I collapsed onto my bed in a state of begrudging triumph. I'd finished contacting the entire list. It might not result in anything, but for now, I had taken a step toward *something*. I'd given it my best shot, and now I'd have to wait to see if it was enough.

CHAPTER SIXTEEN

By the time New Year's Eve rolled around, my anxiety had flared up again. I'd already started to receive rejections from schools who'd long since promised their scholarship money to people who didn't wait until the last minute to get their lives together.

I'd finally texted Brad back, but only to let him know I was alive and that I needed space to process things. I thought it'd help stem the tide of texts I received from him, but instead, it was like he knew I was trying to pull away and doubled down on his attempt to reassure me of his desperate need for me in his life. He'd wanted to celebrate tonight—*a new year together*, he'd said. I lied and told him my parents wouldn't let me go out. Then I'd gone over to Liz's, who was throwing a small get-together because her dad was one of those parents who thought it was safer to let us drink in his house because "you're going to do it anyway." He honestly had no idea how lucky he was to end up with such a goody-two-shoes daughter. In the three years her parents had been divorced, Liz had only had people over to drink a handful of times.

"I guess we should thank Cedar for letting you slum it with us in the Grove tonight, huh?" Rhys's voice cut into my thoughts as he lifted his cup in a sort of mock toast to the fact that I'd resurfaced at Liz's instead of celebrating with the boyfriend no one knew I was avoiding.

I raised my cup toward where Rhys was seated, on a black leather loveseat matching my black leather couch, both of which stood out like black eyes against the painted bright yellow walls. The stereotype of divorced dads lacking style was a cliché, but it was a cliché for good reason. The living room had a giant decal of the Iowa Hawkeye on the wall, for god's sake. It was like being inside a locker room. "Lucky you, huh?" I asked with a sardonic smile.

"Well, *I'm* glad to have you here," Liz said, bumping me with her knee as she perched on the armrest next to me, her body swaying back and forth. "I can't be the only lightweight on New Year's."

Despite being at least half a foot taller than me and probably double my weight in muscle alone, Liz's alcohol tolerance was on par with mine because she rarely drank. The only clue she was buzzed was when she started getting friendly, swapping her usual roster of serious looks for tipsy head bobs and sappy speeches about things she was grateful for.

"I wish Candace were here," she sighed. "I want both my best friends with me on the last day of the year. We should be celebrating together before we all graduate and start going our separate ways, growing apart. What if we stop being friends after high school? I don't want this to be our last memory together."

She was buzzed, all right.

I slapped my knees and stood up. "Okey dokey, lightweight. Let's get you some water." I tried to pull her up but couldn't get her to budge. She wasn't doing much to help.

Rhys sighed heavily, lumbering out of his seat and shuffling across the carpet. "I'll take care of it."

He pulled her to her feet with ease and navigated her toward the kitchen, where everyone else was gathered around the keg—alcohol that Paul had once again conveniently provided. There weren't many people here—just Savannah and the guys and a couple of girls from Liz's volleyball team from fall season—but the house was filled with the noise of a much larger crowd. Especially with Grayson's voice booming dozens of decibels over everyone else's.

I probably should have joined them in the kitchen in the name of being social, but I didn't feel much like it. I'd thought coming here would give me a distraction—a return to the normalcy I'd been craving. But something about the night felt off. Candace was missing, Liz was drunk, and Rhys was, well, Rhys. I could never quite figure out what was up with him.

We hadn't spoken again since our run-in at the park—that is, until his awkward dig about me not being with Brad tonight. I didn't know if that was his way of trying to make a joke or if he was being an undercover asshole about what happened. Both scenarios seemed equally likely.

I pulled out my phone and made the usual rounds through my apps, looking at pictures people had already posted of their night. The people at this party started to trickle back into the room and

I swiped the happy faces off my screen as quickly as I could; I had enough of those to deal with in person. Two girls from Liz's volleyball team plopped down next to me on the couch, their combined weight nearly bouncing me off the cushion and into their laps. I slid as far away as I could, keeping a tight grip on my phone. If I buried my face in it, people might avoid talking to me for the rest of the night.

Coming here at all was a mistake.

I pulled up my email inbox, expecting more rejections from schools. Apparently, music directors had nothing better to do over their holiday breaks than catch up on their emails, judging by the number of nos I'd received over the past couple of days.

But where I'd been expecting the usual *we're flattered by your interest but unfortunately,* my heart flipped at the words *unexpected vacancy we're looking to fill.* I quickly scanned the rest of the email until I saw *we'd love for you to come out for an official visit.*

I read it again, then once more to make sure I hadn't misread it. Someone was offering to fly me out so *I* could see if *I* wanted *them*?

I shot up from the couch like I'd been electrocuted. I needed to reply. Now, before they changed their minds. But the only thing my brain could come up with was just the word *yes* with a million exclamation points after it.

I stumbled out of the living room, my eyes glued to the message for fear it might disappear if I looked away. I needed to get somewhere quiet where I could actually hear my own brain. I slipped down the hall and into Liz's room, careful to make sure no one had noticed my disappearance. I didn't need a scolding from drunk Liz about how I was suddenly the unfun one of the night.

"Close the door," a groggy voice called out.

I whipped my head around, surprised to find Rhys sprawled across the bed.

"Oh. It's you," Rhys slurred, his eyes squinting from the light coming into the room.

I shut the door.

"What are you doing in here?" I asked.

"You know, getting a jump on my taxes. Filing paperwork."

Even drunk, Rhys had a smart mouth.

"Are you just going to stand there and guard the door or are you going to come over here?" He patted the space next to him sloppily.

He wanted me to lie down? Next to him?

My brain on autopilot, I slowly made my way through the dark room—my socked feet shuffling across the carpet, hands outstretched and ready to stop me from crashing into anything in my path.

The mattress groaned as Rhys shifted over to leave space for me to crawl in next to him. I did it as quietly as possible, as though someone outside might hear the slight rustle of sheets and rush in to find us.

In two months of dating I'd never once been in a bed with him, yet now here I was, lying within inches of him like we'd done this a million times before. My mind churned, trying to sort out why I'd agreed to this at all. It wasn't like Rhys was trying anything romantic. He hadn't even seemed to want that while we were dating. Did this mean he wanted to be friends now? Maybe he hadn't been judging me that day in the park like I'd imagined he was.

Up on the ceiling, the faintest of glows radiated off the peel-and-stick stars Liz had put up years ago and never bothered to take down. Instead of a random scattering, she had arranged them to spell out the word *star*. A little on the nose, but that was Liz. At least it gave my eyes something to focus on.

"I got an offer to visit a school," I said. "They want me to come audition."

I didn't know why I was telling him, but saying the words aloud made it more real.

"Wow," he murmured. "Congrats, I guess."

The space between us filled with unsaid words. I imagined him asking me why I was excited to go play for a school when just weeks ago I was happy about the possibility of never having to perform again. I imagined myself answering that it was complicated. We'd only talked about my violin playing a couple of times while we were together, but I'm sure I'd given him the impression I hated it. It was a lot easier to let people think that than the explain the truth.

"It's in Washington state," I added.

"That's . . . far . . ."

"Could be a good thing."

"Because of your parents?"

My parents. Ugh. Having to admit aloud that my mom was right about me not giving up music or settling for UNI was not great. She was insufferable enough as it was. But even if I ended up hating this new school, their interest in me at least proved I wasn't as lazy and unmotivated as she thought I was.

"My parents still want me to go to Northwestern," I said. "Oh yeah, by the way, I got in," I added. "The letter came a few days ago."

"You sound thrilled."

"It's complicated," I sighed, this time saying the words aloud.

Initially I'd been elated; the piece of paper seemed to prove once and for all that I was at least as smart as Wendy. But instead of relieving the pressure, it seemed to double it instead—a constant reminder that admission was only half of the equation. My parents didn't even congratulate me, except to say that I should notify the music director immediately to try and hasten his scholarship decision.

I'd sent that rash of emails in an attempt to flee as far as possible from Brad and any future that put me anywhere near Pine Grove four years from now. I'd sent them to protect myself from my possible rejection from Northwestern. But until five minutes ago, I wasn't sure I believed that any of it would actually work. And now, with the choice staring me in the face, I finally realized what it would mean to go to a school halfway across the country. I wouldn't just be leaving Brad, but everyone who meant something to me. Candace. Liz. And . . . him.

Maybe things were still awkward between us, but the awkwardness was also familiar. At some point it simply became our operating standard. Like spending time with a childhood friend you had nothing in common with anymore except the shared history you didn't want to let go of.

The extended silence between us in the dark room had turned to intimacy, his lack of words finally a comfort. Every other conversation I'd had about college thus far seemed to prompt a barrage of questions—all of them intended to reveal my true self, none of which I was equipped to answer. It was nice to think that for once I had a few inches of space to just . . . breathe.

"Where do *you* want to go to school?" I blurted out. Part of me hoped he would leave too, so I wouldn't be the only one. It was a tricky thing, trying to leave a place no one ever left. There was safety in numbers and, weirdly, I felt a certain solidarity with Rhys. We were AP kids, destined for bigger and better things. No matter how much he pretended not to care about grades or tests or studying, he cared enough to sign up for the accelerated classes in the first place. Surely that meant something.

Rhys paused for a beat before answering, his voice wobbly from the alcohol. "I dunno. Probably UNI like everyone else, I guess. I should probably turn in my application."

"Wait, so you haven't applied *anywhere*? You could go wherever you want. You practically got a perfect score on the SATs. You could probably apply for the Ivies! Why aren't you looking at other schools? Deadlines are coming up!" I could hear myself turning into my mom, scolding as if my future depended on his. Because if he knew how to choose the best option, maybe I would too.

Rhys reached over, his hand finding mine in the dark. I was startled by how normal it felt. How comforting.

Rhys and I didn't hold hands a single time while we were together. Brad and I did, but usually as a sign that we were a couple. Like while he drove, or if he wanted to say something particularly sweet to me. I'd never had someone just rest their hand on mine for reassurance, like stilling a rocking boat.

Nothing except our hands touched, but the rest of me ached to be stilled too—to be wrapped so tightly that I couldn't move, much less think. I wanted to be distracted by the scent of marigolds and pine, my face burrowed into an expanse of warm flannel. I wanted fingers combing through my hair, gently reigning in my brain from the one hundred and one separate directions it was running.

The intensity of my desire fractured as the jumpy parts of me started to creep back into my chest—the parts that made me wonder if I was talking too much or not talking enough or whether I was saying the right thing. This newfound friendship was stuck somewhere between the old me who desperately wanted him to like me and the new me who was hell-bent on being independent and unattached.

Rhys squeezed my hand, like he knew I needed to be reassured. Except all it did was make me feel worse. Brad was out there somewhere thinking I was holed up in a dark room having big feelings about something I'd already nearly erased from my memory, while instead I was in a dark room with my ex-boyfriend talking about our futures like they were more intertwined with each other's than mine was with Brad's.

I was like the fabled girl from Chinese lessons whose story was meant to teach us the shame of being selfish. *Dōng shí xī sù—eating in the east and sleeping in the west.* I hadn't broken up with Brad yet because even though I knew I didn't actually want to be with him, I wasn't ready to let go of the one person who at least *tried to* love me. At the same time, I'd let myself lie here and indulge in the tiny fantasy that there might still be something between Rhys and me because it gave me butterflies. I was being greedy in the worst possible way, my fingers bookmarking the pages of a *Choose Your Own Adventure* book so I could read the developments in every story line without having to actually choose one.

Rhys started to speak, a low rasp where his voice should have been. He cleared his throat and tried again. "My parents took Paul and me to Seattle when we were kids. It was . . ." His voice trailed off for so long I wasn't sure he was going to finish his thought. "Nice," he belatedly finished.

How the hell was I supposed to respond to that? I went with Rhys's usual standby response.

"Okay."

Oh god, is that why he always responded that way to me? Was I usually the rambling, semicoherent person who chatted away about topics long after the conversation had shifted?

A wave of panic seized my stomach as I suddenly remembered the humiliating failure that was *Mission: BJ* at Liz's cabin. I'd broken up with him afterward, thinking he hated me because he hadn't wanted to hook up with me. But seeing him here, drunk and awkwardly sweet, but clearly not himself, I could only imagine how I'd come off to him that night.

What if I'd been the one to ruin it? And for nothing? What if he'd had a perfectly reasonable explanation for why he was gone from school for those four days afterward? Why hadn't I just asked him where he was?

Rhys's hand now felt more hot than comforting—a suffocating heat seeping through my skin and causing my blood to rapidly churn, like agitated electrons jumping to a higher orbital. I needed to get out of here before I asked a question I wasn't sure I wanted to know the answer to. I'd made enough mistakes without plunging myself back into the special hell that was trying to decipher Rhys's feelings.

I snatched my hand away more forcefully than I intended, which jolted Rhys from a shallow sleep.

"Did I miss it? Is it midnight?" he croaked, his head lifting an inch off the pillow, eyes barely open.

I chewed on my lip, trying very hard not to think about what would happen if I was still here lying next to him in bed when midnight struck.

"Go back to sleep," I whispered. "I'll wake you up when it's time."

Satisfied, his head sank back onto Liz's pillow and his heavy breathing became regular. I slipped out of the room, making my exit from the party a few minutes later, well before the ball dropped and people started eyeing each other for midnight kisses. Back home safely, I ignored the incoming texts from Brad, clutching my phone to my chest and staring at my ceiling, wishing I could disappear into the vast blankness above me.

CHAPTER SEVENTEEN

I was a terrible person for breaking up with Brad in a text, but I just couldn't face the thought of another in-person breakup where the guilt would show on my face. He called, demanding an explanation for something that "came out of nowhere." Like it wasn't immediately obvious we weren't compatible the moment he'd suggested it might be a good idea for me to have a baby while I was still in high school.

I had let him prey on my weakness—convincing me that I was being stubborn and selfish not to let him love me. He'd played me against myself, squeezing himself between the cracks of my self-esteem, making me believe that *he* was the thing that made me whole. Like I'd fall apart without his constant reassurance because I had no one else.

Well, I was still in one piece. And after an hour of him crying on the phone, pleading with me not to leave him—reminding me of every time I'd ever told him I'd loved him—I was finally free. Not without some serious reservations about my judgment when it came to relationships, but free nevertheless.

The new semester started straightaway and Rhys and I didn't have class together anymore, so there was no reason for us to talk. So we didn't. Instead, we passed each other in the hallways, half smiles and retracted waves serving as our only methods of communication. We were like neighbors who'd forgotten each other's names, with too much time passing for us to reintroduce ourselves. Either he was upset about what happened between us on New Year's, or he'd been too drunk to remember it.

I didn't have time to dwell on it—I still had my parents to deal with.

It was impossible to schedule an official visit to Washington without my parents' sign-off, seeing as they might notice if I disappeared for a few days, so I broke the news to them at dinner one night. They didn't say much of anything.

I expected yelling or for them to forbid me to go—even a quick lecture about disappointment or one of their other favorites. Instead, nothing. So I blabbered on and on, telling them about how this program found me and how it would be a shame to waste an opportunity to just *see* what they were offering.

In other words, I lied. But it seemed more likely they'd be impressed a school had sought me out rather than admitting I'd emailed clips of myself playing Metallica to dozens of colleges in the middle of a mental meltdown after a pregnancy scare. Besides, it was the same story I'd told Liz and Candace, and it was easier to keep track of the same lie than new ones for each person. I couldn't afford to have them veto this opportunity—not after the tumultuous few weeks I'd had.

When I finished talking, they continued eating as if I'd said nothing, my mom not even bothering to look up from her bowl as she fed herself one vegetable after another without pause.

"Well . . . what do you think?" I dared to ask, my fingers clutching my chopsticks so tightly they were liable to snap in half.

"I'm not sure how the academics of this school compares to Northwestern, considering we've never heard of it before now," my dad said.

"That would kind of be the point of visiting, don't you think?" I tried to keep the annoyance out of my voice. I'd done everything they'd asked of me thus far, including emailing Northwestern's music director to let him know I'd been accepted and ask whether he'd had a chance to look over his budget for next year. It wasn't my fault he hadn't replied, not that my parents cared about correctly assigning blame.

I took a steadying breath and made my final plea. "Look, I know you guys want me to go to Northwestern. But it can't hurt to have more options. Who knows? It might even end up being a better fit."

My mom kept her eyes focused on the plate of sautéed green beans in the middle of the table as she plucked them off and into her mouth one by one. "I forget to mention, I run into Cindy's mom the other day. You know Cindy, the one who always beat you, her older brother is a doctor? Her mom say she get into Julliard. But she choose Yale. Better choice. Going to become a lawyer. Maybe one day a judge. Julliard not provide that."

If we'd all been characters in a Batman movie, my mom would have been The Riddler—always speaking in codes to get her point across as passive-aggressively as possible. The fact that Cindy—a player so hardcore that she had her cast taken off her broken hand three weeks early so she could still compete in MTNA Regionals—would give up *Julliard* showed just how much influence Asian parents had over their kids' life decisions. Not that going to Yale was a concession.

"Yeah, well, Yale doesn't give merit scholarships," I said defiantly.

My mom liked to pretend she'd be proud of me if I went to some highly prestigious school, but there was zero chance she would still be pushing Northwestern if they'd said there wasn't any money to offer me. In theory you could get into any good med school if you graduated with top grades and a high enough MCAT score. There was no way she thought going two hundred fifty thousand dollars into debt was worth it. Even for Yale.

"Southern California does," my mom said pointedly.

"So what? Who's going there?"

The words came tumbling out before I could stop them. My mom had tricked me—turned me into an unsuspecting participant in her game of Guess Whose Life is Better than Yours.

"Pervy, Parvi, whatever. You know, the Indian." She waved away her concern for accuracy.

"Her name is Parvati, Mom. It's not that hard to remember." I threw my hands in the air in frustration. "And you can't refer to someone as 'the Indian.'"

My mom feigned innocence, her eyebrows skating all the way up to her tidy hairline. "Why not? She's not Indian?"

I gave an exasperated sigh. The widely known, little-talked-about secret among Asians was that they all seemed to keep an internal hierarchy of cultures in which East Asians believed they were superior to South and Southeast Asians, then ranked each country within the East Asian community itself. Unsurprisingly, in my mom's estimation, Taiwan always managed to come out on top. I'd tried to tell my mom a million times how racist this was, but she'd always dismiss the accusation. In her mind, how could she be racist if she was only using the comparison of other Asians to illustrate how much better at life they were than me?

There was no point in arguing with her now. She'd deny it, my dad would tell me to stop attacking her, and we'd end up sidetracked into a conversation about something that had nothing to do with whether or not I could visit Washington.

"Your mom's point is that all the other girls you know are signing with good schools," my dad intervened. "Well-known schools."

Never mind that most of the girls I knew were actually from Pine Grove and none of them were headed to "well-known schools." In my parents' minds, the only people I should compare myself to were other Asian girls who were better at violin than I was.

"It's just a visit," I pleaded. "I thought you'd be excited that someone was scouting me."

My mom sighed heavily as if I were throwing a tantrum and not politely pleading my case to possibly accept a college scholarship. "You miss Chinese New Year."

I tucked my hair behind my ear with a guilty swallow. "I know, but it's getting late, so if I put it off any longer they might offer it to someone else, and the director said it was the first weekend he was available, so . . ."

My parents exchanged a quick look, my dad giving the signal that the final call was my mom's.

She gave an almost imperceptible shrug, unable to care enough to raise her shoulders all the way up. "If you don't care, why should I?"

I didn't want to give her a reason to change her mind, but the fact that she was going to let me go with so little challenge seemed unlikely.

"There are a lot of colleges. Just because you've never heard of it doesn't make it not a good school," I insisted.

My mom looked up at me, her signature gaze staring through me like I were a transparent pane of glass. "Méi zuò kuī xīn shì, bú pà guǐ jiào mén," she said. "A clear conscience does not fear a knock at midnight."

CHAPTER EIGHTEEN

When I'd agreed to a long weekend in Washington over Lunar New Year, I'd expected to miss the festivities altogether. But the minute I'd met my host, Amy—a sophomore violist from the Bay Area—she asked if I celebrated the holiday, and when I confirmed that I did, a look of relief swept across her face. She explained that she and her friends had made plans to go out to celebrate long before I had booked my visit.

After that it was impossible not to notice the number of Asian faces we passed on campus. It was strange, but in a good way. Like for once, I didn't have to wonder when people stared at me if they were doing it because I was the only nonwhite person they'd ever seen. Wendy used to laugh and claim she assumed they stared because she was beautiful. Yes, really.

A quick appraisal of Amy's and my respective outfits shelved that idea. If anything, they were staring at *her*. I don't know how she wasn't freezing cold in nothing more than paper-thin, above-the-ankle pants and a cropped motorcycle jacket, but she looked so fierce I nearly walked into a garbage can because I kept stealing glances at her.

"It seems like there are a lot Asian people here," I said, hoping she didn't notice my awkward stumble around the trash. "What are the demographics of the school?"

Amy shrugged but kept walking, her demeanor all business. "I don't know the specific breakdown; you'll have to take an official tour for those kinds of stats. I can tell you it's nowhere near any kind of majority, but we have a decent number of international students here from Asia at least. It's still mostly white. You'll see, the main cafeteria is all pizza and burgers and white people's versions of burritos with french fries and stuff in them. All the 'Asian' foods are stuffed in one corner, and even that's just cafeteria food without any real flavor. Most of us just eat out for authentic stuff. There are some good spots around town if you know where to look."

My mind tried to wrap itself around the idea of a cafeteria that even *offered* Asian food. The closest we had at Pine Grove were crispy noodles at the salad bar. If this is what "mostly white" looked like to Amy, I wanted her to come to Iowa for a day and watch my friends make gagging noises over my dried squid snacks while they happily downed corn nuts that smelled like sweaty feet. *That* was what it was like being around mostly white people. We didn't even have a burrito place in Pine Grove, french fries or no french fries.

It hadn't occurred to me until right now that I'd been using "white people" as shorthand for "Midwestern," where Kraft

Singles were considered a food category and people were wary of anything new that seemed "weird." Being surrounded by so many Asian people and listening to Amy talk about growing up in a more diverse environment, it finally occurred to me that much of Midwestern culture *was* just white culture. Maybe deep down I already knew that on some subconscious level, and that was why I'd been dragging my feet on going to Northwestern.

Or maybe I was full of crap and looking for a more poetic explanation for why I wanted to go here that had nothing to do with either Wendy or my parents. Either way, I already felt more comfortable here than I ever had at the schools I toured in Iowa.

Amy continued, leading me through the buildings where she had class and pointing out her favorite study spots across the campus before we made our way to the music building. The whole walk took maybe thirty minutes—not even long enough for my body to process that I was forcing it to exercise.

"This is it," she announced outside the building, its exterior an unassuming brown brick. She yanked open the exterior double doors and the faint sound of familiar music floated through a second set of doors, clearly leading into what had to be an auditorium of some kind.

Amy walked toward them like she was preparing to go inside anyway.

"I think there's a performance going on," I whispered loudly, rooting my feet to the shiny gray tile. Walking in midsong was a major faux pas, something Amy would most certainly know.

"There are no scheduled performances," Amy said, pointing to the bulletin board on the wall. "That's probably just Gang. There are pianos in all the practice rooms, but he likes to practice in the auditorium because it has a stage. He's a total show-off." She rolled her eyes before using the full force of her slim body to pull open one of the heavy doors.

The auditorium was larger than it looked from the outside, with a spread of red velveteen seats set between stark white walls with sound paneling and a huge bleached-wood stage. The lights over the audience section had been dimmed, and a spotlight set all the focus on a figure seated at the enormous black grand piano onstage.

Amy led me down the aisle toward the stage, clearly unconcerned with whether or not we were interrupting Gang, whose fingers were cascading across the keys like water droplets on a windowpane. Sleek black hair swayed back and forth as his head moved in rhythm with the music, his torso remaining perfectly erect. A real piano player's posture.

I couldn't keep pace with Amy, the sound of Mozart transporting me back to the privacy of my own room. I'd listened to Mozart—to this exact song—a hundred times. A thousand, probably. I knew every flourish and crescendo, and this was as perfect as if Mozart himself were playing. It was hard to believe this was a simple practice. Between the lights and the rich fullness of the music in this space, it was hard to do anything but stand there and appreciate the artistry.

Amy, on the other hand, charged forward with the same determination she had shown getting through each stop on our tour, slowing only after she tripped on the carpeted aisle near the front, which allowed me to catch up. Finally sensing the intrusion, Gang stopped playing and turned to us, a slender hand shielding his dark eyes from the bright spotlight. Seeing him up close, I nearly lost my breath.

He was a vision, straight from the pages of a magazine: smooth faced, with no trace of hair anywhere on his jaw, and a deep V-neck shirt that showcased a chest equally as smooth. Sometimes guys looked weird with no chest hair, like they weren't mature enough to grow it. Like the Timothée Chalamets of the world. But this chest screamed "male model." As did his hair. His glorious hair—a triumph of superior genetics and expensive product, no doubt—settled to one side of his face in that ridiculously sexy disheveled look, making it impossible not to imagine him getting out of bed like that. Even the way his hand rested oh-so-casually across the top of his forehead, his other elbow perched on his knee, looked as though it was designed to inflict maximum damage to anyone who happened to see him.

If Chris Evans had America's ass, this guy had America's everything else.

"Come to watch me perform, did you?" He smiled, a perfect set of teeth accompanying the kind of accent that announced *I'm rich.*

A streak of irrational jealousy shot through me. Was Amy *with* this perfect specimen of a person? Is that why she'd brought me here? In the hallway she'd made it seem like he was going to be some obnoxious orchestra dork, not a movie star who'd left me with what could be tidily summarized as Mù dèng kǒu dāi—eyes staring and mouth blank.

"Recruit. Violin," Amy said, jerking a thumb in my direction. "Gang is the resident pianist, here from Guangzhou. He's in our grad program."

I nodded like, *Sure. Guangzhou.* It sounded familiar. As long as neither of them asked me to point to it on a map I was fine. As it was, I could barely concentrate with Gang's face just sitting there, hypnotizing me like I was a kid looking in an ice cream store window. He was probably used to girls staring. And boys. Anyone, really. Probably even animals. A person this good-looking had to be dangerous. People weren't this hot for no reason.

Gang turned his attention to me, a smile playing on the edges of his lightly pink lips. "Does this recruit have a name?"

I forced down a dry swallow, now aware that my mouth had likely been open this entire time. "June," I croaked, licking my lips before trying again. "June Chu." I didn't know why I added my last name. No one introduced themselves with last names.

"How are you liking our little school so far, June Chu?"

The way he said my name sent shivers down my spine—like we were the only two people standing in the auditorium and Amy had melted away. Which, from the way I couldn't tear my eyes away from him, might as well have been true.

"It's good," I said faintly.

"Okay well, we have to get going," Amy announced, either unaware of or uncaring about the obvious moment Gang and I were sharing. She started toward the door and I gave Gang one last look, my eyes greedily drinking in his form for my own personal memory.

"I hope you find what you are looking for, June Chu," he said, his eyes hooded with insinuation. "I would love to see a talented *violin player* like you around here."

I forced my mouth closed again, then my eyes. *Blink, June. Don't be a weirdo.*

"Thanks," I stammered. "Nice to meet you. Sorry about interrupting your practice."

Finally, breaking the spell by looking away, I fled up the aisle to catch up with Amy.

CHAPTER NINETEEN

I sat on Amy's bed, watching her get ready. She was the same age as Wendy, but everything about her felt more mature. She was like the kind of older sister I wished I'd had growing up. Wendy never even let me in her room without an invitation. She would make me stand at the threshold and ask for explicit permission like I was a vampire who would die if I set foot inside without it.

Amy's dorm room walls were decorated with two large posters of singers whose names I didn't know, as well as an assortment of Polaroid photos taped up around a cheap full-length mirror attached to the sliding closet door. Atop the bureau inside the closet sat her makeup bag, which she went back and forth with to the mirror, applying different layers of makeup.

"Sorry to leave you like this, but Julian is never in town and he's only here for the one night, so I figured you'd understand. Besides, it's only Thursday and there's not much going on anyway to miss out on. We'll go out tomorrow for New Year's. My roommate went home for the weekend, so you don't have to worry about her coming back. I'll leave you a set of keys in case you get hungry and want to go out or whatever. Otherwise, I have some snacks in the Tupperware under my bed."

Amy pulled out a fluffy makeup brush and dusted bronzer over her cheeks and into her cleavage. "Makes my boobs look bigger." She winked when she saw my curious expression in the mirror. "Julian told me about it. He said the stylists draw his abs in with eyeliner so they look more cut in his underwear pictures."

Amy hadn't even mentioned Julian before about ten minutes ago, but now she was talking about him like we were all old friends and I knew all about what I assumed was his modeling career.

My phone buzzed and I looked at the incoming message before quickly tucking it away so Amy didn't think I was texting while she was trying to talk to me.

"Do you need to get that?" she asked, nodding at the phone I was unsuccessfully trying to jam back into my pocket.

I gave a casual shrug. "Just my mom bugging me about practicing. You know how it is. My sister and I always joke it's like shù yù jìng ér fēng bù zhǐ, where my mom is the wind because she never stops."

Amy frowned. "You know there's a second half to that proverb, right?"

"I . . . did not?" I admitted while scrambling around in the corners of my brain for any memory of that fact. It was one I'd heard my mom use on a number of occasions and I'd never stopped to ask the meaning of it—it had seemed fairly obvious.

"Shù yù jìng ér fēng bù zhǐ, zǐ yù yàng ér qīn bú dài—the tree wants peace but the wind won't stop, children want to take care of their parents but the parents don't wait." She stared at me, as if waiting for me to get it. "It's about having your parents pass away before you can take care of them."

Oh. That was decidedly *not* the way Wendy and I had been using it. Amy patted her curled hair one last time, spinning around to face me. "You're okay, yeah? I'll be back in the morning. And you have my number, so you can call me if there's an emergency."

My brain was still processing her last comment but I nodded, hoping I looked as okay as she thought I was. My own parents didn't even trust me to stay home alone. Yet here I was, spending the night alone in a strange place, with my host completely assured that I could handle it.

I straightened up a little more confidently this time. "I'll be fine. Have fun."

Amy blew me a kiss as she headed out the door.

After Amy left, I stripped off both my bra and makeup and settled into her roommate's bed for the night. Except, as I turned my attention to my phone, I realized it was early. Like, old-people-going-to-bed early. Friggin' time change.

I couldn't go to bed this early. I was on a college campus! A college campus I'd fought so hard to find and get to. Going to bed now and missing the opportunity to soak it all up would be an insult to everything I'd been through to make this happen in the first place. I could at least wander around the campus and get a feeling for what it would be like to be a student here.

I shivered at the thought. I was going to go here. I already knew it. Everything about this place already felt more welcoming than home. I could start over here.

In Washington, no one knew who June Chu was or who she was supposed to be. I wasn't Wendy's little sister, or the Asian girl, or even "that nerdy violin chick," as I once heard someone refer to me. No one here knew my parents or the fact that I'd gone to a seventh-grade pool party in a gymnastics leotard instead of a swimsuit because my mom had gotten it on sale and insisted they were the same thing, only to get made fun of by a bunch of girls who actually did gymnastics. This place represented a chance for me to start over and redefine myself the way *I* wanted to. The fact that I would no longer have to stress about Northwestern was just the cherry on top of this already sweet, sweet sundae.

Suddenly I was full of energy. A quick peek out the window showed that the sky had already darkened and the outdoor lights were beginning to flicker on. I threw on my favorite gray hoodie, stuffed my feet into the pair of white Sorels I'd worn on the plane, and headed out into the mild winter weather.

People around me were bundled up in down parkas and peacoats, some even with hats and scarves on, like it was forty degrees below zero instead forty degrees above it. I'd already walked through the whole campus earlier, but now I had time to really savor it without Amy racing me through like we were trying to break some kind of tour speed record. Not that I blamed her. My trip had been planned on such short notice, she probably didn't appreciate suddenly having to play hostess to some high school kid.

The buildings around me were stately, many of them composed of red or tan brick, like oversized colonial dwellings that just happened to house intellectual power. Even now, in the dead of winter, the landscape in front of each building had been impeccably maintained, lush with conifers and sprawling juniper plants that had turned a deep shade of green from all the precipitation.

I wandered through paths, bare oak trees towering above and a damp fog creeping down their trunks. It wasn't exactly raining, but it wasn't *not* raining. Students were still out and milling around, going to and from buildings while others headed toward the street.

This place was magical. I suddenly had the overwhelming urge to call my mom—show her how amazing this campus was. If she could see it for herself, she'd agree. There was no way *not* to be charmed by a campus that had an actual creek running through the middle of it, like the college itself was self-contained as a tiny village. Besides, I was still feeling guilty for inadvertently joking about her demise all these years because of a misunderstood proverb. Even though Wendy had made the same mistake.

I checked the time again. It was still early. Early enough, anyway.

I angled the phone as it rang, checking my own reflection in the video chat box to make sure my mom could see my face when she answered. Otherwise, the first minute of our conversation would just be her yelling into the phone, asking if I was really there.

"Hello? June?" My screen filled with the image of my mom's knitted eyebrows.

"You're too close, mom. Hold the phone away from you."

She tilted her head back and stretched her arm as far away as it could go. "Better?"

I sighed. "Sure."

"Why you calling? You not having a good time?" She sounded a little eager to believe her own words.

"Of course I'm having a good time," I snapped. "Why would you assume I'm not?"

"Why you calling so late?"

"Were you asleep?"

"No."

"Then why did you say it's late? It's not like I woke you up."

Now it was my mom's turn to sigh.

I knew I was being a brat, but it was like I was powerless to stop it. Something about my mom turned me into my worst self. Why couldn't she just have been happy I called?

"So?" she asked.

"Geez, can't I just call to say hello?"

Her shoulders relaxed a bit and she inched the phone closer to her face. "Oh. Okay. That's all?"

"I wanted to show you the campus. It's a little dark now, but you should be able to see some of it." I slowly rotated my phone 360 degrees, giving her a panoramic view. "See?" I asked, turning it back to my face. "Isn't it great?"

I held my breath, waiting for her reaction. I knew better than to expect gushing, but a nod of approval wouldn't be unwelcome. Or at least a smile?

Instead, she waited until I'd done a full turn and my face was back in view. "Buildings look old," she sniffed, her eyes practically daring me to disagree.

"They're not old, they're historic," I shot back, a hot flare streaking through my chest. "This school has been here for over a hundred years."

"Maybe they don't have money to update. No money for buildings means no money for math and science research. Maybe they don't care about these things at art school."

"It's *liberal arts*, Mom. It just means they make sure students learn about *all* subjects."

The fog had coalesced into a drizzly sort of rain and I tugged my hoodie over my head and picked up my pace. If I walked fast enough, the water droplets would probably evaporate off me. That was how physics worked, right? I looked around to see if there was a coffee shop or something I could duck into.

"Yeah yeah, what are all those kids going to do with degrees in history? Or pottery? It's not practical."

"History's actually a pretty important subject," I said loudly, my breath growing short as I picked up the pace of my strides. "A lot of companies are now saying they wish their employees had more of a background in humanities so they're not just emotionless robots."

Out of the corner of my eye I saw a brightly lit restaurant, its neon Open sign glowing red through the drizzle. My mom was saying something, probably about how smart she and my dad had been to choose *practical* careers in accounting and medicine.

"Mom, I gotta go," I cut her off. "I just walked into a restaurant."

She frowned. "Restaurant? Who is open so late?"

"I'm two hours behind you, remember?"

Her frown didn't ease. "Okay, but don't eat too close to bedtime or you get fat."

I closed my eyes for a brief moment and exhaled. It wasn't even worth explaining to her why a comment like that was inappropriate.

"Who is that?"

My eyes flew open. "Huh?"

She tipped her chin. "The boy behind you. Staring at your phone. You know him?"

I spun around to find myself staring directly into the protruding clavicle of one beautiful piano player.

I yelped, nearly dropping my phone before clumsily juggling it back into my hands.

"Gang! What are you doing here?"

He looked amused by my slapstick reaction. "Are you coming in?" I followed the direction of his arm to see that he was holding open a second set of doors leading to the actual restaurant.

I turned my phone back to my mom, who was waiting patiently for me to return to the conversation. "I gotta go, Mom. I'll call you later."

"Aiya, you should brush your hair you look like—"

CHAPTER TWENTY

I hung up before she could finish and stuffed the phone deep into my pocket, as if I could bury my embarrassment along with it. "I was just getting out of the rain," I said weakly, smoothing my hair just in case. I didn't know how my mom's sentence was going to end, but I could guarantee it wouldn't have been flattering.

Gang squinted out the glass door, which had only a couple of thin streaks of water winding their way across the front of a Japanese character and the words *Shiki Sushi*. "Is that rain?"

Great. Now I looked like the kind of person who overreacted to a little drizzle. "I mean, it's not heavy or anything. It's just kind of cold. And damp." I brushed the shoulders of my sweatshirt to illustrate my point. Except now I was bringing attention to the fact that I was wearing a soggy sweatshirt. And winter boots. And no makeup. Oh god, why had I decided to go out like this?

Gang was wearing the same white V-neck as earlier but had paired it with a black blazer, left unbuttoned so the world could gape at how perfectly his clothes fit him. I wore my fair share of T-shirts, and none of them looked like that on me.

"You are not staying?" he asked.

"I'm just getting some food to go." *That way I'll never have to show my face outside the room again.*

"That is unfortunate. I was just sitting down to eat. I was hoping you might provide me with your company."

Who talked like that? Grown-ass men, that was who. I had no idea how old Gang was, but if I'd met him anywhere but on a college campus, I would have guessed somewhere in his midtwenties. I'd probably spend the entire meal saying "like" a thousand times while he sat there in his tailored outfit, speaking like the hottest English teacher imaginable.

I had to hold myself back from mimicking his accent with a *Splendid! I would be delighted to accompany you in a meal.*

"Yeah, okay. Sure."

He gestured toward the counter, where the chefs were busy preparing an assortment of nigiri and sashimi for customers. I walked as lightly as I could, each clop of my Sorels landing on the tile floor like horse hooves. Why had I thought it would be cute to wear my winter boots on this trip? Midwest fashion was not fashion, especially not to someone foreign who wore *blazers* out to dinner by himself.

A waiter came by to get us drinks and again Gang swept his hand, indicating I should go first.

"I'm okay with water, thanks," I said to the waiter.

"We will also take a bottle of Koshu," Gang added.

The waiter returned promptly with two wineglasses and the bottle Gang had requested. He glanced skeptically at me a second time, as if he couldn't quite believe I was old enough to drink, before deciding to set down a glass in front of me. Either that or he was wondering what the hell Gang was doing on a date with someone who had to keep her lips pressed together so he wouldn't notice how chapped they were. Not that this was a date.

After ordering a combination platter from the chefs across the counter, Gang coolly poured each of us a glass. Maybe it wasn't weird to drink underage in public places where he was from. Or did he think I was a transfer student? Was it possible I looked twenty-one?

"Have you had this before?" he asked, holding up the bottle.

I shook my head.

"It is made from the Koshu grape grown in Japan. It pairs well with sushi."

I nodded along, as if I had any idea about how particular wines paired with food. The last alcoholic drink I'd had had been a cup of Milwaukee's Best from a keg. Something told me it wasn't a beer Gang would know.

"I've had sake," I volunteered.

Gang's lips curled at the corners, as if he was amused at my attempt to keep pace in the conversation. "Sake is good too."

I lifted the glass to my lips and took a small sip. The wine was light and sweet. Refreshing, almost. I imagined being one of those wine snobs who swirled the sip around in my mouth before declaring that it held hints of elderberry or whatever.

"How was the rest of your tour?" he asked, leaning back in his chair and crossing one leg over the other.

I leaned back too, hoping to copy his casual demeanor. Except that the pose left a weird deflated spot in my chest area where my boobs should have been. "It was good," I said, shifting my shoulders in an attempt to reinflate them, before remembering I didn't have a bra on and hunching back over. "A little quick, but Amy's a good tour guide. I think we covered everything."

"And the school? It is to your liking?"

I pretended to think carefully, like I had so many other options and this school was one of many that was courting me. As if I hadn't decided in the first thirty seconds that I was willing to cut off my own foot just to come here. An unpleasant reminder that I hadn't yet auditioned for my place popped into my brain and I quickly shoved it away. "It's good."

Our food arrived and I busied myself rubbing the wasabi into a smooth paste with soy sauce. The last thing I needed was to accidentally choke on a glob and have a coughing fit where I spewed fish all over the counter. Not that I'd done that a time or two at home or anything.

Gang watched all of this with interest, not making the slightest move to do the same. Instead, he watched me dip my nigiri in the soy sauce and bite it in half as he placed an entire piece of his nigiri into his mouth. Without sauce. Crap. Was I eating sushi wrong too? I'd never known anyone outside of my own family who ate sushi—at least the raw kind. I'd convinced Liz to try California rolls once, but Candace's face had scrunched in horror when I'd told her the fish was supposed to be raw.

I ate my second half without dip. It wasn't as good.

"So," he said, his voice as silky as his hair. "You play the violin."

I nodded.

"You must be very good to be auditioning here."

"You must be very good to play here," I joked.

He raised a sculpted eyebrow. "You heard me play. You tell me."

I nervously licked my lips. My stupid jokes weren't going to work on someone like Gang. Never mind that he had the extra barrier of speaking English as a second language.

"You're really good," I said finally, hoping my pause in the conversation hadn't been noticeable. "Like really, *really* good." *Stop complimenting him.* "You were playing Mozart, right?"

Gang looked impressed. "I was. You know it?"

"It's actually one of my favorite pieces," I confessed with an exhale of relief. Finally, a topic I was educated on. "I've listened to like, every single recording of it. Did you know Mozart later used the flute and clarinet section in the second movement in *Don Giovanni*? And of all of the six-hundred-some works he composed, that second movement was the only one in F minor? My dad used to make us write reports on the concertos of different composers so we could analyze their style, and I was being a brat so I purposely wrote about piano concertos instead of violin ones because he didn't specify, but then I got obsessed with Mozart and fell down this rabbit hole of research. Did you know it was also Joseph Stalin's favorite piece?"

Oh.

My.

God.

Stop.

Talking.

Did I just tell a twenty-something guy I used to write book reports on dead composers for my parents?

I meekly sank back into my chair, suddenly aware that I'd leaned so far forward during my nerd rant, I was practically in his lap.

What was wrong with me? Why couldn't I act like a normal human being?

Miraculously, Gang didn't seem horrified by my disclosure of everything embarrassing. Instead, he pressed his lips together and swirled the wine in his glass. "You have a lot in common with Joseph Stalin, do you?"

I wrapped my arms around myself protectively as though it would keep me from blurting out anything else. "I don't know why I said that."

Gang leaned forward in his chair a little, a smile tugging at the corner of his lips. "I find it very interesting. You enjoy the same music as Joseph Stalin. Do you share similarities with any other dictators?"

I allowed myself a small laugh. Maybe he understood jokes after all.

"I make everyone I know hang a portrait of me in their house. You know, like Mao," I joked.

He raised one of his perfectly sculpted eyebrows and I briefly panicked that my Mao joke was in poor taste. Was I even allowed to joke about him? But when Gang spoke, his lips curled up into a smile. "This is not such a terrible idea. You are certainly more pleasing to look at."

My face burst into flames as I tried to hide my blushing cheeks under the guise of brushing hair off my face. I didn't know how or why someone like Gang was sitting here, his attention focused solely on me, but I never wanted it to end. Even if it meant risking saying something else embarrassing.

"So, what's your story?" I asked, my voice striving for casually interested. "How did you decide to come here all the way from Guangzhou?" I hoped it seemed impressive that I'd remembered where he was from.

Gang leaned back again, this time with one leg folded flat across the other, his arm slung across the back of his chair. It was like every pose he struck was in preparation for a photo shoot. "I am more interested in hearing about you, June Chu. Hmmm, *chu*." He stroked his chin thoughtfully as if my name were a source of utter fascination. "Is it the same *chǔ* as *master*?" His slender pointer finger swooped through the air, drawing the character in the space between us.

I nodded.

"Tell me. What are you the master of?" he asked.

Not much of anything at the moment. I could barely master my own breathing, let alone a coherent response to that question.

"I don't know. Mistakes?" I laughed.

A small chuckle escaped Gang's lips. "You don't seem like the kind of girl who makes mistakes."

"You must not know me very well."

He unfolded his legs and leaned dangerously close to me. "Well then." His voice dropped half an octave and he spoke almost conspiratorially. "I hope I have the chance to rectify that."

I managed to make it through the rest of dinner without incident, including suppressing my Chinese instinct to insist that he not pay the entire bill. It wasn't like I had enough money on me to cover it. So I politely thanked him and tried not to think about the fact that having him pay made it much more like a date than it was before.

We ambled out of the restaurant, where the rain was still falling at a light drizzle, shooting through the beams of light from the lampposts like tiny comets. "Well . . . I'm going this way," I said, jerking a thumb behind me toward Amy's dorm. I didn't want to linger and make it awkward, but I also didn't want to leave. Being around Gang made me nervous, but also settled in a way. Like I was capable of holding my own with someone like him.

"I can't have you walking home unaccompanied," he said, heading down the path with me.

"I did walk here alone, you know," I said.

"I am not doubting your capability. In those boots I'm sure you could take on anyone who dares cross you." He gave a nod at my heavy white rubber Sorels.

I threw up my hands. "They're waterproof. They're *supposed* to be heavy." Had no one on the West Coast ever seen real boots before?

"I like them!" he insisted. "They make you a little . . . dangerous."

I'd certainly never heard that before. If anything, he was the dangerous one. I'd known it the moment I first met him. I was like a moth throwing itself into a flame—fēi é tóu huǒ. He was addictive. I just wanted to be near him. Stare at him. Imagine running my hands across his chest. Snort his hair product like drugs. All very normal stuff.

I walked back to the dorms as slowly as I could to delay our inevitable split, despite the fact that the rain had started to accumulate in my hair and drip down my face in a way I could only assume was completely unflattering. I'd seen myself step out of a shower before—it wasn't my best look.

Gang, on the other hand, seemed to glow in the rain. His lustrous hair was even shinier than it had been inside, the moisture giving it a more casual, tousled look. Jesus. There was literally nothing this guy could do that would make him look bad.

"So, June Chu, will you be celebrating the new year tomorrow?"

"Yeah. I think Amy mentioned going to dinner with some of the girls from the orchestra so I could meet them. How about you?"

"Naturally. A new year is always cause for celebration. I could use your help collecting resolutions." He arched an eyebrow toward me.

As if *I* could come up with something he needed to improve on? Ha!

"I'm not big into resolutions," I lied. My last New Year's decision had been to crawl into bed with my ex-boyfriend before breaking up with my current one. Good decision-making\wasn't in my repertoire.

"Perhaps *resolution* is not the right word. More like . . . goals. Like where you plan to be next year."

My heart screeched to a dead stop. Was he really asking if I . . . ?

I turned to look at him. He had already stopped walking and now faced me, his tall, slender frame illuminated from behind, casting a shadow over me.

I couldn't answer. Like, physically. Couldn't. Answer.

Gang wanted me.

Here.

At this school.

With him.

In what felt like slow motion, he leaned down and lifted my chin with his exquisite fingers until my eyes met his. Slowly, slowly, slowly he brought his lips down to meet mine. I held my breath.

It was surreal. The rain, the fuzzy light, the fact that we stood alone on a cobblestone path with trees towering over us like we were in the most romantic movie I could possibly imagine.

His lips met mine with the softness of fresh snow, drawing me in close enough to smell a hint of tea tree and orange radiating off him. Soft splatters of rain dusted my closed eyes and ran down the sides of my face, but I wasn't thinking about how I looked anymore.

I wasn't thinking about anything except how I wanted to freeze this moment in time—this kiss—so I could replay it in my head on repeat for the rest of my life. It was perfection.

When I could no longer hold my breath, I gently pulled back, his fingers lingering on my face for an additional moment.

"I should . . . go," I said hesitantly.

My sweatshirt was now soaked enough that I could feel the dampness creeping in toward my skin. My hair was heavy, sodden with rain. Even my legs were damp, the breeze blowing raindrops into the absorbent fabric. The only warm parts of my body were my feet, protected by the infamous boots, and my lips, which burned with happiness.

"June Chu, you are like rain clouds over Wushan," he said softly.

He straightened up and said more formally, "I hope I will see you in the new year. Regardless of what you decide."

Then he strode off in the direction we had come. I turned and sprinted back into the dorm, my feet barely touching the ground.

CHAPTER TWENTY-ONE

My phone rang and I took a deep breath before answering. I was almost surprised it had taken her a whole twenty hours before calling me after I'd hung up on her so abruptly in the restaurant.

I forced a smile across my lips. "Hi, Mom," I said, her round face so close to the screen it felt like she was actually right in front of me, invading my space. "What's up?"

"Just call to see how your trip going," she said.

"It's good. But I called you last night, remember? And I'll be home in two days."

"Ah, yes." She nodded, as if that realization had just hit her. "What your plan for tonight? Your host taking you anywhere for Chinese New Year? Meeting friends? Did you pack nice clothes? You want to make a good impression, you know. Never know who you might meet." Her eyes sparkled with interest when she said "never know who you might meet."

"Oh my god, Mom. Did you really call to pry about the guy you saw last night?"

A guilty look crept onto her face. "Did I say anything about him? No, you just assume."

"Fine. Yes, Amy is taking me out. We're going to dinner."

"I hope you look at the school, not just going out, having fun. You not there to have fun. You should be studying the school. Make sure it's right for your future. You practice for your audition?"

Of course.

Heaven forbid I have fun on a college campus half a continent away from my parents. No no, she had to remind me that no matter how far away I moved, she could still call me and remind me to practice, just to ruin my day. So just like yesterday, I ignored the question about my audition. After last night, I had a good reason to. If my mom found out I was nervous about performing, it would just give her an excuse to push Northwestern again. As if making the orchestra would be any easier there. I definitely didn't want to think about the possibility I could choke and end up with neither. "There's nothing to study, Mom. It's a college. They all have the same things: buildings, professors, landscapes that cost way too much money."

I thought I'd get a smile out of her with that joke, but her eyebrows remained knitted, her mouth a familiar scowl. "If they are same why you go all the way out there instead of Illinois with Wendy? No need to move far away if they are same." She said "all the way out there" like Washington was in Asia and not a couple of hours away by flight.

"They offered me a full scholarship," I volunteered. "Well, sort of. It's mostly academic, but they can offer me some money for music and the rest with grants and an honorarium through the school's fund as long as I minor in music. I can have them call you to explain it. It should cover everything except room and board and books. But I could get a job to cover the cost of those, so it wouldn't be any more expensive," I added quickly.

Her frown deepened. "Why you get a job? How you have time to study if you working?"

I suppressed a smile. We were no longer quarreling over whether or not I could come here, but whether or not I'd have to pay the difference in cost. I felt like a general who'd just pulled off a sneak attack against immeasurable odds.

"It's a really great school, Mom. Their professor-to-student ratio is one of the lowest in the country. And the campus is amazing. They have as many trees as they do students."

"What do trees help? You not going to be arborist."

I sighed. So close.

"I don't know. I just thought it was a cool fact, I guess."

"Good to hear not too many students," she said. "Less competition, more attention."

It was something. She was trying.

"Thanks," I said. "Hey, do you know what the phrase 'rain clouds over Wushan' means?"

My mom's eyes widened.

Immediately I knew I'd said something wrong. "What?"

"Where you hear that?" she asked sharply.

"Nowhere! I don't know. I was just asking," I babbled. "It was just something I overheard and I thought you might know. Sheesh. Never mind."

Stupid, stupid, stupid. Why hadn't I just googled it?

But my mom wasn't ready to let it go that easily. "Did someone say that to you?"

"No! I overheard one of the girls in the dorm talking about it." I came up with the first lie I could think of.

I could see my mom heave a sigh of relief. "Old story. King Chuhuai travel to Yangtze River, a place called 'Rain Clouds over Wushan.' He fall asleep and dream he, *you know*, with the goddess of Wushan." She intoned the meaning of *you know* with her eyebrows. "Before he wake up, she tell him the way to find her is think of rain clouds over Wushan. It's not something nice girls talk about."

Holy. Shit.

I tried to keep my face as neutral as I could, but inside, my heart was floating its way out of my body.

Gang was a freaking poet. For me. He liked me. Truly. And not in a "let me take you home and bang you" kind of way, but in a "kiss you in the rain and leave you coded messages" kind of way.

I could've fainted from happiness.

Except, of course, there was still the matter of my mom to deal with.

"Hey, Mom, I should get going. I don't want to be the one holding up the party."

Her face piqued with interest. "Party? Who will be at this party?"

I eyed her change of attitude warily. "Why do you ask?" Since when did my mom ask for the specifics of my social life?

"Just concerned," she protested. But then she added, "Will that boy be there?"

"What boy?" I asked, knowing full well who she meant.

"Aiya. You know who. The one I saw on the phone. Gang. Probably named for the word *steel*. Good boy's name."

I blinked into the phone in disbelief. "You literally called Rhys the wrong name for two months but you can remember the name of some guy you overheard me talking to over the phone? Are you serious?"

"It's different. He's *Chinese*."

"So?"

"So it's different."

"Since when?"

"Since always."

"Yet you want me to stay in the Midwest for the rest of my life, where there are basically no other Chinese people."

My mom clucked her tongue in disapproval. "You always exaggerate. All I said was eŕ xíng qiān lǐ mǔ dān yōu—mothers worry when children travel far from home. It's not same thing."

I bit my tongue. I had already won the battle of where I'd go to school. She was showing interest in someone I liked. I needed to quit while I was ahead.

"Okay, Mom. You're right. But I do have to go."

Even my mom looked surprised that I'd admitted she was right about something.

"Oh—oh, oh, okay. I let you go."

"Bye! Oh, and xīnnián kuàilè!"

My mom beamed through the phone, wishing me a happy new year back. "Xīnnián kuàilè! Make sure you wear something nice, not too skimpy. Remember, no one likes cows if milk is free!"

———

I zipped up the skirt Amy had lent me and smoothed the metallic pleats. It was about as close to new clothes as I was going to get for the night. All I had packed were leggings and jeans, not expecting to need to dress up quite so fancy on my visit. At least my mom would be happy it wasn't too skimpy.

I, on the other hand, wouldn't have minded if it were a couple of inches shorter. If I was going to balance out my fashionable average on this trip, I would need something hotter to make up for my hoodie/Sorels combo from last night.

"You're okay with drinking, right?" Amy asked, swiping on a second coat of mascara.

"Of course." I tried not to get overexcited at the thought that I might finally get to prove myself as anything more than a wide-eyed kid. Bless Rhys and his brother for their steady supply of alcohol that prepared me for this moment.

Amy pointed to her desk with the mascara wand. "I have Pepcid in the drawer."

When I didn't respond, she took one look at my confused face and asked, "Do you not get the Asian glow?"

"The Asian what?"

"Glow. Like, your face turns red if you drink?"

Recognition dawned on me. "I didn't know that's what it was called! Do only Asian people get it?"

She chuckled as she turned back toward the mirror. "Just trust me. Take a pill now and it'll help you from turning into a tomato later."

I noticed she didn't really answer my question, but I obediently popped a pill out of the packaging and swallowed it. One benefit of having a doctor for a dad was I learned from an early age how to swallow pills without water. It wasn't the most dazzling of talents, but it did come in handy occasionally.

"Is there a reason you have so many pregnancy tests in here?" I asked, holding up one of the pink boxes. "Not to be a snoop or anything."

Amy waved me off. "I'm just super paranoid about getting pregnant so I take a test every couple of weeks just to make sure. I have a bunch of Plan B in the other drawer too. All my friends know to come to me in an emergency." She laughed.

"So . . . have you taken it before?" I asked, trying to keep my voice casual.

"A couple of times. I can't rush off to the doctor every time a condom breaks, I'm a double major—I don't have time to even *think* about what would happen if I ended up pregnant."

She said it laughingly, as if we were discussing something as inconsequential as using the wrong color of nail polish or something. She'd taken the morning-after pill. Multiple times, apparently. And wasn't even ashamed to talk about it.

I closed her home pharmacy drawers and straightened up, a sense of lightness in my shoulders. I'd never felt guilty about what

I'd done, but hearing Amy talk about it so matter-of-factly eased any lingering discomfort. People had sex. Accidents happened. If we had the means to fix those mistakes, why wouldn't we? Broken condoms weren't someone's fault; they shouldn't derail an entire life. People acted like the morning-after pill was only for irresponsible people, but having sex in and of itself wasn't irresponsible. *Not* taking measures to prevent an unwanted pregnancy, like taking Plan B, was the real irresponsible thing.

Amy dotted a white liquid under her eyebrows and along the top of her rounded cheekbones, talking to me as she blended them in with her pinky finger. "So anyway, we'll go out to dinner first with the girls and then to a bar afterward. I'll get you an ID to use."

My mind leapt back to the conversation at hand, my heart skipping with excitement. I was going to a bar. Like it was no big deal. College was even more grown-up than I could have anticipated. No more cold garages, no more cheap forties. I patted my pockets to ensure I had the money my parents had sent me with. I didn't know how expensive drinks at a bar would be, so I'd stuffed it all in just in case.

"Are we meeting up with any other orchestra people afterward?" I asked, tucking in my T-shirt and checking the mirror to see if it looked better. It didn't. I untucked it.

"After when?"

"I don't know, after dinner? Like at the bar?"

"Like who?"

"I don't know. Like Gang? Or whatever." It wasn't subtle, but oh well. I just wanted an answer. I fussed with my shirt some more to make my question seem more offhand. Maybe I could get away with only tucking it in in front.

Amy frowned in the mirror, making the same expression she'd made when I'd misquoted the proverb last night. "Gang?"

I shrugged. "I was just throwing out names. He's the only other person here I've talked to." I'd met a rash of orchestra players when I'd first arrived, but it had all gone by in such a blur, I couldn't remember anyone's face, let alone their name. Except Gang, whose high cheekbones and smooth, chiseled jaw were emblazoned in my mind like I'd been tasked with recreating his likeness from memory, which I was almost certain I could do.

She spun to face me, her shoulder-length bob twirling into her face. "You're not into him, are you?"

"What?" My voice lifted an octave higher than it had been a second ago. "I don't even know him. I was just asking a question!"

She spun back around, taking a final glance at herself in the mirror. "I'm just saying. Don't get your hopes up. Besides, he's only into Chinese girls."

Now it was my turn to frown. "I'm Chinese, though."

She sighed. "You know what I mean. Like, *Chinese* Chinese."

"I don't, actually. I'm *Chinese* Chinese."

She gave a pointed glance at my shoes lined up next to the door. "What about those boots?"

"What about them?"

Amy threw up her hands. "Come on, June. They're a step away from Uggs!"

"They're nothing like Uggs. Mine are actual winter boots. Like, for snow. Uggs were made in Australia." I didn't expand on how the rubber traction on the sole of my boots compared to Uggs, or the fact that my boots wouldn't fall apart in two years.

She rolled her eyes. "Whatever. I'm just saying. They're white-girl boots."

"What the hell are white-girl boots?"

"The kind of boots white girls wear with their yoga pants." She gave a pointed look at the pants I'd worn earlier that were now slung across the back of her desk chair.

"Everyone wears yoga pants! It's athleisure! It's a billion-dollar industry!"

"Yeeeeah," she said, drawing out the word into multiple syllables. "For white girls."

I couldn't believe this. "You're telling me you don't own a single pair of yoga pants?"

Amy gave me an *are you kidding me* look.

"Well, everyone I know wears these," I said, crossing my arms and sinking down onto Amy's bed.

"And everyone you know is white."

What the hell was Amy getting at?

"Not everyone I know is white," I said, my face getting hot and my voice flaring up to match.

She crossed her arms, mirroring my defensive pose. "Name three nonwhite people you hang out with who aren't related to you."

"I know plenty of nonwhite people!"

"I said people you *hang out with*. Not just people you've met in passing."

"That's ridiculous," I scoffed. "I can't believe you're questioning the people I hang out with."

"Name them."

I blustered, trying to come up with three people. Surely I had nonwhite friends. Not at school, but at competitions? Saturday Chinese School when I was a kid? Why couldn't I remember anyone's name?

"Britney Lee!" I cried triumphantly. "And her sister! I grew up playing violin with them. That's two!"

"Same family. That counts as one."

This was bullshit. Why was I reporting to Amy, anyway? It wasn't any of her business who I hung out with.

I shifted back farther onto her bed, trying to put as much distance between the two of us as possible—a difficult feat in the tiny room. "This is stupid. Of course I know mostly white people. I grew up in Iowa. What do you expect? It doesn't make me not Chinese."

She released her arms, busying herself with getting ready once again. "No one said you're not Chinese."

How dare she casually try on shoes like she didn't just insult me? "You did!" I exclaimed. "You said I wear white-girl boots and white-girl pants and all my friends are white."

"Well? Am I wrong? You didn't even know about Asian glow." She put on another heel, looked in the mirror, and tossed it back into the bottom of her closet.

"I didn't know it had a specific name," I spluttered. "That doesn't make me not Chinese."

Amy sighed loudly. "Why do you even care? I thought you said you were Taiwanese anyway."

I didn't know how to explain that in Iowa, no one bothered differentiating between specific cultures. I wasn't Chinese or even Taiwanese—I was just . . . Asian. There was so little representation that I'd naturally latched on to anything even remotely Oriental in origin, drawing connections between my experiences and whatever was depicted, whether it was East Asian, South Asian, or Southeast Asian. I'd never stopped to consider the implications of nebulously claiming *all* Asian cultures simultaneously while hating the fact that everyone around me did the same.

It was an uncomfortable feeling.

"My family is wàishěngrén," I blurted out, hoping that somehow explained everything. I couldn't be blamed for identifying with both cultures if it was literally a part of my history. Even if the sum total of my knowledge about our history essentially began and ended with that very specific term. It had never seemed particularly important to know the details before, but now I wished I did if for no other reason than to be able to hold it up as some kind of armor against these attacks.

Amy flashed her eyebrows north for a second and pursed her lips—making the same face Wendy made when she didn't want to deal with me anymore. "Let's not make a big deal of this, okay?"

"I'm not the one who brought it up."

"Okay, sorry I said anything," she said breezily. "All I was trying to say was that it was different for you because you didn't grow up around other Asian people like the rest of us. Just forget I said anything."

She turned to fish the other shoe out of her closet while I stewed in silence.

The rest of us.

Even in her apology Amy still managed to imply that I wasn't Asian enough. To her, I was just some girl who happened to look like her. It didn't matter that I had two Taiwanese parents or that I was proud of my heritage and identified myself in it. To her, I was born in the wrong location, with the wrong kind of people, and there was nothing I could do to change that.

Screw her.

I already knew Gang liked me, regardless of how "Chinese" I was. And whether or not I saw him tonight, nothing she said could take back the kiss I had with him last night.

I closed my eyes, remembering the rain on my face, the smell of his hair, and the gentle pressure of his fingers lifting my chin. It was more than romantic. It was validation. And I didn't need her approval to savor it.

CHAPTER TWENTY-TWO

We met up with Amy's friends at a Chinese restaurant downtown, where we stuffed our faces with noodles, fish, dumplings, and all the other lucky foods. The other girls were nice enough, the conversation peppered with Mandarin, Cantonese, and English. I couldn't follow along with the Cantonese parts, or even all of the Mandarin ones, but I had enough food to keep me otherwise occupied as I nodded along pleasantly, laughing when everyone else did.

I wanted so badly to fit in—to be accepted as a natural part of this already existing friend group, where everyone seemed to just get each other. These girls, I'm sure, were who Amy considered to be *Chinese* Chinese, somehow seamlessly managing three languages while I still struggled to get past the basics of a second one. And even though I knew I didn't need to prove my Chineseness, I still made a mental note to dust off my old Saturday School textbooks when I got back to Iowa.

After a long dinner and a stop for froyo, we headed to a nearby hookah lounge. Amy had already arranged for one of the girls to pass back her ID to me at the entrance of the club since it was 21+. I flashed it with as much confidence as I could muster at the bouncer, who barely even glanced at it. He just waved our group through with a bored look on his face.

Inside, we ducked under a red velvet curtain, where we were greeted by a Chinese woman in a sheer black dress. Amy spoke to her and the woman nodded, then led us through a maze of overstuffed red velvet booths with round glass tables in front of each. It seemed this was *the* place to celebrate the New Year, because the place was absolutely packed with other Asians, including a pretty singer warming up onstage, a huge, shiny gold hairpiece fastened to the top of her pale, dyed silver-gray hair. I made a mental note of how cool it looked in case I ever summoned the courage to dye my own.

At the back of the lounge we were greeted by Gang and a handful of male companions, who were already sitting in one of the booths. He remained seated while everyone else jumped up to hug hello and wish each other a happy new year. I stood off to the side, ever the outsider, smiling as earnestly as I could as Amy introduced me to the new additions to our party. I'd barely started to remember the girls' names from dinner—there was zero chance I'd remember these new people's names too.

"We reserved all four of these, so you can sit wherever," Amy said to me, her arm sweeping around us.

Gang, who was reclined against a plush red pillow with a thick glass tumbler already in his hand, looked on at us from his booth. He was dressed in a crisp white button-down, slate gray slacks, and shiny black loafers and looked incredible, as usual.

Even Amy's metallic pleated skirt didn't stop my vintage tee from sticking out as being terribly out of place in this very fancy space.

"Why don't you come to my table?" she asked, tugging my arm toward the booth next to where Gang sat alone. Several girls and a guy were already mixing drinks while another guy was already taking a hit off the ornate hookah that was placed atop each glass table.

"Happy New Year, June Chu." My name rolled off Gang's tongue as he stood and leaned across the table, placing his hand on my shoulder for an air kiss to the cheek.

My heart jumped around my chest like ants in a hot pan as I tried to remain casual. Any surge of confidence I'd felt back at the dorms evaporated the second I saw him again, reminding me of just how perfect he was and how imperfect everything I said around him was.

But I had to respond with something.

"Xīnnián kuàilè," I said with a coy smile, sending Gang's eyebrows up into his hairline.

"So you do speak Mandarin," he said.

I gave a little shrug as I tossed my hair over my shoulder, but I was pleased I'd impressed him. So much for Amy's theory that I wasn't Chinese enough.

"Hey, Gang," Amy said in a bored voice.

Gang said something to her in rapid Cantonese and she rolled her eyes at him before leaving us to go sit with her friends.

"Come. Sit." He gestured for me to come around the table, where he handed me a glass before I'd even sat down. I gingerly took a sip from my glass and stifled the urge to gag. The gin and tonic plodded its way down my throat like a wad of cotton balls. *People voluntarily drink this?*

"How do you like it?" he asked.

I nodded and gave a half smile. I didn't want to make it seem like I couldn't drink a grown-up drink.

I sat primly on the edge of the red velvet cushion of our couch and choked down a few more gulps, hoping the alcohol would kick in and soothe my nerves. I didn't know how to act around Gang now that he had kissed me. Was he expecting the same nervous, charmingly innocent girl he'd met at the sushi restaurant? Or could I take him by surprise by acting like Amy—confident and in control of my own sexuality? The second option certainly sounded more appealing. That is, if I could get my nerves under control.

The air was hot and thick, both from the density of bodies inside and the vapor from the hookahs. I could feel dampness coming through my armpits and I moved my arms off the sides of my body, hoping I wouldn't sweat through my shirt. It was dark in here, but not dark enough to conceal pit stains. Especially with Gang reclined next to me, mere inches away from finding out how gross and sweaty I actually was.

I slowly exhaled eight counts, trying to get my pulse down to the low three digits. Right now, my heart seemed to think I was doing laps around a track while being chased by some kind of large, predatory animal. Once I got that under control, I could decide how to proceed.

"Come, June Chu, and cuddle with me."

The low voice of his, gravelly from the gin, sounded exactly the way it had when he'd practically whispered the words *rain clouds over Wushan* to me.

A shiver went down my spine as I thought of what those words meant.

"I'm listening to the music," I demurred, gesturing to the stage and sweeping my hair over one shoulder. The millisecond of breeze generated by my moving hair was a welcome respite on the nape of my neck, where a trickle of sweat was making its way down to my collar.

"Do you need me to translate for you? Perhaps the words are"—he leaned forward and kissed the exposed side of my neck, sending a ripple of goose bumps down my arm—"too complicated?"

I could feel my body starting to melt, the rigidity in my back giving way to a curved spine that wanted nothing more than to sink back into the warmth of Gang's body and let the intoxicating melody coming from the stage shield us from prying eyes. But I couldn't. Not yet. I needed to scan the room again; I needed to make sure the alcohol hadn't tricked me into dreaming the whole thing. Was I really in this sexy, adult nightclub with someone who looked like Gang? Did he really want to spend the entire night talking to only me?

In the span of just two days, I had somehow aged half a decade, my days of drinking cheap beer on friends' couches and in garages a lifetime ago. Iowa, and everyone in it, faded into the background as unimportant. Here, I was powerful. I commanded the attention of the hottest guy in the room, possibly the hottest guy in the entire universe. I was no longer fretting over boys who did or didn't like me, but grown men in suits who recited poetry to seduce me.

Maybe Gang had been right. I needed a New Year's resolution, and I was about to make one right now. New year, new me. No more childish insecurities. If I wanted to be around someone like Gang, I needed to believe I belonged. Amy may have been a bitch, but she was a confident bitch. She would never have settled for being Just Good Enough.

"I speak Chinese too, remember?" I said, playfully swatting at him. Just another excuse to touch him.

He kissed my neck again, sending a shudder through my body.

"Tell me what she says," he whispered into my ear before gently nipping at my lobe.

I gulped and licked my lips, trying to regain my composure before speaking. He'd manage to find my weak spot without even trying. "Okay, I might not be not totally fluent," I admitted, pins of electricity buzzing through my ear from where his lips had touched. "But I can understand some of it."

Leaning back onto his elbow, Gang ran his other hand across my shoulder and down my arm, causing my body to involuntarily shudder again. "Do I make you nervous, June Chu?" he drawled.

Yes. Yes. Yes. Yes.

"No," I lied.

He nestled his head against my chest, the familiar scent of tea tree oil and orange in his hair keeping me from completely passing out. I didn't know what he was doing, but I didn't move an inch, praying he never stopped whatever it was.

"Do you know what qīshàng bāxià means?" he asked, removing his ear from my rapidly beating heart.

I quickly translated the words in my head. "Seven up, eight down?"

A playful smile crept across Gang's lips, their usual light pink hue taking on a deeper tone in the dim light. "It means your heart is very anxious."

I swallowed hard, trying to keep said anxious heart from jumping out of my throat. "Jǐjiā huānxǐ jǐjiā chou," I replied, telling Gang, *while some are happy, some are anxious.*

He threw his head back in laughter. "Ah, June, you make me laugh."

I rubbed my lips together self-consciously. "Why?" Had I misquoted the proverb? Again?

"Because you are irresistible when you speak Chinese," he said, touching the tip of my nose with his long, exquisite finger. "Tell me, what other proverbs do you know?"

This was my chance to impress him. Finally, the past eighteen years of my life were useful for something. I racked my brain for one I was sure I couldn't mess up the meaning of.

"Yǒuyuán qiānlǐ lái xiānghuí," I said. *Fate brings people together from far apart.*

Still reclining on his elbow, Gang raised a sculpted eyebrow as he reached over to pick up his drink. "So it does." He took a long sip before adding, "I think fate has been kind to us."

I gave a cool smile, but I could feel my entire body warming with immense pride. I'd impressed Gang. He'd referred to meeting me as *fate*. And the terribly nervous butterflies in my stomach were beginning to dissipate.

Gang tugged gently on the back on my shirt. "Come, June Chu, speaker of Chinese proverbs and fate. I have spent all night thinking of kissing you and I cannot wait any longer." He slid his hand behind my head to tilt it down toward him. Just before he kissed me, he looked into my eyes and smiled deliciously—like a wolf before dinner.

CHAPTER TWENTY-THREE

I awoke the next morning alone and incredibly thirsty, but neatly tucked under the cream comforter and matching cream sheets in Gang's oversized bed. He had ordered nothing but gin and tonics for us all night, and now it felt like I had a throat full of sand. All I wanted was a glass of water.

My head was pounding, but I rose from the bed and hastily threw on my clothes from the previous night, which were scattered across the floor. The prospect of being seen naked during daylight hours felt much more exposed.

I tiptoed across the stripes of sunlight coming through the window, cracking open the bedroom door to peek out into the living room. The apartment was completely silent, the only proof of life coming from the glass tumblers scattered across the coffee table, presumably from the previous night. How many roommates did he have living with him? I couldn't remember.

We'd drunk and made out until the club closed, at which point Gang decided he'd had too much to drink and called us a cab back to his apartment. It felt sort of weird to leave without Amy, who was officially tasked with looking after me, but as she'd said when I'd asked if she was okay with me going with Gang, I was a grown-up and she wasn't my mother.

I already knew what my mother would have said about the situation.

So I left with him. I didn't quite realize what that meant until we were walking in his door to a chorus of hellos from nameless faces who didn't seem particularly surprised to see me. But when the kissing resumed inside the privacy of his bedroom, I didn't say no. I didn't want to say no.

Instead, I'd kissed him, arching my back until my shoulders grazed the top of his bed, one of his hands firmly encircling my waist. It was everything I never knew I'd been missing.

My problem with Brad hadn't been about not liking sex. It had been about not liking sex enough *with him*. Gang didn't paw at me, trying to get through everything as fast as possible. He took each step slowly, as if savoring the lead-up. It wasn't about what I could do for him, but rather, what he could do for me. I'd never realized just how little Brad cared about my satisfaction until I was with someone who did.

But as the Chinese philosophers warned, Tiān xià méi yǒu bú sàn de yàn xi—no banquet in the world goes on forever. Today was my last full day in Washington and also the day I had to officially audition for my place here. The music director had assured me it was very casual and nothing to get nervous about, but now I had so much riding on it. If I blew it, how could I possibly go back to my life in Iowa, knowing what I'd lost?

Suddenly I wished I'd spent at least some of my time here practicing. Instead I'd pushed the whole ordeal out of my mind as if I could reduce its importance by ignoring it, like teachers tell you to do with mean kids in school.

I took another peek out the door to ensure no one was coming, then paced his room, surveying its contents. If this was the last time I was going be in his proximity, I wasn't in a rush to leave it. Even if the dreaded audition was today. *Especially* because the dreaded audition was today.

Gang's bedroom was tidy and sparse, with only his bed, a desk, and one dresser inside. The closet was neatly organized and full of crisp button-downs and slacks of varying colors, exactly like the ones he'd been wearing when I met him. I wanted to reach out and run my fingers across them, savoring the feel of the linens, but I resisted. Something about touching the fabrics when his body wasn't in them wasn't quite the same. It wasn't the clothes I wanted to touch—it was him.

I crossed over to his desk, which was nearly empty except for a laptop and his passport. I flipped open the passport to a perfectly styled photo and pages full of stamps.

Of course.

But at least now I had his last name. "Wang Gang." I whispered his name aloud. *Steel King.* That was fitting.

I moved to his dresser, where I quietly opened a drawer. Everything inside it was neatly folded and stacked, as though a retail store employee had come and organized his drawers for him. I didn't even fold my own laundry—my mom did. It was as if there was no limit to his superiority over me in maturity and sophistication. He even folded his underwear like a goddamned grown-up.

Along his walls were a few miniature Polaroid photos, similar to the ones Amy had on her walls. Some of the pictures had girls in them, some didn't. I examined the face and body positioning of every girl, my stomach twisting into knots as I wondered if he'd had sex with any of them. Were any of them special to him? Had he whispered any of their names in the voice that made it feel like it was the only word that should ever be spoken? Were any of them in love with him?

I peeked out the door a third time, the eerie silence of the apartment unchanged. Had Gang had gone to retrieve his car from outside the club? Or pick up breakfast? Without his number to text, there was no way to know anything. I hadn't thought to ask for it.

It was better to be gone before he got back. I didn't want to seem like I'd been waiting around for him, even though I'd been doing exactly that for at least half an hour already. Except that meant now I had to get out of here before he reappeared or his roommates woke up and I had to answer questions about where he'd gone.

I hastily tore a page out of a notebook I found inside his desk drawer and scribbled a breezy goodbye with my number at the bottom, just in case. I didn't want him to think I'd slunk out in embarrassment. This wasn't a walk of shame. If anything, I was proud of myself.

I was brave. I was bold. Unlike the first time I'd decided to have sex with Brad, I hadn't done this because I wanted to prove something. I wasn't checking off some box on a list of milestones I wanted to achieve. I'd done it simply because I *wanted* to. There was no chance of starting a relationship with Gang right now, but I'd done it anyway. I didn't need to convince him to like me or to take me seriously or even to worship me like Brad had after we'd started hooking up. Gang liked me before anything had happened between us. And *he* made the moves on *me.*

A shiver ran through me as I allowed myself another second to replay certain parts of the night in my mind. Another minute, really. Then I shook it off, finally ready to devote my full focus to my upcoming performance. Contrary to what my family believed, I did actually care about how I did at competitions. And while I'd stopped *expecting* to win a long time ago, it didn't mean it didn't still sting when I was handed yet another third-place trophy. But I couldn't pretend this one didn't matter to me. This audition was everything, my entire future. If I didn't manage to impress the director, there would be no Lunar New Year dinners, no multicultural cafeterias, no posh bars. And—my heart squeezed at the thought—no Gang. With a slow, steady breath, I gave the room a final sweep and with it came inspiration. I knew exactly what I was going to play for my audition.

CHAPTER TWENTY-FOUR

The audition was casual, as promised, with only the music director and the first chair violinist in attendance. We were in a small practice room, which was mostly empty except for the sets of chairs unevenly stacked along the wall and a few scattered music stands.

The brief moment of panic I'd felt this morning in Gang's room had faded, my confidence soaring as I dragged a chair to the middle of the room. There was nowhere to hide here, no orchestra to blend in with. But I was no longer the kind of girl who needed to apologize for existing. They *wanted* me here. *Gang* wanted me here. I *belonged* here. It was fate. And as Gang had said, fate was being kind to me, for once.

"You can start whenever you're ready," the director instructed.

With a deep breath, I steadied my hands and began to play. Mozart, of course. This time, a bold concerto in G major—a reflection of my mood. In the confined space, the music quickly filled the room, my notes seeming to settle around and on top of the three of us, tiny embellishments unfurling like petals in sunlight.

My parents always frowned upon my little additions, reminding me to stick to the music as it was written. Wendy never embellished. She played like a machine. But right now, in this moment, I was a wind chime swaying in the breeze, adding notes wherever they felt right.

I was a goddess, a musical genius. If music were a mountain, I was standing atop it, gleefully surveying the fruits of my uphill climb.

I deserved this performance. I deserved this moment of triumph after the thousands of hours I'd put into it—tens of thousands of hours, probably. I'd never, not even once, ever felt like this while playing.

It was like I was on my deathbed, moments from my life flashing by. Except instead of regrets, I had only happy memories: mastering "Twinkle, Twinkle Little Star," my first recital dress, finishing my last Suzuki book, discovering I could play along to Metallica.

The notes stretched across the room, growing fuller with each and every pull of my bow, filling the space until there was no quarter from it. I was drowning in music while gasping for more of it.

Then, all too soon, the song came to an end. I kept my eyes closed a few extra moments, loathe to rejoin the real world, where I might be reminded of my less pleasant memories: Wendy taunting me for taking longer than her to get through Book 4. My mom telling me it was a waste of their money for me to compete nationally. Cracking my violin in a fit of rage, then having to lie about dropping it and sitting through a lecture about being careless with my things, followed by having to work off the cost of a new instrument.

How was it possible to simultaneously love and hate the same thing? Violin had caused me so much grief over the years—sometimes it felt like nothing but pain and resentment. Yet at the same time, I couldn't imagine never playing again. It was simply a part of me. Playing had a way of accessing emotions I kept buried, regardless of whether they were positive or negative. Listening to music had a similar impact, but even that couldn't replicate the experience of *creating* it. Listening to a piece as it shifted and changed under my fingers, depending on my mood, was the closest thing I had to finding my true self. And right now I was someone who was full of optimism and confidence because everything was going right in her life.

As I lowered my instrument, I was surprised to see my arms covered with goose bumps.

"Thank you, June. That was beautiful."

The music director's voice pulled me out of my existential crisis, my eyes refocusing on the girl's face next to his. If I'd been hallucinating my brilliance just now, she'd be the one to tip me off. Some people just had a certain look about them.

But to my relief, she smiled warmly. "I think you'd be a great fit here. Our contemporary style really encourages individual touches where they can be managed, and it's clear you can play the hell out of that thing." With a guilty glance at the director, she straightened up and amended her statement. "What I meant to say was thank you for your time. We have some things to discuss."

But on my way out the door, she gave me a wink and a thumbs-up.

———————

Once I'd turned my phone's sound back on, it buzzed with missed notifications. A text from an unfamiliar number.

I missed you this morning. Sorry for disappearing.

A silly grin spread across my face. It could only be from one person.

I began to type *no worries* before I thought better of it. I was always doing this—dismissing things as not a big deal, sweeping away my feelings about something because I didn't want to be thought of as difficult or uncool. It *was* bad that he'd left me without saying anything. I *was* bugged about it. And even though he was apologizing now, that didn't make it okay.

On the other hand, it was silly to pick a fight when I only had one more day to spend with him. And compared to the bullshit I had been willing to put up with when I was dating Rhys and Brad, one tiny slight wasn't really that big of a deal. It wasn't like he'd done something low-key racist, like call me "China."

Ugh. Even *thinking* about it made me cringe. Maybe one day I'd figure out what the hell I was thinking when I let Brad call me that, especially since I couldn't imagine letting my friends do the same. The only logical explanation had to be some girl version of beer goggles for cute guys who love-bombed them. Either way, it made moving away from Iowa look that much more enticing.

I'll let you make it up to me

I typed.

I stared at the phone as the three little dots blinked endlessly, my heart racing to see his reply.

After what felt like a decade, it came through.

Of course. Tonight. You name the location.

I nearly screamed. Grown-up me was flirting, and doing it well!

I clutched my phone to my chest and sank against the wall, wondering how much higher the cloud I was on could rise. As it was, I was already set up for quite a fall the minute I walked out of this building.

Amy had given me instructions to drop off my violin back in her room so we could meet up with her friends for dinner before going out for the night. While things between us this morning had been fine, I was half hoping she'd show more interest in what happened between Gang and me last night. Not just because I wanted to rub it in that he found me "Chinese enough," though I couldn't deny that was at least a small part of it.

I'd never really spoken Chinese to anyone who wasn't either a teacher or directly related to me. My Mandarin wasn't even really good enough for me to feel like I could claim it as *my* language. But being able to rattle off the proverbs my mom had drilled into my head and being able to follow snatches of conversation had given me new life. I finally *felt* Chinese in a way that wasn't defined by the way other people saw the shape of my eyes. Or, I guess, Taiwanese. And all the snide remarks from Amy couldn't take that away from me.

I looked back down at the earlier text messages from Gang, my heart climbing up into my throat as I remembered the way he looked at me last night. Maybe it wasn't crazy to think that this could actually be something. People had long-distance relationships all the time. And it wasn't like there was anyone back in Iowa I would rather be with. In only a few short months I'd be back here permanently, and then we'd have all the time we needed. I just needed one more night to show him how much we belonged together.

———

A quick pass back of someone's ID and a hand stamp later, I found myself in the cavernous front room of the bar, the floor already mysteriously sticky enough that you had to peel your shoes off of it with each step. Amy's friends had mentioned this being a popular spot for students on campus, with its close proximity and live bands. I tried to picture what it would be like to be with Gang in this space. It was certainly a departure from last night's upscale hookah lounge.

A short while later, he finally arrived with the same group of orchestra guys that had been with him the previous night. After a quick hello to the other girls, Gang strode over to me with a kiss on the cheek and his arm around my shoulder. He looked somehow even better than ever, a pinkish striped button-down tucked into gray slacks and black loafers. His hair fell around his face expertly, his jaw and neck freshly shaved and so smooth I wanted to run my fingers over it the way antique dealers assessed finely made porcelain.

I could see the curious looks from the other girls as they tried to decipher how, exactly, I'd swooped in here and caught the attention of someone as incredible as Gang. If I'd been in their shoes, I'd have been desperately jealous of me. I tried to act casual, fussing with my hair to keep me from having to make eye contact with them as Gang went to order drinks for us at the bar. I hoped he picked up on my telepathic thoughts to *not* get gin and tonics again.

The violinist who'd been present for my audition sidled up next to me. "You and Gang, huh?" There was a note of surprise in her voice. "Looks like you two are a music match made in heaven. I always hear him playing Mozart during practice."

I tried to shrug casually but couldn't contain my smile as heat spread across my face. "I guess so."

"You're definitely coming here next year then?"

"If I get the scholarship."

She gave a confident nod. "You'll get it. Beckman already told me he's getting the paperwork together."

A wave of relief coursed through me as the final barrier to my future life abruptly crumbled like the aliens at the end of *The War of the Worlds.* It was wild to think that I'd been stressing over this decision for months, only to have the perfect solution pop up out of nowhere. It was almost too good to be true.

"Now I just have to get through the next six months before I can come back," I half joked.

She sighed wistfully. "I remember that feeling. Like I couldn't wait for all of it to start. Now I'm in my last semester, looking back at how fast it all flew by. Don't worry. It'll all be waiting for you when you get here. Try to enjoy the rest of high school too."

Ha. Like I could possibly go back to Iowa and be satisfied with my life after this.

Gang returned, slipping a thick glass into my hand and his arm around my waist. "Did I miss anything important?" he asked.

"June's decided to come here in the fall," she told him, not bothering to ask if I'd wanted to tell him the news myself.

"Really?" he asked her.

They were both taller than me, so the conversation was taking place literally over my head.

"Really," I chimed in, reminding him of my presence.

Gang looked down at me with a smile, his arm still wrapped around my waist. "Wonderful news. This calls for a celebration."

Even without having taken a sip of my drink yet, I could feel my cheeks beginning to turn red. Why couldn't I skip ahead a year so I could already be here? Right now I felt like a dumb high schooler, sandwiched between the two grown-ups as they discussed my future. If I were actually a student, people might stop looking shocked I was here—that Gang would be interested in me. Why couldn't they see what he clearly saw in me?

"I'll be right back, I'm going to find the restroom," I said, peeling away from Gang's arm. I needed some space to compose myself, or as Liz would say, *get my head in the game*. This was my last night. I wanted him to remember me as the June from the audition this afternoon—how could I get her to make an appearance?

I stood in the back room just outside the bathroom doors, my finger hovering over Candace's number on my phone for what felt like ages. If anyone could give me a pep talk right now, it was her. But what would I even say to her? How could I possibly explain everything that was at stake right now?

Slowly I slipped my phone back into my pocket. I'd wanted to be a grown-up. I'd need to get through this on my own like a grown-up.

I wandered back toward the front of the bar where I'd left everyone, making my way through the crowd of people who'd arrived while I was hiding out in the back. Gang and the violinist were still chatting, both of them with their backs turned toward me.

". . . so I'll be moving to Canada this summer," she was saying.

"Very exciting," Gang responded. "Canada is a wonderful country. And much less gun violence than here."

"What about you? Are you staying in the States over the summer or are you going back to China?"

I snuck back a few steps, grateful neither of them had spotted me, and flattened myself against the bar behind them. I knew it was wrong and weird to eavesdrop, but I couldn't resist the opportunity just to know *anything* about Gang's personal life. He hadn't even told me about his love of Mozart.

My ears strained to catch his voice, praying this wasn't the moment everyone suddenly decided to order a drink. Maybe Gang was planning to stay around here. I wasn't going to be due back until August, but there wasn't a reason I couldn't come out early. Some of the girls in the orchestra had apartments nearby. Maybe I could stay with them and—

"I will go back, naturally," Gang said. "My girlfriend is there waiting for me. We like to travel and go wine tasting in the summers."

All the air in the room disappeared.

Girlfriend.

Wine tasting.

The sweet Koshu wine he'd ordered with dinner the night we met.

Blood rushed through my ears like a tidal wave.

Gang wasn't opposed to long-distance relationships—he was already in one.

The violinist must have been as shocked as I was, because when my ears finally cleared, I heard her say, "I didn't even realize you had a girlfriend. I was under the impression you had this little thing going on with June all weekend."

I mentally promised to name my firstborn after her. It didn't matter that I didn't know her name; my child would simply be named "tall violinist who stood up for me."

Gang's deep voice rang out clearly, with no sign of hesitation or remorse. "June is amusing, but she is a child. My girlfriend and I have been together for years. We will get married someday. Things with June are just for fun—nothing serious. My girlfriend understands."

My chest felt like it was collapsing on itself. I staggered back toward the wall, unable to find the exit through my blurry eyes.

How could this be happening? He thought I was a child. *Nothing serious.*

I'd let myself run around all weekend believing he liked me. Believing he saw me as an equal. Believing I belonged. Or that I would someday.

Instead, he found me *amusing*. A distraction. Something to entertain himself with while his real girlfriend was thousands of miles away. And she knew! I mattered so little that she knew!

I sank back into the wall and dipped my head to my knees, trying to keep the blood from draining completely out of my brain. My fingernails dug into my thighs, and I willed my legs to hold my body weight and keep me from collapsing onto the dirty floor.

"What are you doing back here? I thought you would be draped all over Gang all night."

I snapped my head up at the sound of Amy's bored voice. She loomed over me, her black leather purse in one hand and a reddish cocktail in the other. Everything about her at this moment stood out as a reminder of just how much older she was than me. The shiny black stilettos that weren't trying too hard. The way her yellow blouse was tucked into her jeans. Even the strapless clutch purse.

"I accidentally splashed my drink in my eyes," I said, using the lie as an excuse to quickly wipe away the moisture that had collected in them.

Amy's face shifted into an expression of concern. "Oh shit, I've done that before. It stings. Are you okay?"

As if on cue, Gang appeared. "Ah, there you are." If he sensed that I'd eavesdropped on his conversation, he gave no hint of it.

"She got something in her eye," Amy explained as I blinked rapidly, willing my eyes to stop producing tears. "Do you need to go wash it out in the bathroom or something?" she asked me.

Both of them hovered over me like I was an injured child.

"I'm fine, I'm fine," I insisted, fighting against my desire to be swallowed up by the floor and die. This was all so humiliating. The girlfriend, the tears, the concern over my fake injury.

Gang wrapped an arm around me protectively and tried to lift my chin so he could look into my eye. Like he wasn't the exact thing I needed to extract from my body.

A torrent of emotions swelled inside me like a tornado. Anger. Hurt. Embarrassment. Shame. Deep, searing, burning shame.

He'd made me believe I was special to him.

I wanted to shove him off of me, to slap him across the face, to scream at him to stay the hell away from me. I wanted to throw my drink on him and cry in the bathroom, to run away from everyone who was staring at us while pretending they weren't.

But all that would do would prove how immature I was. How I was a child. How I didn't really belong here after all.

So, I let him. I let him look me in the eye before he declared everything looked okay. I let him kiss me in an attempt to make me feel better. I let him wrap his arm around my waist again and lead me into the room where the band would be performing. All the while, I smiled and made small talk with the girls and sipped my drink, feeling nothing but the steady drip of my own blood as it leaked out of my slowly blackening heart.

CHAPTER TWENTY-FIVE

I had a blessedly early flight the next morning, sparing me the agony of meaningless chitchat over breakfast with Amy. She knew. She had to. How else could I explain her little side conversations with Gang when I was around? Why else would she roll her eyes every time she talked to him? Gang had no interest in me beyond a weekend fling and she didn't think it was worth mentioning. She probably agreed with him. I wasn't Chinese enough, I wasn't old enough, I wasn't good enough.

June is a child. Nothing serious.

I was ashamed at my own inferiority. *Zì kuì fú rú,* my mom would say whenever I complained about the praise they seemed to lavish on Wendy. Why, for once in my life, couldn't I rise to the occasion? Of all the losses I'd suffered in my life, this one stung the most.

I'd gone from Just Good Enough to Not Good Enough. I had been fooling myself, thinking he actually cared about what I thought. Looking at me like I was the only person in the room. Making me feel like *he* was the one who was lucky to be with *me.*

June is a child. Nothing serious.

The words played on a loop in my head, taunting me.

I'd thought I was so mature, running around a college campus, pretending I belonged. Drinking in bars and going home with a strange man, acting like I knew what I was doing. I thought it meant something when he whispered poems in my ear and told me I was *xiù sè kě cān—a feast for the eyes*. I'd wanted it all to be true so badly I'd believed it.

If it hadn't been me, Gang probably would have done the same thing with another girl. Maybe he already had. Maybe he did this to all the recruits. Maybe Amy thought she had been warning me and that I didn't care. Maybe, maybe, maybe. I'd never know now.

I was such a fool. I couldn't go to Washington now. If I did, it would look like I was chasing Gang, following through on his bullshit about wanting me to be there with him. What a line. And I fell for it.

It had all been a fantasy from the beginning, and I'd let myself indulge in it. *Xiǎng rù fēi fēi*, the Chinese called it. I'd let myself imagine that I'd fit in with Amy and her friends, I'd completely blown off the now-seemingly-reasonable assertion that maybe growing up in Iowa gave me less in common with people actually *from* Asia, and I'd deluded myself into thinking someone like Gang would see a future with me. Why? Because I'd charmed him with my gawking eyes and use of Chinese proverbs? Because I'd slept with him? He didn't even think it was worthwhile to tell me his last name. Imagine if he found out I had no clue where Guangzhou was. *That* was how far apart our realities really were.

I'd spent the rest of my last night in Washington with a cool detachment as Gang seemed to squeeze me tighter and tighter, determined to keep me by his side. I couldn't bear to prove Amy right. To prove my own inner doubts right. I let him hug me and kiss me and whisper sexy things in my ear all night, hating myself for every twinge of weakness. I knew he was lying to me. I'd heard it with my own ears. And yet, when he asked me to come home with him again, I nearly said yes.

I wanted so desperately for it to be true. That he liked me enough to want to be with me. That I'd magically convince him to break up with his girlfriend and be with me instead.

But the memory of Brad's tears haunted me, reminding me what it looked like when someone was so desperate to hold on that it oozed out of them, contaminating the very air around them. I didn't want to be that girl. I *couldn't* be that girl. I needed to go home with at least the appearance of dignity to cover for the fact that I no longer had any.

So I'd said no. I blamed my early flight, even against his protests, and managed not to let on that I knew about his girlfriend, even when he bid me farewell with a "see you soon."

My parents picked me up from the airport, suddenly chatty about everything from the weather variations in the Pacific Northwest to a full financial breakdown of the tax implications of accepting grant money. I pretended to sleep the whole way home so as to avoid them, my brain screaming the words I'd heard over and over again.

June is a child. Nothing serious.

CHAPTER TWENTY-SIX

Staying in my house was impossible. Everything I touched reminded me of Gang. My violin? I would have burned it if I could. My bed? All I could see were flashes of Gang's sinewy chest, hovering over me like a panther in motion. Leaving my room was a nonstarter. My parents were both home, waiting to pounce all over me and force me to have conversations about my future. Like I had any idea what that would look like right now.

I did the only logical thing—I fled.

Both Candace and Liz were out as safe options. I didn't need a lecture from Liz about the risks of sleeping with a stranger or a "look on the bright side" take from Candace that I'd at least gotten sex out of the situation. I needed someone who wouldn't talk, someone who wasn't eager to give advice.

I texted Rhys.

> I need to be alone but not be alone

Was all I said. He didn't ask questions. He told me to just come over.

No words were exchanged as we made our way to his room

in the basement, where I laid down on the far side of his bed and used my phone to queue up the second movement of Mozart's Piano Concerto no. 23 in A major—the same piece I'd heard Gang play in the auditorium. I wanted to lose myself in an ocean of grief and drown in my own tears. I wanted to suffer through every indignity and pore over Gang's words for the millionth time.

She is a child. Nothing serious.

I deserved it. I deserved it for letting myself believe someone like Gang could ever be interested in someone like me. I deserved it for letting myself get my hopes up over something that was so obviously *not serious*. And while I might have never said aloud what I wanted, I knew deep down I had been hoping Gang would find me . . . worthy.

I *was* a child.

Tears silently slipped down the sides of my face, running into my temples and matting my hair against my head. I didn't wipe them away. I deserved the tears too.

Amy was right. I wasn't enough. Maybe I'd never be enough. I was naive to think I could fit in there. They were probably all laughing at me—the little high schooler cosplaying as someone who could fit in with the *real* Asians. All the proverbs in the world couldn't fool them into thinking I belonged. Even my own mother had been shocked at the idea of me fitting in with other Chinese people.

Rhys reached over from his side of the bed and laid his hand on mine, the same way he had on New Year's Eve. It was smooth and warm, unlike the long bony fingers of Gang or the rough, calloused hands of Brad. How sad that I'd had so few people of note hold my hand that I could actually compare them.

"Do you want to talk about it?" he asked softly.

"No."

He didn't argue. Instead, he kept his hand over mine, listening as I played the movement over and over again, trying to hold together the splinters of my heart as my brain whispered circles around the question I didn't dare ask of even myself: What if the reason things kept not working out was because there was something fundamentally wrong with me?

Eventually my tears slowed and I gathered the courage to speak. "Do you think sex can make people fall in love?" My voice was barely audible over the music.

I could feel his surprise at the question as his fingers twitched ever so slightly, though he didn't remove them from mine.

"I—" his voice sounded creaky and huskier than usual, probably from not speaking for so long. He cleared his throat and tried again. "I guess I wouldn't know."

If I'd asked myself the same question a few months ago, I would have said yes. Yes, I could make Rhys fall in love with me if I just had sex with him; yes, I made Brad fall in love with me by having sex with him. But Gang had come along and messed everything up because I *knew* I wasn't in love with him. In love with the idea of him, maybe. In love with the way I felt around him. But I wasn't silly enough to think people fell in love after a matter of days. Especially when one person had already committed their heart to a girlfriend back home.

So why did I feel guilty about what happened in Washington? Why did I still feel like the one to blame?

Rhys cleared his throat again. "I think, you know, people are going to do whatever they're going to do, but they should be up-front about why they're doing it."

I tried to parse the vagueness of his words, but my brain was too muddled and all that came out was, "Huh?"

"I just mean, some people can do stuff without any kind of attachment to the other person. Some people can't. And it's a shitty thing to do if you're the first kind of person, letting the other person think you're the second kind."

Rhys's words broke open my chest and a flood of righteousness poured out of it, drowning my shame and misery. What happened with Gang *wasn't* my fault. He'd led me to believe he felt something for me, and my decision to have sex with him wasn't embarrassing because there was no way for me to know he *didn't*. If I was naive for not seeing through the façade, then maybe I was a child. But maybe that was better than being the type of person who used someone's optimism and trusting nature against them.

The song ended and I pressed Play again, even though I was barely listening to it anymore.

I'd thought I was in love with Brad when I was with him. But just as easily as I'd fallen for him, I'd gotten over him without so much as a second glance backward. Was he sitting around cursing my name, thinking I'd tricked him into believing he was special to me? Maybe we were all the asshole in someone else's story.

The warmth of Rhys's hand kept me from completely floating away and getting sucked up into a spiral of doubt and worry about every action I'd ever taken in my life. If only I could hide out in this bed forever, ignoring the fact that I eventually needed to make certain decisions about my future. This space was safe.

Warm. Well, warm for a basement.

"Why do you sleep in the basement?" I asked, suddenly changing the subject.

"I dunno, more privacy I guess."

Privacy from whom? As far as I knew, his parents gave him all the space he needed. My mom, on the other hand, still "cleaned" my room at unexpected intervals and confronted me about anything semipersonal she found. It was how I'd learned never to keep a diary.

I glanced around the bare-bones room—the hard, concrete floor, the unpainted walls, even the unvarnished desk that sat in the corner. All the other times I'd been in his room, I'd been so preoccupied with what we would or wouldn't do together, I'd never really noticed how odd it was that he'd willingly moved out of a normal, carpeted bedroom for this. The ceiling wasn't even finished—studs peeked out between the gaps in the drywall that seemed to have been placed with no particular order in mind. I knew next to nothing about home repair, but even I could see this was done by someone who probably didn't care enough to find out the right way to do it.

"How come everything is unfinished?" I asked.

"I'll get to it eventually. Maybe after graduation, when I have more time."

"You did all this? Yourself?"

Rhys chuckled like he was embarrassed at my incredulity. "I had some help from Paul."

I'd only met his older brother in passing, but he didn't appear to be the handiest guy. Then again, neither did Rhys. The heaviest thing he hauled on a daily basis was his backpack, and even that was nearly empty half the time. Knowing he could fix things—even haphazardly—was oddly appealing.

A blurry image flashed across my mind, of Rhys making repairs on a rundown house like Ryan Gosling's character in *The Notebook*. Rowing in the rain. *It wasn't over. It still isn't over.*

I shook it off.

"Doesn't it get cold?" I asked.

"Not really," he replied. "But if you're cold you can get under the covers."

My free hand searched the space next to me, landing upon a scrunched pile of flannel—so weathered and worn it no longer even held a fuzzy texture but had become soft and supple like a thick, sturdy cotton. Sheets like this would definitely keep you warm, even in a basement in Iowa in the middle of winter. It was especially warm right now, Rhys's hands serving as a hot coil around mine.

Despite all the time I'd spent here, everything about this place right now—this situation—was foreign to me. The way the bare light bulbs on the ceiling cast a harsh light over the room. The slight dampness in the air. The unfinished quality of it all, right down to the fact that the bed had only two flattened pillows, heavy from years of use.

Nothing about this was like my house, but somehow it felt like home.

I fell asleep, our hands still touching, until it was time for me to leave.

CHAPTER TWENTY-SEVEN

"Two weeks from Friday. Liz wants to go to the cabin. You in?" Candace asked as I dropped my plastic cafeteria tray onto the table with a *clank*.

"Can I have a second to think about it, or do I need to answer right now?" I asked as Liz reflexively reached over, pulling the stray hairs off my back and dropping them onto the floor. I could probably nest a family of gorillas with the amount of hair I shed every day.

Candace swirled a french fry in a mix of ketchup and mayo before shoving the entire thing into her tiny mouth. She liked to brag about how she'd been doing it long before Heinz got the idea and marketed it as "Mayochup," the world's worst product name. "You need to answer right now."

I sighed, pulling out my phone and checking my calendar. "Can't. I'm visiting Wendy that weekend to tour the school."

Liz and Candace exchanged a look of disbelief, Liz even setting down her tuna sandwich before she'd finished it.

"What happened to Washington?" Liz demanded.

"I can look at more than one school," I said defensively.

Candace narrowed her eyes. "You said it was perfect."

So, I'd omitted a few details upon my return. Namely, anything having to do with Gang, his conspicuous silence since I left, or the number of hours I'd devoted to obsessing about whether or not I counted as a real Chinese person. I was like Panda Express—somehow mocked for being not "authentic," but was in fact created by a Chinese chef, with roots in Chinese cuisine, and delicious in its own right.

Which then led me to the begrudging realization that Amy's comments had only reflected the same truths I'd realized about the overlap between the Midwest and white culture. And whether I'd adopted some of those tastes and habits out of the necessity of assimilation or because I just *liked* yoga pants and heavy metal music, maybe it wasn't the most offensive thing ever for her to assume I wouldn't share cultural touchstones with people who grew up somewhere else.

None of which was easily explainable to my very Midwestern and very white friends.

"I don't know if I said it was *perfect*," I backtracked. "I said their music program was a good fit and the campus was nice. I just want to make sure I'm exploring all my options."

It was too embarrassing to admit that no other schools had replied in the intervening weeks, thereby limiting my options to facing Gang again or living in Wendy's shadow for the next two years—both of which were still vastly more appealing than admitting I'd spent hundreds of hours throughout high school on AP classes and violin practice only to end up at UNI like everyone else from Pine Grove. I was running short on both solutions and time, not to mention my parents' patience. I'd had a hell of a time explaining why I was now hesitant to accept the offer from Washington, and I only managed to deflect suspicion by claiming I wanted to visit Wendy before making any decisions.

If my parents had paid even a modicum of attention to anything I'd said previously, it should have been an immediate red flag that I was stalling for time. It was hard not to feel a pang of sadness that my friends could easily pick up on what my parents didn't care enough to notice. But now was not the moment to confess that my entire future was one good shake away from collapsing completely.

"Northwestern is one of the top schools in the country," I said primly, parroting the same language my mom always used when pretending not to brag to other parents.

"It's always been one of the top schools in the country," Candace said pointedly.

"I guess I realized it would be stupid to not even consider it. I mean, I already got accepted. Besides," I added, "if I go there, I'll only be a few hours away from you guys. I can even come back to help Candace cheer you on at games." I grinned wickedly at Liz, who gave a half laugh, half groan.

"I have to make the team first. I called UNI and they said tryouts for walk-ons will happen after school starts. But if I don't make it, they have intramural teams and stuff too.".

"What about housing?" I asked. "Are you two going to try and room together?" I felt a sudden stab of jealousy at the thought of the two of them having fun together while I was busy interviewing candidates to fill the role of New Best Friend like some tragic reality show character.

My choices for people I knew at school were currently limited to either Amy or Wendy. So much for the idea of reinventing myself at college.

Candace shifted uncomfortably in her seat, pushing the french fries around her tray and avoiding eye contact with both Liz and me. "I don't really know if I'm going to go," she said, more to her food than to us.

"What do you mean?" Liz and I asked at the same time, doing a double take at each other and shouting "Jinx!" at the same time.

"Are you still considering Eau Claire?" I asked hopefully, referencing the school in Wisconsin that Candace had been eyeing before she started dating Dominic.

She shook her head. "No, I'm just not really into the whole college thing."

Liz's jaw dropped open, revealing a mouthful of half-chewed tuna salad.

I tried, repeatedly, to blurt out some kind of reply, but no sound came out.

Candace had certainly *been* into "the whole college thing," as she put it. Last summer she'd taken two classes at Kirkwood Community College that counted as credit for both high school and college as a way to get ahead without taking on the heavy workload of AP classes during the year.

"Not everyone has to go to college, you know," Candace said defensively. "Plenty of people do just fine without it. Besides," she added before either of us could speak, "college is expensive.

People are graduating with these massive loans and no jobs. I already have a job and no debt."

"You took that job to save up for college," I said, finally finding my voice.

"Well, now I can use it for something more . . . useful," she spluttered.

"Like what?" Liz had also now recovered, sitting next to me like we were a powerful inquisitorial squad against Candace's defiance of common sense.

"Like an apartment for Dom and me."

"Are you kidding me?" Liz screeched at the same time I exclaimed, "You're giving up college for *him*?"

Any trace of shame Candace had seemed to feel was now gone, her posture haughty and drawn up as high as she could make it, which wasn't a lot.

"I'm not giving it up for *him*. It's for myself."

"He just so happens to benefit by not having you go away and break up with him when you see what else is out there," I shot back.

"You two haven't made a secret of how you feel about my boyfriend, but this is my choice and I don't need you judging me for it."

"Then why did you bother telling us?" Liz muttered.

"I *thought* you were my friends," Candace retorted, her face now reddening with anger as she stood up to leave. "And real friends don't judge each other."

"That's not true. We judge each other all the time, the rest of us just usually do it inside our own heads." I'd said it sarcastically, half joking about the fact that Candace should have been the last person to criticize anyone else for being judgmental, what with her "tell it like it is" attitude toward everything.

"Thanks for finally telling the truth," she said crisply, her blue eyes boring into me for a moment before she whirled back around and stalked out of the cafeteria.

———

The rest of the day I stewed over Candace's massive declaration. How could she throw away her entire future for a guy? I felt both sick and triumphant, my gut instinct about Dom validated. What kind of twenty-three-year-old was interested in a high school kid anyway?

The realization hit me so hard I nearly choked, my mind anywhere but on the English Lit essay I was supposed to be writing. I was doing the same thing as Candace. I wasn't giving up college entirely, but I'd written off a place I'd been desperate to go to, all on the say-so of one guy. Why had I thought Gang was any better than Dom? Because he was hot? Foreign? Cultured? I could pretend all I wanted that Gang hadn't known I was in high school, but the fact was, he probably didn't care. I had been so awed by him—so flattered he'd even take an interest in me that I was more than willing to do anything he wanted, no pressure necessary.

I couldn't believe I hadn't seen it earlier. *Dom likes it when I wear my hair down. Dom only likes watching horror movies. Dom says it's best for us to work the same shifts.* She'd gotten swept up, trying to be the person he saw her as—something I could certainly relate to. Maybe it was easier to let someone confident dictate our narrative instead of fighting to carve out our own. And that was assuming we even *knew* what kind of person we wanted to be.

The second the bell rang, signaling the end of the day, I sprinted out into the hallway and straight to Candace's locker, where she was packing up to leave.

"I have something to tell you," I panted, out of breath from the exertion of running fifty whole feet. Sometimes it was a wonder Liz and I had ever become friends.

Before she could cut me off, I told her the whole story about Gang. Every grisly detail, including the part about me rifling through his drawers in his room after we'd slept together, hoping to gain a clue about how to further his interest in me. It was humiliating, but it would be worth it if I could just get her to see how similarly we were reacting.

"Don't let what he wants eclipse what you need. He is very dreamy but he is not the sun. You are," I concluded, pulling the quote from the one show I knew could convince her. We'd watched every single episode of *Grey's Anatomy* together, even well past the point at which we should have quit. "He should see that you deserve the future you planned on," I stressed.

Candace didn't respond but closed her locker quietly, swinging her backpack over a shoulder without looking at me. "I'm late for work."

I followed her down the hallway and out the back door into the parking lot. "Is that it?" I demanded. "Everything I said? You have no reaction?"

She pulled a scarf out of her pocket and began winding it around herself, covering her neck and half her face until all that was visible was a tiny diamond stud and a pair of round blue eyes. "I'm sorry you had such a bad experience in Washington." Her muffled voice was stiff—formal, almost. "But you had a choice about your actions and so do I. Just because you regret yours doesn't mean I'm going to. This isn't some one-night stand. Dom and I are building a life together. It's not the same thing."

"What life?" I exploded. "You're eighteen! We haven't even graduated high school yet! Or did you forget that because *Dom* decided to have you skip five years of your life so you'll end up exactly where he is?"

Candace pierced me with a cold stare, her blue eyes barely peeking out over her scarf. "And that is?"

"Somewhere you don't need a college degree."

She regarded me slowly, her words coming out one at a time, like Pringles being carefully dropped back into their tube from a height. "For someone who spends so much time complaining about how her parents want to control her life, you sure are quick to do the same to your friends. Other people are allowed to disagree with you, you know."

"I'm not the one telling you what to do! I'm trying to help. This is what *you* said you wanted!"

"Obviously I don't anymore."

"Is it that obvious?" I pressed. "Because I'm your best friend and it's not obvious to me at all that you're convinced."

Candace fished out a large jumble of keys from her purse, the ridiculously oversized key chain Liz and I had given her for her sixteenth birthday swinging back and forth as she fumbled through the mass for her car key. When at last she'd found it, she pointed it in my direction, as if to prevent me from stepping any closer to her.

"Maybe you're not my best friend if I have to convince you," she snapped, climbing into her car, slamming the door, and peeling out of the parking lot.

CHAPTER TWENTY-EIGHT

The following weeks with Candace were awkward—a mixture of stiff small talk and pure avoidance as Liz flitted between us and her soccer teammates during lunchtime, leaving Candace and me alone together more often than not. I started eating lunch with Rhys and his friends on a semiregular basis just to escape the prospect of yet another meal of quiet chewing and finding neutral topics to discuss that didn't carry any reminder of Dom, my parents, or anything related to college.

Was this how our friendship was going to die? I always knew it was impossible to stay close with all your friends from high school, especially if you split off into separate directions, like, say, one of you moving across the country by yourself to a place where the only people you knew didn't even like you. My heart pinched every time I thought about it.

But I always thought I would have Candace. We were too much alike to ever outgrow each other. She was supposed to be my *person*. Yet it was Rhys, not Candace, who texted me the day of my drive to Northwestern, telling me to have fun and wishing me luck.

I arrived while it was still light outside, the large parking garage easy to find from Wendy's highly detailed directions. She had insisted I call her when I was five minutes out so that she was waiting for me when I arrived. The sight of a familiar face smiling and Wendy's enthusiastic waving, flooded me with relief after an hours-long drive filled with nothing but my tortured thoughts about everything I'd done wrong up until now. I tumbled out of the car and hugged her fiercely, the top of her thick hair tickling the bottom of my nose.

It was clear my hug took her by surprise, a little "Oh!" dislodging from her throat as I squeezed her. She disentangled herself gently, smoothing the outsides of her long jacket as if I'd wrinkled her. "You're a hugger now, that's new."

I shrugged happily. "You'll get used to it."

She shouldered my duffel bag, leaving me to carry my violin case as we headed off across the sprawling campus. "Is this all you brought? How was the drive?"

I shrugged again, tightly wrapping my arms around myself to keep the gusts of wind that kept blowing by from going straight through me. "I'm only coming for two days. And the drive was fine. A little too much country music for my taste, but it wasn't terrible. I'd probably bring a Bluetooth adapter next time."

"I can't believe you really drove," she said, shaking her head. "Flying is so much easier."

"Well, your music director said he didn't have the budget for a flight, so Mom asked him to reimburse her for mileage instead," I said.

"Shut up!" Her eyes looked at me accusingly, as if I would make up a lie this embarrassing.

"I swear. I told Mom he wouldn't want to buy the cow if the milk had to drive itself practically for free."

That earned a snort from Wendy. "Well, Jeff *is* a real cheapskate. I'm surprised Mom was even able to negotiate with him. Did I tell you he put a restriction on the amount of rosin each player can order per year? Like we're desperately hoarding it for some other purpose. I talked to him about your scholarship and even though he swears he can't offer you as much as me, I got him to pull some money from other parts of the budget. It'll cover more of your living expenses instead of tuition because it's easier to manipulate that than having to go through the university bursar. It should be enough to make Mom and Dad satisfied, anyway."

I cocked my head, confused, and my lips pressed into a frown as the wind lashed against my face. "I . . . I didn't realize you were talking to him about my offer. I haven't even auditioned yet." I lifted the case at my side as if to reiterate my point.

Wendy gave a little laugh. "I'm first chair and you're my sister. If I say you can play here, Jeff is going to believe me. No further proof necessary."

"Really? Just like that?" I was both flattered and annoyed. After all the teasing while we were growing up about how much better than me she was, it felt at least a little bit nice to think that Wendy actually believed I was good enough to play at a top school. But if she truly believed in me, why would she keep me from auditioning?

She shrugged. "I promised him we'd both major in music."

She glanced at my wide eyes and before I could respond, she waved away my concern. "It's fine, I'm still keeping my biology major. And I was already doing a minor in music, so it's just a matter of adding some classes. Really," she added with another glance at my doubt-filled face.

"Mom and Dad will love that," I muttered.

My parents, for all the time, effort, and money they had expended toward making us top-tier violinists, didn't actually want us to pursue music in any meaningful sense. It was just something Asian parents did. Their kids played piano or violin or occasionally another stringed instrument. It was why, despite the fact that I had no Asian classmates, my violin competitions were made up mostly of Asian kids. We were like Texans and football, or rich white kids and private school—somehow playing the piano or violin was just ingrained in the culture.

It was probably because learning an instrument required high levels of discipline and focus—skills that could be easily transferred to any other parts of life. Like, say, medical school. And there was no better way for Asian parents to brag than by having a kid who was both a concert-level musician who went to school for free *and* a doctor.

If Wendy heard my comment about our parents, she didn't reply. She stretched her arms out as we walked, impervious to the cold in a thick down jacket while I shivered next to her, the wind blowing my hair into my face every few steps. "Well, this is it," she said. "I might as well start your tour on our way to the dorms."

Wendy looked at me, expecting me to be awed or excited or something, but all I could manage was a grunt and half a nod as I pulled a chunk of hair out from where it had blown into my mouth.

"Oh yeah, the wind," she said. "You get used to it. Just tie your hair up." She pulled an extra hair binder off her wrist and handed it to me. "So, there are two campuses, one here and one twelve miles away in Chicago. There's a shuttle that runs between them. This campus is two hundred forty acres. We have three libraries—"

"Yes, I read the website too, thanks."

She frowned at me. "Rude. If you're such an expert, you can figure out the rest yourself." She flounced ahead, her chin held unnaturally high, as if it made her look taller.

I quickened my pace to catch up. "Don't be such a baby. All I'm saying is I expected to hear what *you* think of the campus and the school. I don't need the official school version."

Wendy frowned, her brows pulled together in a look of concentration. "What *I* think of the school? I don't know. It's fine. It's a good school."

I stared at her expectantly. "That's it?"

"I mean, I could look into the ceramics department for you now that you're into that kind of stuff."

I hip checked her off the path and into the snow-covered grass, where she laughed hysterically before attempting to shove me back, missing, and falling off the path again herself.

"You deserved it," she panted, finally giving up on trying to physically bully me. "I still don't know what you were thinking. How did you manage to get an A in the class? You're a horrible artist."

"Thanks," I said drily. "I cried to my teacher about how it would mess up my GPA for college and she felt bad so she changed it. Said she was giving me the grade for effort."

Wendy laughed harder. "You didn't!"

"I had to! It's not like it matters, I'm never taking another art class in my life."

Wendy shook her head, a smile emerging. "I always knew you were faking it all those times you cried to Mom and Dad about how mean I was to you."

"You *were* mean to me!" I protested. "I have a permanent bruise from where you used to hit me. I swear, it was like you knew how to hit in exactly the same spot every time." I rubbed my upper arm, the memory of Wendy's bony knuckles making contact with it emblazoned in my memory.

She shrugged. "Whatever. I have a scar on my belly button from where you bit me and you don't hear me crying about it."

"I was six!"

"Exactly."

She yanked open the door to her dormitory, took us up the elevator, flung open the door to her room, and dropped my duffel bag in the middle of the floor. "Ta da."

I stepped into the room, which felt less like a dorm room than a floor model of a dorm room. Unlike Amy's room, which had been comfortably overstuffed with glossy photos, throw rugs, and pillows, Wendy's room was tidy to the point of pathological. Her bed was lofted with a small desk underneath, and a mini fridge stacked with a microwave anchored the other side of the small room. In the corner was a slim push vacuum—the kind our dentist used to keep in his office. Even that had felt homier than this room.

"Don't you miss having a roommate?" I asked, spinning around to get a complete view of just how blank and undecorated the single room was.

"No. I had one last year and all she did was make calls to her boyfriend every night for hours. *I miss you. No, I miss you more.* Blech. Not going through that again."

I thought of the way Liz and I rolled our eyes every time Candace got on the phone with Dom as they exchanged similar cutesy longings. Hearing it come out of Wendy's mouth sounded a lot meaner than I expected and a pang of guilt fluttered in my stomach.

"Maybe she misses him," I said simply. "I'm sure it's hard to go away to college and leave your boyfriend behind. But she still did it."

Wendy gave me a dubious look. "If all she was going to do was sit around and moan about missing him, she shouldn't have come. Either break up with him and move on, or move back. It's not that hard. Some of us have more important stuff to worry about."

Wendy's famous decision-making matrix: yes or no, black or white. No room for uncertainty or ambiguity. Even without knowing her former roommate, I felt a rush of sympathy for her.

"I'm sure she's happier now too, not living with someone so judgmental," I said. "Just because you've never dated anyone doesn't mean—"

"She left school. Moved back home to be with him at the end of the year," Wendy said flatly. "Anything else?"

I clamped my mouth shut. There went that theory.

"So. What's the plan for tonight?" I asked brightly, clasping my hands together. "What's for dinner? And where am I sleeping?"

Wendy frowned. "Are you hungry already? You're sleeping on the floor. You didn't bring a sleeping bag or anything, so I'll have to see if someone has one you can borrow."

She was so good at saying things that inspired guilt without having to rely on dramatic tones to get her point across.

"You didn't tell me to bring stuff to sleep on," I said defensively. "I assumed I would just sleep in the bed with you."

"It's fine," she said airily. "I'll take care of it. Keep your jacket on, I'll take you across campus to my favorite café."

"What kind of food does it have?"

Wendy frowned. "I don't know. The edible kind. Didn't you say you were hungry?"

"I'm sorry Miss Rice and Beans, I didn't realize you were so open about food now."

Wendy rolled her eyes. "Whatever. Fine. We'll walk to downtown Evanston. There's a Korean bowl place I really like."

"There you go," I goaded, nudging her with my elbow. "See? That's something that didn't come straight off the website."

"You're so annoying," Wendy sighed.

"Watch out or I'll hug you again," I joked, throwing my arms open.

She rolled her eyes again, but she was smiling as we headed out the door and back across the campus, the bundled people and snow-covered trees so reminiscent of the place I'd just come from.

CHAPTER TWENTY-NINE

The next morning, I pried my eyes open and let out a large, indulgent, jawbreaking yawn. I felt like I'd slept for a week, but was simultaneously tired from having done it on the hard, barely carpeted floor. I knew I shouldn't have stayed up for so long after Wendy turned out the lights, but there was also no way I was going to fall asleep at ten thirty like she did.

Even from my spot on the floor, I could see Wendy's bed tidily made up, so I pulled my phone out from under the pillow and nearly dropped it when I saw the time. It was after noon already, and I had a text message from Wendy telling me to call her when I was finally awake.

By the time she'd arrived back in the room, I'd managed to get dressed and ready, throwing a spare jacket of Wendy's over my hoodie. Once again I'd underpacked for a college visit. Except this time, instead of needing dresses and heels, I was short on thermal layers and proper winter gear. It's not like it wasn't cold in Iowa, but we were smart enough not to *walk* everywhere when it was.

"Where have you been?" I demanded the moment she walked through the door.

She looked up, as if recounting her steps through the morning. "Let see, I got up around seven, had breakfast, went to the library for a bit to work on a paper I have due next week, then I had rehearsal, went to the coffee shop to meet up with some friends, and now I'm back."

She'd done more in one morning that I did in a single day.

"Why did you get up at seven?" was all I could manage to get out.

"I always do. But I know you like to sleep late so I didn't want to wake you."

Again, the feeling of being both appreciative and annoyed tugged me in opposite directions. I *did* hate waking up early, but it was starting to feel like I was in the way.

"But now half the day is gone and we haven't done anything. Don't you think it would have been helpful for me to see what your rehearsals are like?" I asked.

First no audition and now no rehearsal. I hadn't even met anyone else from the orchestra. By this time in Washington, I'd already toured the music building and met half the players. If it wasn't for Wendy's preference for efficiency, I might suspect she was purposely keeping me from the entire department. As it was, she probably thought she was doing me a favor. Like I didn't need to see things with my own two eyes because her word passed as gospel with everyone else.

She shrugged nonchalantly. "It's just a rehearsal. It's not like you don't know how they work. Come on, if you're ready we can go grab you some food." She eyed my outfit with a critical eye before adding, "You're not going to need that jacket."

I pulled it tighter around me. "Yes I will, I was freezing yesterday."

Wendy's eyes danced in amusement. "Okay, suit yourself."

She took me back down the elevator and around a corner, where a large cafeteria opened in front of us. Wendy burst into laughter, her hands flying up to keep her glasses on her nose as she watched me realize we didn't even have to leave the building.

"Very funny. You could've just told me," I shot, refusing to take off the jacket now even though I was starting to sweat underneath it.

"And miss your reaction? No way."

She paid for our meals and we sat down, the space full but not overly crowded. After my last college visit, I couldn't help but take note of the fact that the diversity of this school lagged behind the last one I'd been to, and not just when it came to other Asians. Maybe it was just that basically all of Amy's good friends had been Chinese and that skewed my view of the school, but walking around the campus in Washington had given me an instant feeling of solidarity I had yet to feel here.

Then again, it turned out they didn't really feel solidarity with me. Maybe I was better off in a place where I was still considered enough of a minority that no one would question it. This was still the Midwest, after all. And I knew how to get along with people from the Midwest, whether or not they looked like me. They were certainly too polite to ever tell me to my face that I wasn't Asian enough.

I turned back to Wendy, who was carefully slicing a piece of chicken into perfectly equal-sized bites. "What's the plan for today?" I asked. "Well, the rest of the day, now that you let me sleep through half of it?"

I thought I saw her stiffen, the muscles in her soft jaw flexing ever so slightly. "No plan. Just whatever you feel like doing."

Hmmm. Something was definitely up. Wendy loved plans. She loved them so much she even kept a paper day planner in high school *in addition to* putting reminders into her phone.

"Okay, great," I said with feigned enthusiasm to counteract her sudden awkwardness. "In that case, let's go streaking."

Wendy's eyes flew open, momentarily magnified behind her cat-eye glasses. "Very funny," she muttered, re-collecting herself.

"You said we could do whatever I felt like doing."

"You're being annoying."

The laughs and jokes of ten minutes ago had been sucked out of the room, fun and relaxed Wendy replaced with her more familiar twin—easily irritated and impatient Wendy.

I turned back to my food and we ate the rest of our meal in silence, the air around us punctuated with the sounds of other people talking and generally enjoying themselves. As we wrapped up, clearing our dishes and throwing away our trash, I figured enough time had elapsed for her mood to have settled to ask, "No, seriously though, what *is* the plan for today?"

She exploded, her hands flying up into the air in exasperation. "I already told you! I don't have one. Do I have to come up with everything?"

I took a step back, too well aware of the damage those bony knuckles could cause on impact. "I guess I figured you're the one who goes to school here so it kinda made sense that you would know what to do?"

"So, you figured you could just show up and I'd take care of everything like I always do?" She was leaning in toward me, her eyes murderous.

What the hell was going on?

But Wendy wasn't finished. "That's how you've always been. Everything is a big joke to you. You didn't even plan your trip out here until it was almost too late, and *I* was the one left scrambling to make sure there was even a spot left for you!"

I glanced uncomfortably around at the students passing us with curious glances, but Wendy didn't seem to notice them, her face reddened with anger and eyes laser focused on me.

"We should get out of the hallway," I suggested, reaching over to steer her at least toward the door or a wall—anything to get us out of the middle of a major thoroughfare.

She yanked her arm away from me as if I'd tried to burn her. "I don't care if people hear me," she snapped. "You don't even know any of them. What do you care what they think anyway? You don't care what anyone thinks. You don't care about anyone but yourself. I'm done helping you."

My desire to avoid a public confrontation with Wendy cracked, and a violent anger exploded in me. "I don't care about anyone but myself? Are you kidding me? Are you even listening to yourself?" My voice was loud—louder than Wendy's had been. This would certainly test whether she didn't care about people listening like she claimed. "No one asked you to butt into my business. Do you think I *want* you coordinating my future behind my back? Planning it all out so I don't even have to audition because what, you think I couldn't make it in without your help? You're so convinced you're the martyr here, you can't even acknowledge that you do it to yourself."

Wendy shoved her glasses back up her flat nose so hard they crashed against her forehead and slipped down again. "I do this to myself?" she screeched, a hollow, disbelieving laugh echoing in the hallway. "Why don't you ask Mom and Dad all the things I've had to do for you over the years? Why did we have to quit figure skating? Oh, because *you* complained and couldn't handle the cold, so we *both* had to give it up. 'Wouldn't be fair to June, Wendy'," she said in a close impression of our mom's voice.

"Or what about when you decided you hated violin and refused to play at your lessons so our teacher fired us *both* and *I* got lectured about keeping you in line?" she continued. "Even this whole trip! Do you think I *want* you to come here? So I can be stuck looking after you for another two years? This is *my* school! *I'm* the one who earned the right to be here. They didn't want you. But Mom asked me to talk to Jeff and I did it because I'm *responsible*. But you don't care! You just show up and expect everything to be planned for you like it always has been. You're such a child."

The words stung, bringing to the surface the memory of Gang repeating the same words about me.

She is a child. Nothing serious.

"In case you haven't noticed, you've been gone for the last two years and I've managed my life just fine, no thanks to you," I retorted, my voice quavering dangerously.

"Oh yeah, just great," she spat. "Didn't you almost get pregnant a few months ago?"

My hands tightened themselves into fists, my heartbeat pounding in my ears as my eyes stung with tears. I couldn't believe she was going to throw that back in my face right now. Except that I could. That was exactly who she was and would always be. The fact that I ever thought, even for a moment, that I could trust her not be the person she'd always been was entirely my fault.

"Fuck you, Wendy."

Wendy's eyes flew open at my words and she gaped at me for a full second, as though she couldn't believe I'd actually said that to her. I stared back, refusing to blink, willing my tears to stay welled up in my eyes and not spill over.

Without replying, she turned on her heel and stomped outside, the slamming open then closed of the heavy doors echoing down the hall.

CHAPTER THIRTY

Equipped with nothing but my phone and a heavy jacket, my only choices were to sit and wait for her to come back or to roam the campus. Far too agitated to sit, I opted for the second choice.

The weather was just as cold and windy as it had been the day before, but I was so worked up as I paced the walkways, I barely felt it. How dare she accuse *me* of being selfish? This, coming from the girl who sucked up every bit of time and energy from our parents; the girl who dominated every weekend schedule with her extracurriculars and every conversation with her plans and opinions. The entire Chu family revolved around her, and the fact that she still managed to see herself as the victim in all of this just showed how self-absorbed she was.

I huffed my way around and across the grounds, past massive buildings and stretches of undisturbed snow, swerving around clusters of students and away from anyone who sounded like they were enjoying themselves. I walked and walked, looping around the landscape until I eventually reached the lakefront, which was mostly deserted in its windswept cold. I looked out over the water, its surface frozen solid and dusted with snow, as if promising a clear path to the glittering Chicago skyline in the distance.

This lake was like my entire life in one metaphor—the illusion of a way forward, when in fact the ice would most likely crack and I would drop to an icy death if I stepped foot on it. Not that Wendy would care. She would probably point out the fact that she could have gotten across it just fine and that it was my own fault for not using snowshoes or something.

Why had she even bothered to get me a spot here if she didn't really want me to come? I didn't understand why she would stake her reputation on my potential, especially if my potential was so limited that she wanted to keep me from auditioning.

I thought about her other comments—about my getting us yanked from both skating lessons and our violin teacher, whom I hated anyway. Was it really my fault she had been forced to give those up? I wasn't the adult who made those decisions. If my parents had just been willing to let us each pursue our own interests, none of that might ever have happened.

But what *were* my interests? Outside of, say, gossiping with Candace and Liz, or flirting with boys I liked, I didn't really have any actual hobbies. And now I wasn't even speaking to Candace. I'd channeled so much of my energy into resisting whatever my parents told me to do, I never took the time to figure out what it was I'd rather be doing instead. Wendy had been the one to pick the violin. And figure skating. And student government. And whatever organization that took her down to Nicaragua. Somehow she'd been born knowing exactly what she wanted to achieve and the steps she needed to take to get there, while I'd been tugged along behind, resisting every step of the way. No wonder she saw me as deadweight.

Maybe I really was, as my mom described it, dé guò qiě guò—muddling through life without ambition. I had no idea what I wanted out of life, out of my family, even out of my relationships. The only thing I knew how to do with any degree of certainty was to act like I didn't much care about anything—as if my limited success was due to talent and not from keeping my feet rapidly flailing below the water's surface. Like it was somehow better to have people envy you for natural talent than to let them know you'd worked for such paltry achievements. After all, my parents had forced me into the same practice requirements as Wendy and I still couldn't match her success. What if I had tried harder, but ended up with the same results?

I was terrified of *wanting*—of earnestly pursuing something, only to watch myself fail. It had happened with Rhys, my humiliation after Liz's birthday weekend so deep I'd broken up with him rather than admit I just wanted him to care about me. I'd done it again with Gang, refusing to confront him about his girlfriend, hoping that my casual attitude might prove how worthy I really was. As if it was possible to shame the shameless.

Each time I failed, I'd pretended to be detached from the situation, so that it might hurt me less. Like I could build a wall around my sadness to keep anyone else from consoling me and finding out just how weak I really was. That if I could just show everyone I was fine, I would actually *be* fine. Because who was I if not the person other people thought I was?

A gust of wind blew in from the water and I pulled up the collar of my borrowed jacket, the cold a sharp reminder that regardless of how prepared I might have *looked*, I was freezing inside. I needed to be more than my appearance—more than what I thought I *should* be. The only problem was I had no idea how to properly identify what was real and what was pretend anymore.

Everything seemed to be jumbled together—my feelings about college, music, my family, even the boys in my life. And every decision I'd made up to this point only served to further obscure the path forward. I'd put forth not-quite-maximum dedication to the violin, only to discover I actually liked it and was now stuck with limited options to continue playing in any meaningful capacity. I'd found a school that could potentially be a great fit, but only if I could manage to swallow my pride and face the two people who'd humiliated me. And now I'd cursed out the one person still trying to help me, even at the expense of her own happiness.

I shoved my hands farther into the pockets of my jacket, pacing faster now to warm my blood. Even if I still wasn't sure what I wanted, at least now I knew what I *didn't* want, and that was to let someone else choose for me. I might have been a tad overdramatic when I wrote my Smash the Pots and Sink the Boats essay for the Northwestern application, but choosing a college *was* a big decision—one that would, in fact, affect the rest of my life. And I couldn't let it be made by my parents, Gang, or even Wendy.

I let out a big sigh, thinking once again about what was said between us earlier. We'd both stalked off in anger without any discussion of how we'd find each other once we'd cooled down. But that's the thing about sisters—they'll still be there for you even when they hate you.

Sure enough, as I navigated my way back through the maze of buildings, I spotted her on the horizon, bundled up and leaning against the exterior of her dorm, her eyes scanning the grounds for me.

———

We didn't say much to each other on the way back up to her room, except for her quasi-apologetic explanation that her quartet had a performance that evening and I was welcome to attend. Some kind of networking event, but there would be food. I nodded and got dressed without question, not wanting to ask to borrow clothes for the occasion. The end result was an oddly mismatched pair, her in a black floor-length gown and me in an embellished cropped hoodie and high-waisted jeans. At least I'd picked up some makeup tips from Amy. I slicked on a dark shade of plum lipstick to give me a more put-together vibe and air kissed my reflection. *Every Asian looks good in plum*, she'd said. I guess she'd decided I was Asian enough for that.

On the way to the venue, Wendy briefed me on what to expect and how long the event would run, and she handed me her keys in case I wanted to leave early. "Just make sure to text me if you go somewhere other than the room so I can get my keys back from you when I'm done," she said. I didn't know where she thought I'd go, but I nodded obediently and slipped them into my pocket.

The inside of the building was overly warm with the swarm of bodies, and within a few steps of entering, I'd already taken off my jacket and slung it over the crook of my elbow. Careful not to bump anyone with it, I wove with Wendy through packs of people and standing tables draped with purple tablecloths. After making a quick introduction to the other members of her quartet, Wendy was off and I was on my own.

I decided to stake out a spot in the back, close to the doors where the hors d'oeuvres came out so I had first dibs on them. Eating had the added benefit of giving my idle hands something to do, making it less obvious that I wasn't really here to network. As if that wasn't already clear from my jeans and hoodie combo, compared to everyone else's bleary uniform of business-casual khakis or slacks and ill-fitting button-downs. Somehow in the hundred years women had been allowed to work in offices, no one had yet figured out how to properly account for boobs.

The room was slowly becoming uncomfortably hot, and I unzipped my hoodie and grabbed a cup of semiwarm, flat pop from a passing waiter. A quick stop outside in the cold would probably feel amazing, but I didn't want to risk having Wendy see me leave. We'd returned to a stiff sort of truce, like we always did, where one misstep could upset the whole thing. I wasn't going to be responsible for that.

"So, I've been reading Sun Tzu's *The Art of War.*"

I turned to find a white guy leaning against my table, his hand wrapped around a cup of Sprite as if it were a whiskey tumbler.

"That's nice for you," I replied, my tone implying that it was anything but.

"It's really an intriguing text," he continued, undeterred by my uninterest. "It's considered essential reading for even business majors these days. Have you read it?"

Ugh. He was one of *those* people.

For some bizarre reason there was an entire cadre of people who made it a point to mention their interest in random Asian things as a way into a conversation: martial arts, pad Thai, anime, Mortal Kombat. Wendy and I were once asked by our dental hygienist if we'd kept our grandparents' illnesses a secret from them, like in *The Farewell*.

I shifted a step to the right, pretending I hadn't heard his question, which put Wendy into my sightline. She had a fierce, concentrated look that created deep grooves between her eyebrows, like she was trying to intimidate the pages of sheet music into turning themselves. But that was the same face she made whenever she was really into whatever she was doing, even if it was something as simple as watching a movie. I relaxed when I was enjoying something—Wendy got more intense. It was like I already knew on some subconscious level, always cracking jokes to try to get her to lighten up. And she'd always taken it as a sign that I couldn't be serious.

I looked at her again, and she seemed to come into focus for the first time. Sure, I resented how much pressure my parents put on me to emulate Wendy, but so much of the reason I'd been able to avoid actually living up to their expectations had to do with the fact that she'd already been successful enough for the both of us. Even though Wendy got offers from ten different schools, my parents immediately pegged Northwestern as the top choice.

Whether Wendy had actually chosen it for herself or whether she'd done it to please them, it was impossible to tell. Maybe she herself didn't even know.

I thought about how I'd called our mom from Washington, desperate for her stamp of approval on the school campus, and how disappointed I'd been when it didn't come. And despite my embarrassment over her nosiness about Gang, I'd been secretly pleased she was so invested. I couldn't help but wonder if that had been part of my fascination with him. Maybe my desire to win my parents' approval ran so deep it was subconsciously affecting all my decisions—even the ones about who I liked.

Yet another issue I'd need to sort out in my quest for self-actualization.

Meanwhile, my lack of a response to Asian-Fetish Guy hadn't deterred him in the least, and he was expounding on his thoughts with the gusto and length of a Wagner opera. At least I no longer needed to pretend to be polite. If I was going to start drawing a hard line between what I wanted and what I thought others expected of me, this was a great place to start.

"Have you read it in its original language, though?" I asked, cutting him off from a particularly long passage about how to evaluate the intentions of others while moving through hostile territory. "Because so much of the meaning gets lost in translation, don't you think?"

While he scrambled for a response, I casually stepped away, grabbing a mini quiche and popping it into my mouth to keep from laughing aloud. But his message had struck me anyway, because I realized that's how I'd been treating this entire trip—as if Wendy were my enemy and this was her turf. I'd bought into the competitive narrative our parents had set for us, only seeing my life through the lens that I was copying Wendy or not copying Wendy. I hadn't even bothered to question whether the two of us naturally wanted some of the same things.

I had less than twenty-four hours left here. If I was serious about starting fresh, about trying to assess things for myself on my own terms, I needed to start now. I needed to have started the minute I got here.

I glanced around the room at people's faces painted with smiles that were a little too big and head nods that were a little too vigorous. It wasn't the ideal place from which to judge, but at least I could count on everyone here to give me *some* kind of answer to my questions. Namely, what this school had to offer besides its name. Because as tempting as it was to revel in the fact that I'd been accepted into a university that made it onto most people's dream school lists, I'd never much cared about the status of it all. I just wanted a place where I could be myself.

Stuffing a final canapé into my mouth, I wiped my hands on a purple cocktail napkin and launched myself into the crowd of people, determined to give the task as genuine an effort as I could muster. I couldn't magically become earnest on command, but I vowed to make my newfound enthusiasm last at least until the end of the event.

CHAPTER THIRTY-ONE

I waited until the next morning before attempting any kind of real communication with Wendy. After the event wrapped up the previous night, she seemed exhausted, and I used her tiredness as excuse to chicken out. The two of us had never been great at the kind of conversation we desperately needed to have, but I didn't want to go home with old resentments still hanging between us. I'd spent the past couple of weeks having nothing but awkward interactions with my best friend because neither of us wanted to acknowledge the fact that we might have said shitty things to each other we couldn't take back—I didn't want to be responsible for doing the same thing to my sister. So, after I had a brief meeting with Jeff, the music director, Wendy walked me back to my car to drive home and I blurted out, "Thanks for your help in getting this trip arranged. I had a great time."

"Great time" might have been a bit of a stretch, especially considering our fight, the aftermath of which nearly gave me frostbite, but I had liked the school a lot more than I expected to. And Northwestern was large enough that I could conceivably limit our crossed paths to orchestra-related activities if I got here and realized Wendy or I still needed more space.

Wendy looked slightly taken aback by my sudden outburst of gratitude, but I could tell she was mostly pleased. "It wasn't a big deal," she said easily. "I like planning things."

"I know, but you didn't have to. And you didn't have to carry my bag either. But I appreciate it." I had to force the words out, compliments between us rarely given without at least a hint of sarcasm. But I was still proud of myself for saying them.

Wendy fidgeted with the strap of my bag slung over her shoulder, twisting it several times before giving up and switching it to her other shoulder instead. "It was nice having you here," she said. "And this really is a great school."

"I did get, like, four offers to meet someone's *good friend* who played for the Chicago Philharmonic or was in a Broadway musical."

My small joke lightened the atmosphere a little.

Wendy rolled her eyes. "I know. The people at those networking things can be super annoying about the name-dropping, but making connections is supposed to be one of the benefits of going here. You should have told them you're looking at getting into med school—then at least they might actually do something useful for you. I've been trying to find the right people to write letters of recommendation for my application."

Wendy already had more plans in motion for her future two years out than I did for the coming fall. I swallowed the small, familiar bubble of resentment that had worked its way to the surface.

"Good for you," I said, hoping my words sounded genuine and not sarcastic. "I don't think medicine is for me. I don't really know what is—I just need to find something before I break the news to Mom and Dad."

I could tell Wendy was wrestling with this new information, probably thinking about how yet again I was doing what *I* wanted and not what was expected of me. But instead of looking annoyed about it, she gave me a little shrug, pushing her glasses up her nose. "Well, it's not like you have to declare a major your freshman year. Just don't say anything about it while you get your generals out of the way. I'm sure you'll figure it out."

I bit back a smile so Wendy wouldn't think I was laughing at her. I knew this was her way of apologizing to me. And whether or not she actually believed in me, just saying she did was the nicest possible compliment she could have paid me.

It was funny—I had been so furious with Gang for essentially lying to me about not having a girlfriend while desperately wishing my own family would take the trouble to lie to me at least some of the time, like Wendy had just done. Yet somehow, I chose to escape from my family's brutal truth-telling by having two best friends who did nothing *but* tell me their unfiltered truth at all times.

But as my fight with Candace had demonstrated, sometimes people just wanted you to be on their side. And that's what Wendy was choosing to do for me now.

I flung my arms around her again and this time she tried to reciprocate, her arms half pinned to her side as she wrapped her hands around my sides and patted them.

"Thanks," I told her.

She took my violin case from me and set it next to my duffel in the trunk, the way a mom would carefully pack her child's things before a road trip. Even though she had complained about it, I knew a part of her would always relish being the one to take care of me. There were just some things older siblings weren't willing to relinquish.

"Text me when you get home so I know you made it," she called out, just before I drove away.

———

The drive home seemed to fly by much faster than my drive there—and before I knew it, I had crossed the state line back into Iowa. I'd spent my time assessing the criticisms Wendy had leveled at me about how I only ever thought of myself. Candace had said something similar during our fight. Was it possible that my entire life was one giant Reddit AITA post in which I was, in fact, the asshole?

I'd done to Candace exactly what my parents had done to me—pushed a single narrative about what someone's future should look like. Candace was right: not everyone needed to go to college. And without the benefit of scholarships, or parents who'd trained you your entire life to earn them, college *was* prohibitively expensive, especially for most Pine Grove kids. Even if I wanted something more for Candace, it wasn't my job to get her there. I needed to stop telling myself I was pushing her for her own good and start reminding myself that all the good intentions in the world didn't make up for the fact that I'd hurt her by insulting her boyfriend. Even if I still thought he deserved it. Best friends were supposed to be supportive. And she'd always been supportive of me. Not to mention, it wasn't like I had a track record of stellar decision-making.

I checked the time. She should still be at work.

With a quick detour off the highway, I was soon pulling into the car-wash parking lot. The door to the retail space jingled as I opened it, and I gave a little sigh of relief to see Candace standing behind the counter, outfitted in her much-detested company-issued orange polo shirt.

"Hey," she said, with a confused frown. "What are you doing here? You don't get your car washed."

It was true. My parents would never spring for something as wasteful as a car wash, especially when hose water cost only pennies, as my mom once explained to me.

"It has recently come to my attention that I don't have any hobbies outside of violin," I announced to Candace after taking a quick glance around the store to make sure I wasn't interrupting any actual business. Luckily, the store was empty. "And that's less of a hobby and more of required activity. At least most of the time." I was getting off track.

"I went to visit Wendy this past weekend," I continued, making my way through the aisles of candy and other impulse items the business was hoping to entice people into buying while waiting for their cars to be washed. "And it turns out she has more of a life than I do. I mean, not necessarily a life I want, but there are things she actually enjoys doing. So I figured I could take up something like, I dunno, stamp collecting. Or becoming some kind of influencer. My dancing-in-place skills are pretty on point." I gave a few bouncing shoulder shakes to demonstrate. Her face remained uncharacteristically stoic. "I thought you could join me?" I added.

She arched an eyebrow. "Stamp collecting?"

I shrugged. "I considered taking up Scientology—you know, for Tom—but I don't think they'd let me in because I don't fully understand what a thetan is. Plus, I watched that documentary about how they make their bad members scrub the floor with toothbrushes, and we both know that would end up being me."

It was obvious that Candace was suppressing a giggle—I could tell by the fierce way she was chewing on her bottom lip, her arms firmly folded across her chest—but she didn't crack.

I heaved a sigh and threw up my hands. "Okay, look, I'm not good at apologizing, okay? I know this about myself. Can this be over between us now?"

Candace wrinkled her nose, her head cocked to one side. "It's not my fault no one ever taught you how, but you owe me a decent apology. Not whatever the hell that was."

"Are you seriously going to make me do this?"

"Yes."

"You know I feel bad! Why do I have to go on and on about it?"

"Consider it practice. With that mouth, I'm sure you'll have plenty more people to apologize to in the future." She snapped her fingers. "Chop-chop. Let's go."

"Okay but after I do this, *then* can we find a hobby? Because I really think if I had one I might have been able to avoid this quarter-life crisis in which my only outlet is also the thing that causes basically all my stress."

"A quarter-life crisis happens when you're twenty-five."

"What do you call it at eighteen then?" I asked. "A one-fifth life crisis? What's eighteen times five?"

"You're stalling."

"Okay, okay. Just give me a sec."

I'd never had Candace call me out on my bullshit this hard before. I didn't like it, even if I deserved it.

I cleared my throat before throwing one arm out in front of me and clutching the other to my chest like a Shakespearean actor, my head tipped back in dramatic fashion. "Dearest Candace, my rose, my sweet, my pint-sized soul mate. I have acted in the most egregious manner and can only beg your forgiveness. Please, o resplendent one, for I cannot live without your companionship. You complete me."

I bowed my head, twirling my hand to signal the end of my speech.

Silence.

I looked up. Candace was still staring at me with an unimpressed expression, arms folded over her chest.

I blew out a puff of air. "I'm sorry. I really am. I was being judgy and awful and a complete Owen Hunt about your choices. I need you. You're my person. And I should have been yours. It won't happen again."

It wasn't an apology that would work on everyone, but like I'd said, Candace was my person. And if there was one thing that bonded us together, it was our mutual love and hatred for

Grey's Anatomy. Besides, it seemed poetic to apologize using the same show I'd used to instigate the argument. I just hoped she appreciated my attempt at sincerity. I really was trying.

Her face relaxed. "God, Owen really is the worst," she agreed. "Now. What the hell is *resplendent*?"

I gave her a grin. "Pretty good, huh? It was the dictionary word of the day on Friday. I was bored after Wendy went to sleep and started looking stuff up."

Candace shook her head. "Good lord, Juje, you *do* need a hobby."

"Does that mean you're in? Even if I pick something really random, like bird-watching or something? You know there's a contest every year to see who can spot the most birds."

"Shut up. Just shut up." She pretended to wipe away a tear, now in full *Jerry Maguire* character. "You had me at 'hello.'"

CHAPTER THIRTY-TWO

I spent the subsequent weeks buried beneath an avalanche of AP tests and polite rejections from the last of my spreadsheet schools. Without any more scholarship offers from their music directors, I hadn't bothered to apply. Even though I still thought my parents' full-ride requirements were ridiculous—we weren't football players, after all—I wasn't willing to risk getting cut out of the family and saddled with a bunch of loans just so I could move to Maryland or wherever. Besides, I was actually enjoying playing music again. I wasn't even upset when I ended up with yet another third-place finish in my last-ever junior circuit tournament. The fact that I had two solid college choices had me feeling optimistic about the future. Even if I still hadn't decided which one I'd go to.

I'd tried creating another spreadsheet—this one with the pros and cons of each of the two schools—but it was impossible to accurately weigh what essentially boiled down to a feeling. Of course Northwestern was a "better" school, according to the rankings, but I'd never cared much about that. How was I supposed to evaluate the schools' various programs if I had no idea what my major was going to be? Would I want the scrutiny that came with small class sizes, or would I prefer to blend into a crowd of hundreds in a lecture hall? And how much did it really matter whether or not I was surrounded by people who looked like me?

Eventually I gave up trying to logic my way into a decision and prayed for a miracle, promising my increasingly impatient parents that I'd have it sorted out by the time prom rolled around. But even that snuck up on me with the speed of an Asian auntie grabbing the check at dinner, and before I knew it, I was dressed up and posing for photos at Candace's house.

I'd never thought of myself as a school-dance type of person, but, surprise of all surprises, Liz desperately wanted to go to prom. Something about final high school memories and the thrill of dress shopping. The three of us decided to go with each other to save Liz and me the trouble of having to find dates, which suited me just fine. We were all continuing to pretend the whole "Dom told Candace she didn't need college" thing never happened and that she had truly made the decision by and for herself, but she still made the call that prom would be more fun if it were just the three of us.

I'd convinced my parents to let me sleep over at Liz's afterward, which meant that I'd stay in the room Liz's "cool dad" had booked us at the hotel where the dance was being held. So after a short stop to drop off our overnight bags, we were back downstairs, outside Ballroom C, being greeted by a *Mahalo Pine Grove Senior Class* sign next to a table full of cheap plastic leis.

"Yikes," I muttered.

"I think they're kind of cute," Liz said, running a finger over the flowered leis. "Look, this blue one matches my dress."

"I just thought when the flyers said 'tropical-themed' they meant like, plastic flamingos and palm trees. Not . . . this." I wrinkled my nose in distaste.

"Isn't Hawaiian tropical?" Candace asked.

"Yeah, but it's also like, a specific culture," I said. "It's like having a Mexican-themed prom and giving everyone a sombrero when they walk in or something."

The whole thing reminded me of when Savannah got a tattoo of her name in kanji on her eighteenth birthday. I couldn't quite put my finger on why it bugged me at the time, but the past year had helped me realize how many times I'd let things pass without comment. Like I had just accepted these microaggressions as a part of life instead of something that deserved to be called out. And this deserved to be called out.

Liz's mouth pulled into a thoughtful frown. "I hadn't really thought of it like that."

Candace, on the other hand, had already snagged three leis. "They give these out to tourists when they arrive in Hawaii, so it seems like it should be fine. It's not like we showed up in hula skirts and coconut bras. Which I would look amazing in, for the record."

"I don't want one," I told her. "You can wear mine if you want it."

She shrugged and threw the second lei over herself while Liz still seemed to be absorbing the idea that she had almost been guilty of cultural appropriation.

"Candace, don't wear that," Liz scolded her. "Didn't you hear what June said? It's offensive!"

"Yeah, and didn't you hear when she said it was fine if I wear hers? If you don't like it, don't wear it," Candace replied, piling the third lei around her neck. "We should totally get some of these for graduation. Those plain gowns are so boring."

Liz looked to me for support. "June, can you make her take those off? She'll listen to you."

"Let's just go inside, okay?" I said brightly, hoping to get out of answering Liz. "We're already here."

On one hand, Candace's "sure this is bad but it's not as bad as this other, worse thing" justifications were annoying, but so was Liz's insistence that I morph into some kind of racism teacher every time something offensive came up. It wasn't like I was an expert on Hawaiian culture, and besides, they were both more than capable of googling the topic. Right now I just wanted to get to the dance.

Before they could continue arguing, I pushed open the doors to Ballroom C and was welcomed by an explosion of paper palm trees, inflatable pineapples, and oversized fake flowers. Clusters of chairs for sitting on one side of the room had been fitted with grass skirts, and the DJ table had been decorated to look like a tiki hut. If not for the hip-hop blaring out of the giant speakers stationed on either side of the makeshift stage up front, it would have been a convincing, albeit stereotyped, island fantasy.

Candace let out a whoop and immediately pulled us into the line for the photo booth, hurriedly sorting through the available props on a table overflowing with large sunglasses, glittery crowns, and mustaches on sticks to decide who would wear what in our pictures. Eventually she settled on four for each of us, with instructions on how to quickly shift disguises between each shot. She was nothing if not dedicated to getting the best possible pictures.

When we'd finished, the photographer printed out a strip of our photos that Candace promptly folded up and tucked into her bra to be divvied up later.

"What? It's not like I was going to carry a purse all night," she said to Liz, whose expression was horrified.

"You could've brought them upstairs to our room!"

Candace shrugged, yanking up her strapless silver gown and sending a dusting of decorative glitter to the floor. "Now we have more time to dance. Let's go!"

Without waiting for either of us, she plunged herself into the middle of the dance floor, with Liz leading me on our way to catch up since she was tall enough to see over most people. The dance area was packed with bodies, people flailing and half screaming the censored lyrics every time the music bleeped them out—people I'd never once heard utter a swear word in four years now screaming the f-word from the safety of the crowd. It was like being in a very dressy, less-violent-than-expected mosh pit.

Before long we were sweaty, thirsty, and covered in glitter from every time Candace shook her head and it came flying out of her hair. Liz pointed to her throat and croaked out, "Water!" So we made our way out to a table stacked with paper cups and jugs of ice water. As I guzzled down my fourth or so cup, I spotted Grayson, Rhys, Tommy, and Drew making their way into the dance.

"About time you showed up," Candace yelled, waving her arm frantically to catch their attention and bring them our way.

Grayson pulled his wraparound sunglasses off his head and searched for a place to put them, pulling out various items from different pockets—a flask, his vape pen, and a wallet—before settling on wrapping them around the back of his head. Why he was wearing sunglasses this late in the evening in the first place was another question, but his bloodshot eyes likely provided the answer.

"You guys miss us or something?" Rhys said, his eyes catching mine before he broke out into a loopy grin.

"I'm surprised they even let you in, you're so late," Liz commented, giving each of the guys an appraising look. She took a step closer to Grayson, sniffed the air, and wrinkled her nose. "I thought they said they'd be screening people at the door."

Tommy gave a cocky smile, each of the dimples in his cheeks deeper than the whole of his personality. "You're looking at the guy who took the school's hockey team to State for the first time in a decade. You think they're not gonna overlook a little weed?"

"Wow, I had no idea the next Wayne Gretzky was here," I said sarcastically. "I'm surprised no one's asked you for your autograph yet."

Tommy scoffed. "Calm down, Covey. You bang one hockey player and all of a sudden you're throwing out names like you're some kind of expert."

I wanted to blurt out a snappy retort, except Brad *was* the only reason I knew of Wayne Gretzky. I couldn't help but sneak a glance at Rhys, who thankfully seemed just glassy enough not to be fully paying attention to the conversation at hand. For once I was grateful for his inattentiveness. It was silly to still feel weird about the mention of Brad in front of Rhys, but I didn't like calling more attention than necessary to the reminder that I had sort of dumped one for the other.

Luckily, Liz and her love of Taylor Swift songs caught everyone's attention as she shrieked loudly at the change of music. "Come on! We have to go dance!"

Drew looked like he'd rather do literally anything than dance, and Tommy was already gearing up to say something about the music that was probably unflattering, but Grayson responded with an enthusiastic "Hell yes!" and he and Rhys happily followed her back into the fray. For a moment the rest of us looked at one another—we were the oddest possible foursome of the entire group.

Before Candace could claim him, I grabbed Drew's hand and dragged him onto the dance floor, Candace reluctantly following without touching Tommy. Even though we'd all purposely come without dates, the music was just a little too slow to dance to alone.

"I feel like I'm in middle school," Drew chuckled, the two of us a full arm's length apart as we danced, arms resting on each other's shoulders.

"I never went to a middle school dance," I confessed.

"Really?"

"The only dance I ever went to was freshman year homecoming, and that was because Wendy made me because she helped plan it."

Drew nodded with appreciation. "I went to Sadie Hawkins last year but only because I didn't have to ask anyone. I asked a girl to winter formal once and she asked me if I could get Tommy to ask her instead."

I winced. "Oof. That hurts."

He grimaced. "Tell me about it. But I'm glad I came tonight. I know we've never really hung out without Rhys there, but I'm glad we're cool. I feel like we're still friends, even if we're not that close."

I stepped closer, enveloping him in a hug. "Thanks. That means a lot."

The song ended and I turned back toward the group, who'd formed something of a circle. I felt a gentle elbow in my ribs and saw Rhys grinning at me, his eyes lidded and sleepy. "You and Drew having a moment there?" His voice was low and just a little slurred.

"Maybe. You jealous?" I said it as a joke, but to my surprise, Rhys responded, "Maybe."

My stomach lurched a little like I'd missed the bottom step on a flight of stairs.

Racing through my mind was a litany of questions. *Are we flirting? Why is he flirting? Should we be flirting?*

But before I could form a sensible answer to any of them, I recklessly plunged ahead.

I reached into the inside of his coat pocket, fishing out a flask I'd seen him drink from earlier. After a quick scan for chaperones, I took a quick swig, the smoky liquor forcing out a fit of coughing.

Rhys grabbed my wrist, yanking me into him while extracting the flask with his other hand. "You see, that's what you get for stealing people's stuff," he growled before taking a swig of what tasted like liquid burnt firewood, his hand still gripped firmly around my wrist.

My heartbeat had picked up its pace considerably, maybe from the shot of alcohol, or maybe because I was now standing close enough to Rhys to smell his familiar woodsy scent, this time with just a hint of the spiced liqueur.

We stared at each other—for a second, or it could have been ten minutes, I couldn't tell—before Tommy's brash voice interrupted us. "Jesus, you two, not again. I thought you guys moved on."

My cheeks erupted into flames as I broke away from Rhys, pretending to busily fix my hair as I hoped everyone would look away from me.

"Speaking of moving on," Candace loudly announced, as if she could effect a conversation reset if she just talked loudly enough. "Has everyone decided where they're going next year?"

Liz looked around in confusion. "We're going to talk about this right now? Here?"

"I just really want to know what everyone's long-term plan is," she replied, her words purposefully aimed toward me and accompanied by a glare.

I knew what she was doing. Candace had conspicuously avoided talking about the future for the past two months, and suddenly she was bringing it up in the middle of a dance floor? It was obviously a glaring reminder I was running out of time to make a decision about where I was going to school, and that I shouldn't be spending my mental energy on Rhys. I got the message, loud and clear.

But it didn't mean I had to like it.

"Why don't you start?" I said to her with the sweetest smile I could muster.

"I'm going to Kirkwood," she replied, citing the community college near Pine Grove.

I felt the fake smile slide off my face, replaced with astonishment. "What? When did you decide that?"

She shrugged as if it was no big deal. "Decided I needed to think about what was best for my future. Like we all do," she added pointedly.

I was so proud of her I could burst. I didn't even care that she was being less than subtle at the moment.

Unaware of the unspoken conversation going on between the two of us, Drew chimed in next. "Gray, Rhys, and me are all going to UNI, but I think Rhys is going to commute." He turned to Rhys. "Right?"

Rhys nodded, and before I could ask any follow-up questions, Liz exclaimed, "I'm going to UNI too!"

Tommy scoffed. "I'm getting the hell out of here. Already signed my letter with UND to play there next year."

"What about Iowa?" Drew asked. "Didn't they make you an offer too?"

"Eh. Screw Iowa," Tommy replied. "Besides, they're DII."

So Tommy was going to be the only other one of the group to leave, and on scholarship, no less. Who would've guessed?

He waved off all our offers of congratulations with the proclamation that he wasn't nearly drunk or stoned enough. "Rhys is being a little bitch about sharing his whiskey, so gimme your vape pen, Grayson."

Ugh. Whiskey. No wonder my throat was still on fire from the one sip I had.

Grayson drew an arm protectively across his jacket. "I'm not giving you shit, Blondie. You can go back to the room and get your own. You're always talking about how you're in shape, go run your ass up there if you're so athletic."

"Rhys'll do it," Tommy said, nodding his head in the direction of Rhys, who was starting to sway ever so slightly, his eyes fixed somewhere off in the distance. "He still owes me for saving his ass. *Even if he doesn't listen to me*," he added, each word punctuated with something like a glare between Rhys and me.

What the hell did that mean?

"Aw, if you send him, he'll just end up falling asleep. It's what he always does," Drew complained.

"Look, whoever is going, can you at least bring some back for us too?" Candace asked distractedly, her eyes buried in her phone. She was probably texting Dom.

Liz looked aghast. "Since when do you smoke?"

Candace shrugged. "Not that often, but I'm not opposed to it. It works faster than trying to get drunk."

"I'm not doing it," Liz declared, as if we'd all tried to peer pressure her into it.

"What am I supposed to be getting?" Rhys asked dazedly, unaware that he was at least two minutes behind the conversation.

Grayson shook his head. "Take June with you, man. She'll know what to bring."

Candace's head shot up from her phone and she fired off a sharp look toward Grayson. "No, June shouldn't go with him. We need her to stay here, don't we, Liz?" she said with an elbow to Liz's side.

"Ow!" Liz exclaimed, rubbing the spot where she'd just been jabbed.

"It'll be fine," Grayson reassured her. "It's just an elevator ride."

"Don't worry, Covey here will probably get bored and leave him before they even reach the room," Tommy chimed in.

"Do you have a problem with me?" I demanded. "I mean, outside of the fact that I'm Asian and you're racist?" I'd been holding in the accusation for months, and it felt good to finally say it aloud.

Tommy scoffed. "What, the Covey thing? That has nothing to do with you being Asian. Didn't you watch the movie?"

"I don't know what's going on but whatever it is, can you all just hurry up so we can get back to dancing?" Liz asked. "June, if you're going to go, just go."

That was as close to getting permission as I needed. I grabbed Rhys's hand and dragged him out of the room, calling, "We'll be back in five!"

Tommy yelled after us, "We'll know what you're doing if you're not!"

CHAPTER THIRTY-THREE

Rhys was silent on the ride up the elevator, the only sound between us the quiet ticking of the floor numbers as we climbed steadily higher. Rhys was leaning against the silver wall, his head tipped back and eyes closed, long dark lashes in contrast to his pale skin. With his tux jacket pulled open and white collared shirt unbuttoned and slightly crumpled, his long arms and legs crossed, he took on the appearance of those overly thin high-fashion editorial models, his gaunt features highlighted in the fluorescent lighting.

I stared at him, my mind turning over Tommy's words downstairs. He'd implied that I was somehow a mistake he'd saved Rhys from. When? Back in November, when he'd seen me with Brad? Or was there something more recent?

I'd always assumed he'd called me Covey because of my looks. But if he was telling the truth, that meant I mirrored the character in some other way. Naïve? Maybe. Overdramatic? More likely. But neither of those things seemed so terrible that someone would need saving from them.

The elevator dinged and the doors parted. Rhys took an extra moment before opening his eyes and stumbling out of the car. "Where are we going?" he asked. "Oh yeah, room. Sleep."

"Not sleep, refreshments," I corrected him, steering him away from the wall he was running his hand along for stability. We arrived at his door and I held out my hand. "Key."

"I can do it, I can do it," he insisted, taking out the key card and attempting to jam it into the slot several times without success. "Okay, I can't do it," he admitted, handing it over with a wavering hand.

"Nice of you to finally admit I'm better than you," I teased, opening the door on the first try.

I pushed my way into the room, where a small lamp on the desk partially illuminated the space. Crumpled beer cans were scattered across both the desk and the dresser top. At least now I knew how he'd gotten so drunk. Why he was the only one in that state, however, was another matter.

I flipped on the overhead light, then rifled through Tommy's hockey duffel, looking for his pen. I found it without too much trouble, then turned my attention to how best to smuggle more alcohol back into the dance. "Do you guys have anything other than whiskey left?" I asked, turning around to find Rhys lying on the bed, his shoes and jacket having been flung off in opposite directions. "Hey!"

Rhys opened one eye sleepily. "I'm just lying down for a minute. I'll get back up, I swear. Just turn off the light first, it's so bright." He flung his arm over his eyes, shielding them.

"Come on, time to get up," I said, walking over and tugging on an arm to try and rouse him off the bed. "We need to get back or everyone's going wonder what's taking so long."

And by *wonder* I meant *assume*. Tommy had even said so.

Rhys groaned. "I don't care what they think. Let's just lie here for a minute."

I continued tugging on his arm, to no avail. "I'm going to leave you," I warned him. "Then Grayson will come up here and toss you over his shoulder and carry you back like the skinny little twerp you are."

With a sudden display of strength, Rhys pulled me onto the bed. I let out a little yelp as I crashed into his body, rolling across him and into the adjacent empty space.

"Then I'll just have to keep you here with me while I can," he said.

My heart fluttered again just as it had when we were standing next to each other downstairs, my brain going fuzzy from the smell of pine and marigolds. For a moment I was back in the space where time stood still, only this time I was staring into his eyes instead of up at a ceiling.

"We do have to leave eventually," I pointed out. "Don't we?"

He smiled at me—a loopy, sleepy smile, his eyelids fighting to stay open. "I want you to hear something. One song. Then we can go."

My curiosity outweighed my angst about how long we'd already been up here, and I flopped back onto the pillow as he clicked around on his phone, looking for whatever he was planning to play.

Finally, finally, the opening notes came. They were slow and melancholy—completely different from what he normally listened to. He didn't say anything, letting the whining drone of singing about sadness and distance fill the space between us as his chest heaved up and down with noisy breaths.

Listening to music had always been Rhys's thing, but usually he told me why he wanted me to hear a song. I still didn't understand why he was playing me this one.

The song petered out, silence stretching several long seconds while we each waited for the other person to speak. Any hint of flirting or banter from earlier was gone, an expanse of nostalgia unfolding in my stomach instead. But it didn't make sense to be nostalgic about a song I'd never heard before.

"Play it again," I said softly, not quite ready to let the moment end.

I didn't know what I wanted from it, or him, or even myself, but music had a way of burrowing itself under your skin, and something about this song made me want to do nothing more than lie here and listen to it again.

He hit Play and the song began again, its lyrics about raincoats and phone calls and plane rides and sunburns as if it were about the Pacific Northwest, and suddenly I knew. I'd known it from the moment I'd set foot there—I'd just let myself get distracted. After a lifetime of being told I wasn't enough on my own, I'd begun to believe everyone who had told me the same thing. But regardless of Gang or Amy or even my family, the one time I'd felt unequivocally *enough* was playing in that tiny practice room for an audience of two. And I'd had no one there to help me.

Maybe I'd be able to replicate that feeling or maybe I wouldn't, but I knew I'd never get there by staying in the same life I'd always had.

"I'm going to Washington," I said.

I said it so quietly, I didn't know if he'd even heard me.

But after a long pause, he murmured, "One thousand, seven hundred twenty-four."

"What?"

"One thousand, seven hundred twenty-four miles," he repeated, his voice thick and fuzzy. "I know the song says three thousand, five hundred miles, but it's wrong. You're going to be one thousand, seven hundred twenty-four miles away."

I fell into a stunned silence, wondering how and why he knew exactly how many miles away my school would be when I hadn't even decided I was going there until two minutes ago. He knew. Somehow, he knew. He knew before I did that I would leave.

I was never going to Northwestern; never going to be within driving distance. I'd be halfway across the country, one thousand, seven hundred twenty-four miles away.

A sadness wound its way through my insides, settling heavily on my chest like I was trapped beneath a thousand weighted blankets. I should have been happy. After months of angst and worry about making this decision, it was done. But lying here, the full impact of what it meant to leave home finally hit me. I was leaving him. My friends. My family. Everyone that made my home *home*. I would be far away, out of reach, and starting over. No connections, no friends—only phone calls and raincoats.

One thousand, seven hundred twenty-four miles away.

Maybe I wasn't Lara Jean Covey after all. Maybe I was Margot.

And I was leaving behind the one person I'd allowed myself to cry in front of. The one person I'd turned to when I was unable to make a decision, who didn't pressure me and just gave me space to breathe. The one person who held my hand, who never let go first, and who could one day fix up a house for us to live in. The one person it was never over with.

Seven months of trying to sort out my feelings for him, and I could just now figure out the words that had been dancing around in my head all along. Right after I'd decided to leave. But I said them anyway.

"I love you," I whispered.

I waited for a moment to see if Rhys would react, but all I could hear was steady breathing next to me. Without waiting for the song to end, I quietly rolled off the bed and grabbed Tommy's vape pen before slipping out the door.

CHAPTER THIRTY-FOUR

The rest of the night passed quickly, especially once Candace got stoned enough to turn sleepy. Liz was annoyed about it, but I was partly relieved to have an excuse to take Candace back to the room and fall asleep while Liz stayed up with some of her volleyball friends. The way I woke up, however, was less than ideal.

The air-conditioning had dropped the temperature of our room to somewhere near the level of a meat freezer, my throat felt like I'd swallowed sand, Candace's elbow was planted firmly in my chest, and the majority of our comforter was wrapped around her and only her. For someone with such a small body, she had still managed to take over the entire bed. Liz, on the other hand, was comfortably sprawled out across the other double bed, buried under a pile of fluffy white pillows.

A cursory look through both Candace's and Liz's bags yielded no liquids of any kind, so I threw on a hoodie and headed to the lobby in search of water I didn't have to suck out of a bathroom sink. I wasn't about to get charged four dollars for a bottle out of the mini fridge. For some reason, cheap hotels always gave you everything for free while nicer hotels charged for everything.

I wandered around the lobby, consciously swiping under my eyes for signs of runny mascara, until I found a pitcher of water next to the front desk, two sad slices of lemon floating haphazardly atop a couple of half-melted ice cubes. I poured a cup and guzzled it down as I listened to a woman at the checkout desk try to complain her way into a partial refund.

"I couldn't sleep all night; this place was a circus!" she exclaimed, taking great pains to show the uninterested hotel clerk the bags under her eyes.

"Yes ma'am, we had a prom and a wedding here last night," he tried explaining patiently.

At the reminder of the word *circus*, last night's events in Rhys's hotel room were dragged back to the forefront of my mind. So much had happened, yet I still wasn't sure what any of it meant. I shot off a quick text to Rhys before escaping the stale, suspended air of the lobby for the crisp, spring air outside.

The sunlight was too bright to step out into, but if I shaded my eyes with my arm, it was just bearable enough that I could sit on the wooden bench that faced the unremarkable view of the parking lot. The constantly overcast, drizzly sky of the Pacific Northwest would be a change—especially on days like this. But at least I'd escape the months of snow. Spring was the only semistable season in Iowa. The summer was unbearably hot and the fall was liable to tumble into a premature winter at any point. I would, however, need to invest in some lighter rain boots.

I'd only been sitting there for a few minutes when the doors behind me slid open again and I turned to find Rhys, disheveled and sleepy-eyed, standing in the doorway. "Hey," he croaked, raising an arm to shield his own eyes from the bright sun. "I got your text. What are you doing out here?"

"Enjoying the view, obviously," I replied, gesturing to the scores of cars lined up next to one another.

His hair was wilder than usual, dark curls tumbling down over his forehead and softening the angular features of his face even as he squinted hard at the horizon. "Am I still drunk or is this just facing the parking lot?"

"You're still drunk. That's clearly the ocean."

Rhys gave a small chuckle and settled onto the bench next to me. The sleep was visible on his face, his jawline littered with dark stubble and pillow lines etched into his pale skin, goose bumps dotting his bare arms. But at this close distance, the unmistakable woodiness of his cologne filled the air and the familiar tug of wanting to be closer to him—the lure of being together in a dimly lit room with nothing more to do than stare at a ceiling—nearly overpowered my already sleep-deprived brain into making me simply lie down, my head in his lap.

But a lot had happened in the last twenty-four hours, and restarting from where we were seven months ago wasn't an option. This wasn't a Tom Cruise movie and I certainly wasn't Emily Blunt.

"I didn't mean for you to get up right when I texted," I apologized. "Sorry if I woke you."

"It's fine. I think I got a little more sleep than everyone else anyway." He grinned.

It was now or never.

"I have a question for you," I said, gripping my hands together to keep them from fidgeting.

"This sounds serious."

"It's not," I rushed to say. "Well, it kind of is, I guess. I don't know. Maybe it is."

Rhys shot a glance at my hands, which were currently twisting themselves into knots without my realizing. "Just spit it out before you have a heart attack."

"Why did you play me that song last night?" I blurted out.

Rhys paused, one eye squinting as if he were trying to remember. "Song?"

My heart dipped. There was no way he didn't remember our entire interaction. He'd been loopy and sleepy, but not blackout drunk.

"The . . . the song. I don't know what it's called. About raincoats and three thousand miles. You played it last night in your room." My words tumbled out together, barely forming themselves into coherent thoughts.

Rhys gave sort of a bewildered shrug.

Jesus Christ.

I'd been tying myself into knots trying to figure out how to talk to him about my leaving and he didn't even remember me telling him.

"Okay, I guess it doesn't matter then. We had a conversation and I told you I was going to school in Washington. But you don't remember the rest of it, so." I stood up, both annoyed and embarrassed that I'd made this into such a production.

"Wait," he said, and his head dropped down into his hand as his other hand ran through his unruly brown curls. "Sit back down, I know what song you're talking about."

"So you lied when you said you didn't remember," I said, perching myself on the farthest corner of the bench away from him.

"I didn't lie, I just didn't answer."

"Thanks for the clarification, it really helps here," I said sarcastically.

We stared out at the parking lot as a large bird flew by, swooping up and down above the cars and squawking at the two of us. It was as if it knew we were struggling to communicate and was yelling at us to just get it over with.

"Why did you play me that song?" I tried again.

"It's a good song," he replied.

"That's not an answer."

"It's *an* answer."

I sighed with exasperation. "Fine. It's not an answer to the question I asked."

"How do you know?" he asked with a raised eyebrow.

I stood up again. "You don't want to talk about it? We won't talk about it."

"You want to talk about it?" he challenged, now fully alert and no longer avoiding eye contact. "Let's talk."

"Answer my question," I said.

"Mine first. Why did you decide you're going to the school in Washington?"

I furrowed my eyebrows. "What?"

"Oh, are you pretending not to understand now? I thought that was *my* role."

"I understand the question," I replied with a hint of annoyance. "It's a little out of nowhere."

"I thought we were talking about last night. So did you or did you not decide where you were going last night in my room?"

Somehow the entire conversation had flipped, with me being on the receiving end of the interrogation. "I did," I replied hesitantly.

"Okay. Why?"

I gave myself a moment before answering. I hadn't yet composed my bullet point list of reasons—that would come later, before I had to present the decision to my parents. And Wendy. Oh god, I'd have to tell Wendy all her effort was for nothing. "Because—because"—my brain worked furiously, trying to think of all the things that had made sense the night before—"because it felt right."

Rhys's eyebrows floated up in disbelief. "That's your answer? It *felt* right?"

"I don't have to explain it to you!"

He leaned forward, hands clasped together, elbows resting on his knees. Perfectly calm, perfectly infuriating. "Then what exactly is this conversation supposed to be about?"

I slumped back down on the bench. "God, you're annoying."

He didn't say anything, but shifted his position, the wooden slats of the bench creaking beneath us.

"I know Northwestern is a better school," I began. "I know that logically it's the better option. It's a higher-ranked school that would lend more prestige to any postgrad application I decided to pursue. I'd be close to home and could visit my friends a lot more easily. I'd have Wendy there as a support system. It'd make my parents happy." I ticked off the items listed in my pros column. "I have a really clear picture of what my future would look like there."

"But . . . ?" he prompted.

"But I don't *want* my future mapped out right now. I want to have the chance to do things for myself. Explore. I want to be somewhere that's *mine*. Somewhere that wants *me*." It was hard to explain that this wasn't about a bruised ego over Wendy having to secure my spot, but more about being seen for the kind of violinist I was. I wasn't going to Washington to play because I *had* to, but because I *wanted* to.

In a way, it was the best possible outcome for everyone. Wendy got her own space without having to betray her sense of duty, my parents got another four years of material to complain about, and I got what I'd always wanted—freedom.

Rhys shook his head, a sound of annoyance escaping from his throat. "I knew you'd move all the way the hell out there the *second* you got that offer. Do you want to know how I knew?" He didn't wait for me to answer. "Because that's just who you are. Forget anyone or anything else that might already be waiting for you, even if it's the better choice—you go wherever you want because it *feels* right in the moment."

"What the hell?" I could barely get the words out, I was so shocked by his sudden outburst.

"Go ahead, deny it."

My mind spun, trying to come up with a coherent response to the accusation Rhys had just made. It was all so out of nowhere I could scarcely believe he'd even said it.

"You have no idea how hard this was for me," I said. I'd probably spent more time agonizing over the decision than I had on all of my college applications combined.

"So hard you made it in a split second. On a *feeling*." Rhys's disdain was obvious.

"According to you, you already knew it was going to happen, so I guess it wasn't that split second, huh?" I shot back.

That silenced him.

"So that's what the song was about, then?" I asked, my agitation stirring my courage. "Proving to me how smart and logical you are so that you can scold me for making what you consider to be a bad decision? So you can yell at me for leaving? Why couldn't you have just asked me?"

Rhys scoffed, his head once more buried in his hands. "Forget it. Forget I said anything."

"Not super hard to do, considering you basically never say anything anyway," I muttered.

Rhys's head flew up at my dig, as if he were ready to say something but seemed to reconsider. He just shook his head again, his shoulders slumping back into their usual hunched position.

"No no, let's hear it," I goaded him. "Or should I go get you some shots first since apparently the only time you can talk to me is when you're drunk?"

"Is that why you thought you could tell me you were in love with me last night? Because you thought I wouldn't remember?"

My eyes widened, my voice reduced to a faint squeak. "I thought you were asleep."

"So you didn't mean it?" he demanded.

Crap. What was I supposed to say to that?

I bit my lip, debating my choices.

I couldn't very well deny it. And even though I was mad enough to strangle Rhys at the moment, I didn't really *want* to deny it, either. Those words were a hell of a lot braver than anything he'd ever said.

I raised my chin defiantly. "I meant it. So what?"

Rhys's pink cheeks reddened with outrage. "What kind of person says that to someone and then picks up and leaves town?"

"It's not like I'm leaving tomorrow."

"No, yeah, you're right. It'd be way better to drag this out over the summer, *then* have you leave."

His sarcasm was so biting I almost felt guilty for a moment.

But I didn't have anything to feel guilty about. I'd admitted my feelings—something he'd never actually done in seven whole months. Meanwhile, he sat there talking about us as if there was an *us* without there actually being one. Regardless of how he'd acted while we were actually dating, there had been a number of occasions since then where he easily could have done . . .

something. Or had I imagined the intimacy in holding hands, lying next to each other?

I began hesitatingly, "We broke up months ago—"

"About the time you met Brad, right?"

Ouch.

My teeth sank into my bottom lip as the full force of that remark rolled over me.

"That was out of line, I'm sorry," Rhys apologized, his hands tugging at his hair agitatedly.

"No, I deserved that one."

Rhys continued tugging at his hair as I sat there staring at my hands. Funny, they'd been so restless earlier, twisting themselves into knots at the idea of this conversation. But they were perfectly still now.

I had exactly one chance to have this conversation—I couldn't waste it being too nervous to say what needed to be said.

"I know it's probably too late to apologize, but I hated the way we broke up. I'm sorry it happened the way that it did." I still hadn't quite mastered the art of apologies, but I thought I was showing marked improvement regardless.

Before he could say anything, I plowed ahead. "You can think it's dumb for me to make decisions based on my feelings, but it's those same feelings that made me go to your room last night and say the thing you pretended not to hear. So yeah, I haven't always been the best person to you. I'm sure I've hurt you in ways you'll never tell me about. But what I'm not going to do is apologize for wanting to be with someone who's capable of expressing their emotions. Someone who's capable of telling me they want me in their life."

Rhys's eyes were downcast, his feet kicking at a nonexistent spot on the ground.

I waited for him to say something—anything—but he continued to stare at the ground, saying nothing.

And if that wasn't the entire problem.

I stared at his hunched shoulders and his long arms curling over onto his knees like the outline of a moon gate. I'd always loved those distinct circular doorways—their Chinese origin always sent a surge of pride through me. Like Chinese people were the original architects of class and style and Europeans were just snobby pretenders.

Moon gates were special. They required a certain degree of knowledge to create and significant patience to execute. They were markers of excellence. And as much as I hated my parents' hypercritical standards, the truth was, they were right to want excellence in their lives. Or at least people's best efforts toward excellence.

I'd fooled myself into thinking Rhys was Noah Calhoun from *The Notebook*, toiling away behind the scenes, patiently waiting for me to realize he was the love of my life. Except I'd been completely wrong. He'd never fix up a house for me. He'd never write me letters. He couldn't even say the damn words back. "I deserve to be with someone who tries," I said simply.

Rhys looked up and for a moment it seemed like he might say something. But he dropped his head back down, content to give his focus and attention to the weeds growing through the cracks in the pavement.

It was unsurprising, but disappointing all the same. And if this had been at the beginning of the year, I might have internalized it as a reflection of my own personal failure instead of seeing it for what it really was: no longer my problem. At least now I could stop wondering *what if*.

I stood up, giving myself a few extra seconds to dust off the back of my pants before heading back inside the sliding doors and into the stale air of the hotel lobby. Rhys never said a word.

CHAPTER THIRTY-FIVE

The first thing I did when I got home was jump directly into the shower, turning the water up as high as it would go until my skin nearly broke out in hives from the heat. The day was only half over but I'd already used up all of my emotional energy, which didn't bode well for the conversation I was going to have to have with my parents about the decision I'd made.

I wanted to not care about their opinion on the matter—on any matter, really—but I didn't know if that was ever going to be possible. My mom would probably still be trying to impress my ahma if she hadn't died years ago. I would just have to settle with sticking to my plan, regardless of their reaction.

The final minutes of my shower were spent practicing my "serious" face—the one that most closely resembled Wendy's "focused" face. It was as if they couldn't believe anything I said if it looked like I was too happy about it, so I always did my best to seem grim when there was something I really wanted.

The opportunity came sooner than expected when my mom burst into the bathroom just as I was stepping out of the shower, my towel draped haphazardly around my body.

"Augh! Privacy!" I yelped, pulling the towel more tightly around me.

"Eh. You don't lock the door," she replied, waving off my concerns as she busied herself looking through the cupboards.

Wendy had always insisted that showering didn't require a locked door because we shared a bathroom and the other person could use the sink and toilet instead of having to wait. The habit of leaving the door unlocked had been so ingrained I didn't even realize I was still doing it until now.

"You come home later than I expect," she said, continuing to rifle through the cabinets, eventually emerging triumphant with a box of generic cotton swabs. "Don't forget you still need to do your practice today."

Right. Because something like a literal once-in-a-lifetime dance wasn't an excuse to take a day off. I could be half dead, lying in a coma, machines beeping my weak existence, and she'd be raising my mechanical hospital bed so I could sit up and practice. Never mind that I no longer had any competitions to be preparing for.

"Don't let Dad catch you with those," I warned as she swabbed around one of her ears and threw it away, reaching for another one. If I had to sit through countless lectures about the dangers of using cotton swabs in my ears, I could at least use this opportunity to remind my mom that she, too, made reckless decisions on occasion.

She scoffed. "I'm not scared of Daddy. If he doesn't like them, he doesn't use them." But she carefully covered the discarded swabs with toilet paper and tucked the box back into the cabinet. I seriously doubted that just because my mom was the type to snoop through the trash my dad would have similar instincts, but it was funny to think about the ways she snuck around behind his back like a teenager.

She turned and gave me a long look, her thumbs moving up to my face to rub the stubborn mascara stains under my eyes. "You look tired. Too much makeup. You want me to get the Ponds?"

I batted her hand away, along with the idea that her actions were anything like mine. I hid things from them out of necessity; she hid things from my dad because it was easier for her that way. "I'm fine. Can I just have some privacy?"

"Aiya. What privacy? You think you have something to hide?"

"No, Mom. Some people just don't want to be naked in front of their moms. That doesn't make me the weird one here."

"You not naked. You have a towel!"

I suppressed an internal sigh. It was like she could make anything into an argument just for the sake of being right.

I figured I might as well get the conversation over with. At least then I wouldn't have to take on both of my parents at once. Maybe if I caught her off guard, I wouldn't be subject to the third degree.

"Hey, so I need a check this week to send for my housing deposit," I said casually, as if we'd already been discussing the subject.

Her eyes perked up at the mention of college, and she practically broke her hand scrambling to grab the cell phone from her pocket. "I call Wendy and have her go pay for you."

I cleared my throat uncomfortably. "I'm not going to Northwestern." I tried to straighten up and look as confident as possible, which was difficult to do while covered in nothing but a towel.

My mom's signature gaze bore into me, a frown forming at the corners of her mouth. "You decide this all by yourself. Just like that."

I shifted uncomfortably. "Well, obviously I put a lot of thought into it. It's not like I just decided right now. I can go get my list of reasons if you want."

She stared at me, unblinking, daring me to break down and confess that I had not, in fact, compiled a concrete list of reasons beyond the fact that going there would make me happy. Personal happiness didn't rate very high on the list of acceptable reasons for, well, anything in my mom's mind.

"What Daddy and I think doesn't matter. Only you matter. You decide." She said it so matter-of-factly, like it was absurd for my own opinion to carry more weight than hers.

"You've made it perfectly clear what you think," I said, pressing my arms into the sides of my towel in an attempt to stay calm. "If it hadn't been for your guilt-tripping I probably could have decided a lot sooner."

"Me?" she asked, pointing to herself. "You think I guilt-trip? How I want best things for you make you feel guilty?"

"It's not about you wanting things for me and you know it."

My mom feigned innocence. "I don't know. I don't know why you so angry all the time. Blame me for everything. You don't like your life? Fine. Go change it. Move to Washington. I don't care." She waved her hand at me like she was already shooing me out the door.

"See? You *act* like you don't care, but then you're just going to spend the rest of the summer making passive-aggressive comments about how my school isn't as good as Wendy's school."

"Your school *not* as good as Wendy's school. Why I pretend it is?"

I let out a sound of exasperation. Screw staying calm.

"What is it with you? Do you just enjoy being as mean as possible to your own children? Do you get some kind of sick joy from seeing how many negative things you can say to me before I break? Is that what you want?" My voice cracked, tears beginning to prick the backs of my eyes.

First Rhys, now my mom. It was like I'd removed every last barrier I'd erected to keep me safe, words tumbling from my mouth like maple syrup from a bottle whose opening was too big, drenching everything in a sticky mess.

My mom clucked her tongue with disapproval, shaking her finger at me as if I were a poorly trained dog. "Aiya. So dramatic. You not made of porcelain. You won't break. In Taiwan we say mà shì ài—scolding is love. You want me to pat your head, say *Oh, good job for trying*? This way you never learn. Never get better."

"That's what you think you're doing?" I screeched. "Making me better? So you're admitting there will never come a point where you'll actually say 'good job' for anything. *Nothing* I do will ever be good enough. But for some reason, your main worry is

323

making sure I don't get complacent by experiencing any kind of happiness, ever. God forbid you show me even a sliver of affection in my lifetime. I'm sure it won't damage me in any way for the rest of my life."

My mom blinked several times, as though what I said had stung her. Her normally impenetrable façade flickered with pain, and I felt a brief stab of regret. "Jīn wú zú chì, rén wú wán rén— there is no pure gold, no perfect person. We do the best we can. Sorry not good enough for you." She shrugged her shoulders, suddenly looking so much older and more slumped than normal as she exited the bathroom.

The steam from my shower had long since dissipated, leaving me with nothing but my own reflection to stare at. Who would I be if I had different parents? Would I be happier?

My parents' constant criticism affected me in ways I was only starting to fully understand. If I'd felt more loved and accepted at home, maybe I wouldn't have spent so much time trying to find it in other places. Their impossible standards made me desperate to please everyone but myself, hiding my own pain just to preserve the pretense that I was doing okay so I wouldn't be rejected again. Dǎpò ményá wǎng dù lǐ yàn, the Chinese called it—swallowing a broken front tooth.

At the same time, it was impossible to deny that my parents were a major factor in my success. Without them always pushing me to do better, I probably wouldn't have developed the skills I needed to get my scholarship in the first place. They chose the violin for me, they set up and enforced my practice habits, and they instilled in me an unflinching understanding of what was possible with enough hard work. And, as Wendy had recently pointed out, they'd even given me more control over my future than they'd ever given her.

I thought about the proverb I had quoted to Amy and the discovery of its real meaning. *Shù yù jìng ér fēng bù zhǐ, zǐ yù yàng ér qīn bú dài*, she'd said. *The tree wants peace but the wind won't stop, children want to take care of their parents but the parents don't wait.* Chinese proverbs were funny. Most of the time they were unnecessarily poetic, and my mom employed them like an overdramatic thespian when a simple "I would prefer you do this" would suffice. But every once in awhile, I was caught off guard by their impact.

I'd always envisioned myself the tree in that proverb, one of those oddly twisted ones, growing sideways from decades of heavy blows. I'd congratulated myself on surviving the eternal wind that was my parents' pressure and expectations. Except, as it turned out, I'd completely misunderstood it. I'd spent years struggling under a wrong understanding of the true cultural divide between us—I wanted peace; they wanted to take care of me before they couldn't any longer, even if their idea of "care" was misguided.

My feelings were no longer about anger or even guilt at this revelation. Like Amy had said, things were different for me because of where I grew up. I would probably never see eye to eye with my parents because of where *they* grew up. And I could spend the rest of my life hoping they'd change their ways to better support me, or I could choose to appreciate the small ways they already did. Starting with the fact that they were letting me move halfway across the country from them in a few months.

I quickly got changed before finding my mom outside, plucking weeds from the garden with the same intense scowl across her face that Wendy got whenever she was concentrating.

No wonder those two understood each other so well.

I plunked myself down next to her, watching her methodically pull weed after weed from the ground, shaking the excess dirt from the roots before piling them into the bucket next to her. Even here, not a single cent would be wasted.

We sat in silence as she pulled, shook, and discarded again and again. Finally, she spoke.

"I hear from Mrs. Kim her daughter Ashley, you know, the one with the bad skin. She going to some school called Smith," she offered, her sight still trained on the ground in front of her. "In Massachusetts. I ask why not MIT but her mom say it's good school. I guess good enough for Koreans."

I sighed. Even when she was trying to be nice she couldn't just *be nice*. Maybe Liz had been right after all—I had a responsibility to say something. Maybe not to everyone, but at least to the people I had influence with. Otherwise she'd just keep saying stuff like this.

"Smith is a good college for everyone, not just for Koreans, Mom."

"I just mean—"

"I know what you mean," I cut in. Then added more gently, "And I hope you don't think someone telling you my school is good enough for Taiwanese kids is okay."

She frowned, but at least she looked like she was thinking about it.

"Your school better than her school?" she asked hopefully.

I leaned over and wrapped my arms around her. "Thank you," I said, squeezing her bony shoulders. "For everything."

She patted me with the back of a gardening glove before disentangling herself. "Don't forget to practice today. Don't want your new school disappointed when you show up."

CHAPTER THIRTY-SIX

After prom, it was only a handful of weeks to the end of the year. But with college acceptances settled or post-high-school jobs lined up or both, the entire senior class seemed to collectively slide toward the finish line with all the speed of Arvo Pärt's *Spiegel im Spiegel*—a piece of music so lethargic you could take a short nap between notes and still not miss anything.

Everyone seemed to be focused on only two things: graduation and the subsequent party being held at someone's family's sod farm outside of town. If there was one thing Pine Grove knew how to do well, it was how to throw a party. I'd already prepped my parents by telling them we'd be spending the night at Liz's dad's cabin. I didn't even feel guilty about lying anymore. I'd just accepted that we would always have the kind of relationship that required me to hide certain things from them and that they probably liked it that way. For as nosy and "concerned" as my mom was, she never actually asked me about anything she wanted the real answer to.

Things had gotten a bit better since I'd told her about my decision, though mostly because I tried to stop letting her comments get under my skin. She'd continued to make offhand remarks about how much more prestigious Northwestern was and how *no one* had ever heard of my school, but I just had to remind myself that meant she was at least talking about me to her friends. Because no matter how much she complained, I knew she would never tell them something about me that might paint her parenting in an unflattering light.

"One more week," Candace sighed, flopping backward onto the armrest of my parents' green microfiber couch. She lifted her head and peeled the plastic cover off of it before laying her head back down, discarding the cover onto the floor.

"Don't let my mom see you do that or she'll yell at you," I warned. "Can't have people actually enjoying or using the furniture properly. Might depreciate the value."

A fun by-product of my mom's profession was that she constantly calculated the depreciation of any large assets, regardless of whether she ever planned to sell them. Her car's passenger side door didn't even open properly and you couldn't drive it above sixty miles per hour, but she insisted it was unnecessary to get a new one because apparently new cars lost up to 20 percent of their value the moment you drove them off the lot.

"Mrs. Chu would never dream of yelling at me," Candace said, wiggling around until she'd settled into a comfortable position, her feet stretching almost to the armrest of the opposite end of the compact loveseat. "I'm her favorite because I'm the short daughter she never had. You'll never understand. We're kindred spirits."

Sitting next to me on the longer couch, Liz snorted. "Ha. Good luck. I'd love to see you kindred spirit your way into this house."

Candace craned her neck around, her eyes settling on the spread of shiny gold trophies across the mantel. "Oh yeah, I forgot about all that achievement stuff. Never mind, I'm good where I am." She giggled and wiggled her toes, burrowing even farther down into the couch like a little mole. "Wake me up when it's time for my graduation party."

"Hey! My party is first!" Liz exclaimed.

"Okay, wake me up when it's time for your party."

The two of them launched into a more detailed discussion of what food they'd be serving at their parties and how they planned to spend the money they'd get as gifts while I tried to look interested and excited. Of course my parents didn't understand why anyone would throw a party for clearing the low bar of graduating compulsory schooling, let alone get money for it. *You can ask for money when you get married*, my mom had told me.

Wendy wandered into the room, having arrived home for the summer the week before.

"Mom's going to freak out if she sees your friends taking the plastic covers off the furniture," she said, looking up from her phone.

Liz shot Candace a triumphant look and Candace made a face back at her before straining to reach the floor where she'd tossed the cover aside.

"What are you guys up to?" Wendy asked.

"Just talking about graduation next week," Liz replied. She turned her attention back to Candace and me. "It's going to be so weird not to have either of you with me at UNI next year."

"You'll have Rhys and those guys," Candace offered.

"You'll have half of Pine Grove," I added.

"Rhys . . . Rhys." Wendy repeated the name, her eyes tipped toward the ceiling as she searched her brain for a memory of the name. "Didn't you used to date him or something?"

I shrugged off the question. "Kind of. A long time ago."

"Oh, wait, I remember!" Her eyes lit up with recognition. "He was the guy you liked! I thought you said he wasn't interested."

For all the strides Wendy and I had made in our relationship, we obviously hadn't yet cleared the hurdle of not humiliating each other in front of other people.

I cleared my throat, trying to put as much dignity into my voice as possible. "Actually, you made that up. You made a rude comment about me being not cool enough for him to like me, which was not true since we did actually date. And *I* ended things with *him*. Twice."

Wendy stared at me, her tortoiseshell glasses slipping down her nose. "Oh my god, are you still mad about that? I was joking!"

Liz and Candace exchanged an uncomfortable glance, clear that this was something they did not want to be in the middle of. But I couldn't let Wendy get away with just shrugging off something so incendiary, especially after it had caused so much anguish all those months ago.

"That's convenient," I replied smoothly. "And no, I'm not mad, but jokes are usually funny, which that wasn't."

Wendy furrowed her eyebrows, her mouth turning down into a frown. "Okay. Geez. I can tell when I'm not wanted."

She left the room and the tension eased, with Liz letting out a nervous sort of laugh.

"That was awkward," she said, her eyes still darting back and forth between Candace and me, like she was waiting for one of us to say something.

"Good for you," Candace said to me, a smile spreading across her face. "Wendy can be such a bitch sometimes."

"Hey now, that's my sister. Only I'm allowed to say stuff like that about her," I warned. "Besides," I added brightly, "she's trying. In the past she would have just kept going. One day she might even acknowledge she's wrong about something!"

Liz just shook her head, but Candace nodded like she understood. "See? This is how I feel about Dom! I know he's not perfect but he's trying and he's been really understanding about me wanting to go to Kirkwood and stuff. He even came with me when I went to register. So, you know, baby steps."

I had to physically bite my tongue to keep from pointing out that Wendy was born into my family and therefore I *had* to learn how to deal with her, whereas Candace was in a voluntary relationship with a guy she just commended for letting her go to college. But like she said, baby steps.

Liz clasped her hands together, her eyes now signaling she absolutely wanted to bail on this conversation. "Let's go get DQ. I think we could all use some ice cream right now."

Candace pulled herself up from the couch. "Fine. But only if you promise not to tell us again about how you learned how to make the swirl on top when you worked there."

"It's all in the wrist!" Liz called as she ran out of the room, and Candace threw a couch pillow after her.

————————

By the following Wednesday, the weather had turned blazing hot, which made for a less exciting graduation experience than everyone had hoped for. For one thing, we were assembled outside on the football field—row and after row of wobbling plastic chairs baking in the heat, our parents stuffed into the bleachers like overdressed fans. For another, we were assembled alphabetically, because even after four years at the same school, the administrators didn't want the responsibility of having to know our actual names.

This meant that instead of getting to sit with my friends, I was trapped between Chelsey Chelsea, whose parents basically committed a hate crime when they named her, and Dan Coolie and his unrelenting BO, which was now amplified in the stifling afternoon heat. To the left of Chelsey sat Rhys, whose flimsy gown hem was clownishly short and rose almost to his knees— which jutted out so far, they nearly touched the chair in front of him.

His hair was wild and unruly as usual, dark brown curls leaping off the top of his head every which way, but a pair of white cuffs and black dress pants peeked out from under the red gown. His mom had probably insisted he dress up. Mine had certainly weighed in about my outfit, worrying about whether the shorts I'd chosen were appropriate for the occasion because of their length, despite the fact that literally no one could see them and I'd probably pass out from heatstroke if I wore any more clothing.

There were about a thousand speeches to get through, none of them inspiring or even noteworthy, though Principal Blackburn kept emphasizing the incorrect syllable on the word *graduates*— *grad-OO-ets*, she kept repeating. I heard a series of soft snapping sounds and I turned to find Rhys signaling for my attention, his long arms stretched across the back of Chelsey Chelsea's seat. He mouthed the word *grad-OO-ets* at me, his mouth making the exaggerated O shape, and I had to cover my mouth to keep from laughing aloud.

And for a brief moment, everything felt exactly how it used to. The rush of the life I was leaving behind flooded back— inside jokes, our mock arguing, the intense feeling of safety he brought. The nostalgia washed over me, magnifying all the things I was giving up. He would go to UNI and have those things with someone else. Some other girl who didn't demand quite so much.

But I was now free to find those things with someone else too. And I refused to be wowed by the bare minimum of simply *not* being an asshole. Just because Rhys had been the best of the three boys didn't make him a good choice in his own right. Maybe he was okay with settling because he didn't know how to ask for more, but I wasn't. Not anymore.

I was definitely doing the right thing.

I turned my attention back to Principal Blackburn, who was now warning the audience to hold their applause until each student had received their diploma—a futile effort, as the first graduate's name was called to an eruption of cheers and clapping. The entire ceremony was like that, the names barely heard over a steady beat of clapping and yelling, until an hour later it was finally over.

Four years of high school, gone just like that.

Any flutter of sadness I had about the passing of time was shoved to the back of my mind as a buzz of excitement ran through my limbs instead. I was done! Actually, for real, done! For all the time I'd spent preparing for this moment, the reality of it all still caught me off guard.

I made a beeline toward my family, weaving through throngs of sobbing parents who had flooded the field to present their graduates with huge bouquets and weepy hugs. My mom and dad, on the other hand, offered me a nod and modest congratulations on fulfilling my obligation while reminding me of the four years I had ahead of me. To them, a high school diploma was no more an achievement than a middle school or elementary school one, but merely an expected step to be taken on my journey toward a medical degree.

"Congratulations," Wendy said, surprising me with a small hug. She whispered in my ear, "I know Mom and Dad act like it's not a big deal, but this is a milestone. You deserve to celebrate."

"We did it!" Candace shrieked from behind me, her voice so loud and guttural I saw my mom wince.

Liz pumped her fist in the air. "We're free!"

I broke away from Wendy and the three of us jumped up and down on the grass, our arms intertwined and our unzipped gowns flying behind us like capes. "Pine Grove! Pine Grove! Pine Grove!" The chant all around us was infectious.

After we settled down and finished taking a million and one pictures with anyone we might still want to remember in a year, my friends said their greetings to my parents, who offered them much warmer congratulations than the one I'd received.

"You girls come to the house tonight," my mom told them, her voice indicating it was less of an invitation and more of a directive. "I make dinner for everyone."

My friends glanced at me nervously. It was a nice gesture from my mom, especially considering how little she thought of this whole affair, but we had a schedule to keep. None of us wanted to arrive late to the campsite only to find all the good locations claimed. This was probably going to be my last big party in Pine Grove.

Wendy intervened. "They should probably leave before then so it's not too late when they get to the cabin. Don't you think?" she added, her eyes turning to me.

Seeing Wendy come to my rescue sent me into a temporary daze, but I pulled my attention back to the conversation at hand. "Oh! Right! Yeah. It'll be much safer if it's still light out on the drive," I said, much more impassioned than it needed to be.

Wendy rolled her eyes at my lack of subtlety.

With my mom's attention focused on Wendy and me, my friends fled back to the crowd before they could be coerced into coming over. They'd seen firsthand how insistent she could be when she wanted to feed someone.

My mom rolled her eyes, shooing me away. "Yeah yeah, fine, go. Make sure you eat something before you drive. Not safe to drive on empty stomach."

I gave her a small kiss on the cheek, my dad declining his with a nod of his head instead. "I'll be back tomorrow."

As I turned to walk away, she added with a frown, "Aiya. You still wearing those shorts. Zip up your gown so no one sees. Don't want people to think you giving milk for free you know." She raised her eyebrows in insinuation.

"Yes Mom, don't want people confusing me with a cow and looking for the udders."

She shook her head in disapproval, but a hint of a smile was peeking through. "In those shorts, they might find them!"

THE END

Acknowledgments

I once had a fully grown adult try to get me fired from my job for making a list of names using commas instead of bullet points, so it is impossible for me to write acknowledgments—which will inevitably contain lists of names—without thinking about that. Suzanne, wherever you are, I hope these commas haunt you.

First, I have to thank my mom. Mostly because she insisted (she actually wanted the book dedicated to her), but also because she always answered my calls about the Chinese proverbs found in this book. Thank you for helping me rù mù sān fēn.

I owe a huge debt of gratitude to my agent, Kiana Nguyen. Without her tough love and insistence that I simply delete my entire book and start over, *Boys I Know* would have never made it to publication. Thank you for giving me the push I needed. I am now a ruthless killer of darlings and find myself preemptively editing the f-word from my drafts.

I am also eternally grateful to my editor, Ashley Hearn, who connected with this book from the start. It is truly the most validating feeling in the world to have someone who "gets" your story. Thank you for helping me make this book the best it can be (and also for being what seems like the only person in all of publishing who adheres to deadlines). I hope every writer finds someone who very kindly types 'lol' into the margins of every single joke.

Thank you to the rest of the Peachtree team, especially Amy Brittain, Michelle Montague, Terry Borzumato-Greenberg, and Adela Pons. I adore my cover, designed by Kelley Brady and illustrated by Fevik, and thank you for dealing with my never-ending back and forth about June's boots.

Thank you to Beth Phelan and Brenda Drake for creating the pitch contests that connected me to my agent and also to other writers, who have made this journey a group celebration. My absolute favorite people in the world, aka the people who both inspire me to write and actively prevent me from writing almost every day: Naz Kutub, Taj McCoy, Robin Wasley, Traci-Anne Canada, Gates Palissery, Pam Delupio, Tana M, Alaysia Jordan, Paul Ladipo, and our resident doctor and murder expert, Robin St. Clare: I could not have done this—nor would I want to—without all of you. May each of our Pauls see their day in print.

For Anitha, my long-suffering critique partner, who is the fastest reader alive and is magically available at all hours, regardless of her busy schedule. I hope to write as many books as you one day.

Thank you to the yay squad, who suffered through sub hell with me: Steph, J. Elle, Ana, Graci, Sonora Reyes, and Adelle

Yeung. I'm grateful for all of your advice and commiseration. I can't wait to see all of our names in print. And even though I've mentioned all of these people already, I need to give an extra dose of appreciation for my regular Zoom crew, Naz, TA, and Sonora, for forcing me to write, even though I'm technically supposed to be intrinsically motivated to do so. Seeing your faces helped make COVID lockdown so much more bearable, even if we had to listen to what Naz made for lunch every day.

I owe an unquantifiable amount of thanks to my first readers, Joan Minninger and Kirsten Pfleger, for how eagerly you read through an absolute mess of words I slapped together and called a book before I knew what a book should look like, and for giving me encouraging feedback nonetheless. Your support made all the difference. For any and all of the other writers I swapped early drafts with, I am so sorry that I didn't know how to be a proper beta reader and probably gave you useless feedback. Bless you all for the time you spent on my manuscript, and if you want to come back and collect an actual beta read, please do. I feel desperately guilty and I swear I know what I'm doing now.

Becca, Ruby, and Alex: though we may not be a group of feral possums anymore, I'm so happy to have you all in my life. To Rebecca, whose wisdom far surpasses my own. And Kadijah, thank you for being the sole person who rooted for Rhys all the way to the end. Your optimism is contagious.

Thank you to my IRL crew, Kate Eschelbach and Denise Donaldson, who gave me a creative space to write this book in the first place, and who fill me with unearned confidence. I have actively gained ten pounds from our writers' group cheese selection and I regret nothing.

Lastly, thank you to my family for all their support—especially my husband, for his design skills, and my kids, who nobly sacrificed themselves to watch an enormous amount of TV while I wrote. This is my swan feather from a thousand miles away.

About the Author

Anna grew up biracial in the Midwest, spending her formative years repeatedly answering the question, "What are you?" Before finding her way as a young adult author, she was a CPA, a public school teacher, a tennis coach, and for one glorious summer, a waitress at a pie shop. She now lives on the West Coast, raising three kids and writing stories about girls navigating a world full of double standards.

WEBSITE: *ANNA-GRACIA.COM*

TWITTER: @GRAHSEEYA

INSTAGRAM: @GRAHSEEYA